SKIN OF
HER TEETH

SKIN OF HER TEETH

Dorie Turnbull

TEMPLE PUBLISHING COMPANY
London, England

First published in Great Britain 1996
by Temple Publishing Company
Edinburgh House,
19 Nassau Street,
London W1N 7RE

Copyright © Dorie Turnbull 1996

British Library Cataloguing-in-Publication Data.
A catalogue record for this book is available
from the British Library

ISBN 1 85977 016 9

All rights reserved. No part of this publication
may be reproduced, stored in a retrieval system or
transmitted in any form or by any means, electronic,
mechanical, photocopying, recording or otherwise,
without the prior permission of the publisher.

The right of Dorie Turnbull to be identified
as the author of this work has been asserted by
her in accordance with the Copyright, Designs
and Patents Act 1988.

Cover design by Harold King

The characters and situations in this book
are entirely imaginary and bear no relation
to any real person or actual happening.

Printed & bound in England by
Antony Rowe, Chippenham, Wiltshire

PART ONE

Chapter One

Original sin – that's it! Original sin. Not, of course, of the Adam and Eve and apples variety – no thank you; Sara was not into sex, as quite a few of her co-students in Chesley were; Mother Nature always got you in the end, put her screws around your neck and throttled you; unwanted babies, the lot. No, her 'original sin' was duplicity, flap-doodling, throwing dust into her parents' eyes; lies and deceit were words she did not like to use. She'd never had occasion to lie and deceive before, and to her shame, she was finding it delectable, delicious, exciting; leading her family and everybody else up the garden path, her father fondly imagining that the new, small monthly allowance he had so reluctantly consented to, would tide her over from Monday to Friday in comfortable digs to save her the sixty-mile train journey she'd have to make otherwise; Ledingham, oh so different from Chesley, being a wretched, awkward journey with a change of stations.

The 'comfortable digs' turned out to be a small bedsit, shared bathroom, three storeys high, only a street or two away from the sleaziest, poorest, most violent section of Ledingham humanity it was possible to find. She needed at least half of her father's generosity for other purposes . . .

Walking now at five-thirty in the evening, rubbing shoulders with the throng of men and women trudging home from their factories, shops and offices after their hard day's work, Sara heaved her thick roll of canvases more securely under one arm, adjusting her shoulder-bag with difficulty and anxiously gazed down yet again at the two-and-a-half square framed pictures which reached down to her ankles. Three pictures in each hand, roped firmly together by the handles she'd made for them, the thick rope she'd cajoled from Mrs Fish – the owner, overseer, and the landlady of the ten bedsits, its bohemian occupants mostly being a very floating population of repertory actors, jugglers, young aspirants in back rows of choruses of a Christmas pantomime, of musicals on tour at the nearby struggling local theatre.

But Sara Nightingale was of a different mould. She had an 'appointment with destiny' – she was on her way to the very well-known painter's studio – Wolfe Falkland's reputation reaching far beyond the boundaries of Ledingham, nearby Manchester and the north of England generally. He was a famous portrait painter, and portraits, above all else, was what she, Sara Nightingale, wanted to paint and make for herself a splendid career.

'You can't make a living out of portrait painting, Sara,' her father had strongly objected. 'It'd take you years to establish yourself. You've had your two years in college here, I really can't see why you can't do your third year here as well and stay at home. I know your portraits are very good and your Miss Davies thinks you can specialise, but wouldn't it be better to go for design or advertising – that sort of thing?' he finished vaguely. To have an artist daughter on his hands was a bit of a trial . . .

'Oh, mind out!'

'Sorry luv,' a swarthy workman apologised with a rueful grin as he stepped aside, having bumped her frames painfully against her ankle. Everybody called everybody 'luv' in Ledingham and she herself had got into the habit.

Miss Davies was so keen that Sara should get the best possible tuition for this final year that through the means of a cousin connection she'd laboured on Sara's behalf to obtain for her a very poorly paid part-time job as a filing clerk and interviewer in an old-established charitable trust – the Ledingham Charitable Trust Welfare Clinic. This at least pleased Sara's father – her mother scarcely counted. Mrs Nightingale had so many irons in the fire outside the home that Sara scarcely saw her mother.

This determined, artistically God-gifted daughter had enrolled herself for a year's course of evening classes in Wolfe Falkland's studio, living in down-town digs which, if they knew, would horrify her parents, giving over by far the largest part of her father's monthly financial help towards Falkland's fees and keeping a bare subsistence for herself.

This filly, longing to leave the parental home, found herself longing to get back to it, could scarcely wait for the weekends, to return to beautiful Chesley, with its conference centres, laid-out gardens, sumptuous-looking hotels and her own comfortable middle-class family home.

Her arms aching with the weight of her canvases, she cursed herself for not having taken a taxi, or at least a bus, part of the way, but she hoarded her money like a miser. The crowd was thinning out now, people had found their cars, or reached their places in the bus queues, and she carefully put best foot forward through ginnels and alleyways, her high heels sounding loud and clipping as she walked.

Suddenly, her mind switched to the two men in her life who she'd left behind in Chesley, meeting them, enjoying them, only now on Saturdays and Sundays. Neither knew of the other's existence; more original sin! It was catching – this bluffing and flap-doodling duplicity.

It wasn't fair on Howard especially, but she just didn't want to worry him when he worked such long impossible hours at the Chesley Royal Infirmary, swotting for his finals, up to his neck in his Practicals. They'd known and loved each other for two years, Howard – Howard Mallory, soon to be Doctor Howard Mallory he hoped. He was the one she met on Sundays, and in the last six weeks he'd always managed it somehow . . .

Howard and she were exact opposites in physical type and shape; he fair, with tousled hair which so easily blew in the wind, steady clear blue eyes, broad-shouldered, just above average height, typical rugby-football-type frame; she, pale-skinned, thick dark hair tied ballerina style behind her ears, or as now, worn loosely to her shoulders; gleaming, expressive liquid-green eyes, slight, beautifully graceful figure, particular, and elegantly dressed as much as she could afford and when she wasn't trousered in painting gear and overalls. Howard dressed easily and carelessly in sports jackets, but had a particular weakness for extravagantly coloured outdoor jackets. She loved the sound of his kind, baritone voice, his sunshine laugh and his look of exuberant health. They complemented each other perfectly . . .

The new-old space-time everlastingness of two souls touching and influencing each other, the suitor in full cry; she was dumbfounded that the luminosity of her passing glance had caught him so strongly; he was ablaze before she knew how to put out the flames – not that she wanted to, she loved his love for her, and loved him for loving her, it was wonderful to be so loved.

Howard was sun-drenched, saturated, she could almost see the blood glowing within him; he was always so pent-up with all that he was suppressing, his animal spirit devising some gambit to amuse her, like a lyre-bird flapping its wings as it frantically courted its would-be mate; he made her laugh, and he deeply supported her in her passion for portrait painting and her desire to make a career of it. He understood, putting his doctor's hat on, when she told him despairingly about the poverty she'd seen in Ledingham, the sick babies, the shock it had been . . .

Most Sundays, Howard took her to his parents' house, to Wharton in the beautiful countryside, five miles out of Chesley. The fresh air did them both so much good and she liked having tea with his aged father and mother and seeing their billing and cooing after more than forty years of married life. Howard, conceived late, was the only child and 'son and heir to very little', as she laughingly explained. Her own parents never billed and cooed, and were seldom seen together . . .

And Philip? Oh, what a contrast he was. I suppose that's half of the attraction, she thought. But his only interest in me is that I'm his ex-fiancée's kid sister, she confessed bluntly. It was wounding, but one had to be honest with oneself, if one wasn't with anyone else.

She'd met Philip at a disco of all places. It was the last place on earth you'd expect to find Councillor Philip Carver, and he was only there by accident. His car brakes had given up, the car was in the garage opposite, would be repaired in one hour, and meantime out of pure curiosity, he had strolled in to the disco hall, spied Sara and recognised her as Catherine's youngest sister. The engagement was broken off all of ten years ago; apparently everybody knew of Cathy's bout of sexual antics, everybody that is, except Philip. Sara had been Philip's companion the last four Saturday nights, and every time he'd motored her to Manchester for their entertainment — well away from Chesley.

Now on the last lap of her tiring journey to the new studio and the new tutor, Sara asked herself the question, 'Is it possible to be in love with two men at once?' Her deep fondness for Howard was straightforward and honest; she loved his company, he made her laugh and she couldn't imagine her life without him. Then why had Philip Carver taken such a hold on her imagination? That first night he'd driven her home from the disco, stopping the car twenty yards away from the front gate and drive of the pleasant detached house which was the Nightingales' family home. He had never entered that house since Catherine had given him back his ring.

Sara understood at once, stopping any verbal explanation from him, that he would not want to take her right up to their front door; he was smiling ironically and seemed as much intrigued by the situation as she was. Their relationship was clandestine from the start. It was exciting to have this secret between them. She found secrets added spice to life. 'It's the Machiavellian streak in me,' she laughed.

That first evening, saying goodbye in the car, they'd had an extraordinary necking session. it amazed her, and obviously it amazed Philip even more, bowled him over, upset him. Was it that he was indulging in some nostalgic dream, and taking some subtle revenge on sister Catherine in a situation, Sara guessed, he had never been able to resolve?

Over a week ago, Sara had carefully reconnoitred the location of the studio. She glimpsed it at last, from the opposite side-street near the centre of the town which was quite empty now. People had dissolved like ghosts through an insubstantial mist, so absorbed had she been in the respective merits of her two admirers. Enough, enough. She pulled herself together . . .

She knew nothing about Wolfe Falkland other than that he was a well-known portrait painter and an excellent teacher. The studio was his own, and he selected his own pupils. She crossed the road, conscious that the palms of her hands were blistering with the rub of her homemade rope handle. Putting her precious canvases on the concrete pavement, she knocked at the door. Two yards inside was another door, half of it a dirty frosted glass; it whirred like a clock as it swung on its hinges, and she entered at last the sacred portals of the studio. She found herself at once in a large, high room, the ceiling paned out in glass squares which slanted upwards like a greenhouse, and someone in a corner was fiddling with the window cords, hanging in clusters from several fanlights like an old ship's rigging from a mast. Nervousness evaporated a little as the man came forward. He ambled towards her, as red and bulbous-nosed as a superannuated clown.

'Good evening, I've an appointment with Mr Falkland.'

'Eee, luv, you 'ave? I'm Bradley, t'caretaker.' Carelessly, he nodded towards a window to the street opposite. 'Wolfe's just across.'

She watched Bradley shuffle away. Squashy with age, he was like a goalkeeper whose defences were wholly inadequate to ward off time's blows – he'd received every one of them smack in the face.

'Am I expected to 'go across', too?' she wondered.

No, could be a public lavatory or something. She gave herself up freely to viewing with yearning interest the assortment of wall pictures, dirty and faded to the insignificance of past glories and present neglect.

One picture stood out head and shoulders above the others, a small powerful oil painting of two black-skinned figures, a man and a woman facing each other, she in a waist sarong, he in a cotton rag; lustily they stared at each other, utterly absorbed, like wrestlers about to spring into each other's arms. Sara's eyes glinted greenly. God, it's tremendous! It'll be his painting. I've heard he paints like Gauguin. Well, I've got here and I'm here for a year – my final, she exulted, and perhaps a scholarship at the end of it. Miss Davies thinks . . . There were smiles all over her expressive face.

She became very conscious of time; she'd been half an hour walking and gazing round the studio, nerves keyed up to screwing point. Where is the man? I've walked three miles to get here, why can't other people be on time? She stared at the students' unfinished sketches, crude nudes, stuck rakishly on their easels and on the walls.

Mounting anger and anxiety and inner rigidity started to assert itself dreadfully. Damn it all, my appointment was for 6.15 and it's now 7.10, where is the man?

At last there was the rusty noise of the frosted-glass door opening and there came into the room the tallest, six-foot-five muscle-bellied man she'd ever seen. 'Hell-lo,' a rich fruity voice cried familiarly through a luxurious beard. She was winded, knocked over by the amount of height and width this figure took up in space.

Advancing towards her with the strolling agility of a circus lion, he held out his hand. Well! Bitterly hurt, hot and fuming, for a fleeting second Sara glared into his eyes, before diplomatically controlling herself and holding her hand out deliberately limp for him to shake, and which he swallowed up in a huge paw. Robustly, he inquired after the health of Miss Davies whom he knew well.

'Fine, thank you,' she said, not returning his smile. 'It was very kind of her to find me a job in Ledingham so that I could study under *you*, Mr Falkland.'

Let him make what he liked of her tone. She disliked this careless show of the painter's trademarks – the loud red-check shirt, the low-belted corduroys worn oblivious of the season, the mane of black hair and thick wiry beard spread across upper lip as well as chin. He's like a Spanish pirate – all he needs is a dagger between his teeth. Oh hell! She sized him up, she didn't like what she saw . . .

In an instant his whole manner changed. 'If I may be so bold as to ask, why didn't you come before?' The threat of him was unmistakable.

'Miss Davies wrote that you'd be here six weeks ago; I suppose it doesn't occur to you that I've kept out another pupil to take *you* on, Miss Nightingale. Damn it all, that's solid cash to me. D'you imagine you are doing *me* a favour by coming to my studio? That you're the only pupil I've got or the only one who damn well matters? In that case you've another think coming sharp, my pretty one. Thank God I can pick and choose my pupils.'

Well, damn him! Damn him! He was late on purpose. It was deliberate. It was the taste of vinegar when she'd expected champagne. Her heart was in her mouth but poker-faced, she would have died rather than he should see it.

'That's the worst of these blithering students who win a few tin-pot prizes at some piffling little art school. Now let Falkland take me on! They all think they've the right of entry into my studio. I suppose you've been having a high old time, six weeks' dallying, viewing the sights of Ledingham?'

Hastily she opened her handbag, produced a cheque for the whole of his fees and silently handed it to him. He gave it a quick glance and stuffed it into his hip pocket.

She stood before him like Lot's wife, her mind as large and empty as a cathedral, round which those terrifying words echoed and reverberated.

'Be humble, Miss Nightingale. Get down on your knees and pray to the Masters to bring some light to your soul. If it's the artist's life you hanker after, you'll kill yourself by inches. Live a thousand years and it's a bare drop in the ocean to learn anything at all. What d'you think makes a painter tick, eh? It's the thought which pursues you like an army of furies that one day, just for one minute, you'll raise your soul high enough to have converse with God and His angels, and *they* will tell you, *they* will give you the *lapis philosophorum*, the elixir vitae! Believe me, a painter settles his problems in no other way. Are you prepared to give up your sleep and wear yourself out thirsting after the Infinite? Doesn't your mind reel with the immensity of it? And you dilly-dally! Take your time! For six weeks.'

'I'm sorry, I –' she stopped. She couldn't say another word. The feeling of numbness gave way to distressed indignation – how dare he! How could she tell him about her upsetting money problems? The pitiful savings from her pay cheques, her father's little fund towards this first term's fees? How could she, just now, tell him about her job? How in the daytime she'd spent weary hours in a stuffy interview room learning how to cope with an endless queue of apathetic mothers with their wet, smelly babies? How could she, here and now, describe to him her deep shock of what she'd seen in the inner-city area of Ledingham, and how in spite of it, her artist's eye was greedy for more? She'd returned to it one night since, after all, her bedsit wasn't that far away. And she'd taken her sketchbook and, openly when it was politic to do so, and surreptitiously when it was not, she put on paper what she had seen. She led a charmed life, and apart from the good social workers she'd met in the interview room, she had scarcely spoken a single word to a living soul in Ledingham since she'd been here, for six solid weeks . . .

All this flashed through her mind as she remained silent like a naughty child, whilst this grossly insulting man harangued her and reduced her to Tom Thumb size.

'We've finished with the Primitives and you've missed out on Titian, and we're now on to Giotto – wait till you see my slides – as my pupil you might be able to dust the surface.' A faint smell of beer drifted towards her. So 'just across' was a public house. He'd deliberately kept her waiting whilst he swilled himself in beer. Oh, this was the last straw! 'I think I've just dusted it,' chokingly she got it out, her agitated croak at once stripping her, bringing to nothing the dignified, studied blankness of her face. 'You have indeed? Let's see 'em.'

Her legs drained of strength, she did her best to walk unconcernedly to the frames she had left on the floor at the far end of the long room. Taking them out of the parcel of cloth whilst the sudden, taut silence hammered like nails into her nerves, with trembling fingers she brought the first canvas to a nearby easel. 'Painted in Ledingham, so I haven't exactly been wasting my time.' She tried to put grinding venom into the words. Oh, God, I'm making a fool of myself.

He strode over and bent his enormous chest towards the picture as though he was smelling a bad smell.

'My landlady,' she said sourly. Looking at it, Sara was startled that a certain sly lasciviousness had got into the picture which she had not exactly *seen* in the model – but it's not bad. Her own eyes lit up as she studied it, avoiding any glance at the looming, engrossed figure. 'Another,' he said curtly.

She picked up another canvas and dragged across another easel to stand next to the first. She placed the frame on it, moving it to an angle to catch a better light. Show him the cursed lot. Her feelings were still too overwrought to care whether she lived or died. She dragged another easel towards the others making a semi-circle round him, the massive form gazing at them intently, mindless of her.

Quickly, she darted across the aged floor and dragged yet another easel; she nearly ran for her final frame. Behind his back she reset the easel and with a defiant, showman's air, take-it-or-leave-it, she propped up her last picture she'd brought with her from Chesley, of Miss Davies – Dorothy.

Tensely she waited and slowly he turned round. This was the acid test. This was somebody he knew well and seemed to respect greatly. The face gazed at them in shining tranquillity, the neck and arms were living flesh, the gleaming black and crimson MA gown draped the comfortable bosom graciously. Seeing it, Miss Davies had wept and cried aloud that never in one so young had she perceived such an extraordinary command over the medium of oil paint.

All I know is that I want to paint portraits and I *shall* paint portraits. I'll paint them so that I can *feel* the bones under the skin and the marrow in the bones, and the blood in the veins. She felt the stubbornness and obstinacy welling deep inside her.

He didn't move. His face showed no expression. Her heart turned over in deepest trepidation. Oh my God, he doesn't like them. Dorothy's exaggerated, oh merciful heaven they're not any good! They're awful . . . Oh, don't speak, don't *tell* me . . . Frantically, her mind squirmed and floundered, utterly panic-stricken, she herself rushed in to break the silence.

'Look, these eyes are too highlighted,' she touched her landlady's eyes; 'this shadow's a bit smudged and this background is too dense.' Despairingly, her fingers hurried from picture to picture, get it in first. Don't give him the pleasure . . .

The studio door opening and students erupting into the room, distracting her. Old jackets, dark skirts, skinny sleeveless vests, musical motifs paint-encrusted on their jeans. Soon a couple of dozen students had clattered in, most of them her own age – twentyish with a few older, mature students. A motley lot of Ledinghamites, Sara noted, thoroughly downcast, feeling that she'd started hopelessly on the wrong foot and would never retrieve the situation.

'Ja, Wolfe,' 'Wako, Wolfe,' the students uttered disrespectful, cheerful greetings to the tutor and to each other. Quickly, in odd twos and ones and threes the whole class grouped itself with curious eyes and diverse-shaped mouths, like trout come up to feed, before Sara's oh, so nakedly exposed pictures.

'Wot the bloomin' 'ell!' 'Bai Jove;' 'What hev we heah!;' 'Dear, dear – portraits!' Words scattered about like gunshot and Sara's face shuttered down to a bland impenetrable mask; not for one second had she lessened her painful regard of Wolfe Falkland. In deep silence, regardless of everybody, he stared profoundly at her pictures. At last, oh at long last, the voice exploded in the air like a cannon's boom.

'A bloody natural! Would you believe it! A bloody natural!' The hooded eyes narrowed into Chinese slits through which the pupils shone in dark excited brilliance. 'Look fellows, look long at these pictures. She's got it! A chit of a girl! Well, I'm damned!' The mobile mouth widened in a loud belly-laugh. He made a big, helpless gesture of both arms to embrace the little circle of pictures.

'Now, you lot, meet your new student, Miss Dynamite! Miss Sara Nightingale!'

He bowed in obeisance and touched his forehead with the fingers of both hands in mock salaam. In a dream, Sara listened to his rich, yeasty voice expatiating on her canvases.

'Young lady, either you'll go right to the top or you'll fizzle out like a rocket on the moon. Look, chaps, they're full of faults, but look.' He used the occasion to give his flock a crisp lecture on rhythm and symmetry and the mixing of paint.

Relief! Oh merciful heaven, the infinite consummate relief! Sara's heart was reduced to deathly limpness after this baptism of fire. Quietly, she stood aside, separated herself mentally and physically from the press of students packed tightly and silently round the master. She viewed them from a pinnacle of utter detachment: I can see they worship him, ants gyrating round a black beetle . . . Oh hell, this should be my moment of glory. He's extravagantly praised my pictures and I feel as miserable as sin! She still smarted seethingly from the most merciless ticking off she'd ever received in her life.

Falkland at last called the class to order. 'Come on now, get cracking, we can't stand gazing at genius all night.' He came over to her, swaggering, looking thoughtful. 'Will you stay tonight?'

'No . . . I . . .' she looked down quickly at her dark red tailored jacket and dark- and light-grey softly folding dress underneath, her precious black see-through tights and fashionable black high-heeled shoes; she wasn't dressed to paint. Her mind held too much of chaos and confusion; she wasn't ready to paint or to hear that vibrant voice lecturing on Art. 'I – er, I haven't brought my overalls.'

The two students nearest to her paused in the busy business of setting up their easels and greeted the remark with a loud guffaw. 'I haven't brought my overalls,' they mimicked rudely; others quickly took it up, laughing, imitating, eyeing this new poshly dressed student, game for a bit of buffoonery. 'Ha, ha, she hasn't brought her overalls – not brought her overalls – Lord above . . .' Soon the whole class joined in, hooting it, stamping it, feet thundering rhythmically; they smacked their knees, held brushes on high. 'Ya-hoo, whoopee – she hasn't brought her bloody overalls!'

It was Ledingham versus Chesley; town and city rivals in politics, in everything; they didn't get on, didn't like each other. Sara felt like Capulet versus a couple of dozen Montagues – a full Indian war dance was in progress, yelling, roaring. 'She hasn't brought her overalls,' giggling girls and bellowing youths, pandemonium, all hell let loose . . .

What's so funny for heaven's sake? Damned stupid fools! Sara was utterly bewildered, flabbergasted, her startled green eyes imploring them to stop – give it up, finish it. Did these Ledingham barbarians paint cleaner pictures because they had paint sticking all over their clothes? Paradoxically, she knew that many of them did – grubbiness without often went with meticulous order within. Behind the pacifying smile, she got together her bundle of canvases.

'You can leave the frames behind if you like, we'll study them again.' Falkland had at last spoken, grinning widely at her discomfort, his white teeth flashing out of his black beard like a lighthouse flashing its beams in and out of dark rocks. With all the dignity she could muster, Sara walked towards the studio front door, her thick parcels of unframed canvases under her arm. A young, gurgling-throated youth stepped out of the dance and opened it for her with a flourish, gravely bowing her out with extravagant gallantry.

She forced herself to turn round at the door, and looked back at the man in whose care lay her future, her dream of a brilliant career. Black bushy eyebrows shot up and piercing eyes returned her gaze, scrutinising her, his mouth a huge grin . . .

Once outside, Sara stood stock-still, holding back smarting tears of mortification; she, Sara Nightingale, an object of ridicule, cut down to size. Certainly she'd wanted to impress her tutor on this her first encounter; she'd worn her smartest outfit with joy. What a crazy mistake! If I'd turned up in dirty jeans, hand-painted all over with pictures on thighs and bottom, I'd have been all right; that uniform was apparently de rigeur in Ledingham . . .

She sat very still and straight-backed in the bus taking her home, fiercely clutching her canvases, trying desperately to calm herself and take a detached view, as the bus loaded and unloaded itself on the way to the canal, but silly laughter kept ringing in her ears. What a peculiar noise laughter was, she tried to muse philosophically; ha, haw, haa – hee-hee-hee, it was only the human species that made noises like that. She saw their faces in front of her and the portrait painter took over.

He – Wolfe Falkland – had praised her painting lavishly, but that seemed of little consequence. She could manage the students in future – students were the same the world over, but that man? He, like God, had stood on one side, if not paring his nails, making no attempt to bring the silly farce to an end. It hurt the very core of her pride, her dignity. She'd never forgive him – never. And one day, however dim and distant, one day she'd get her own back, see how he'd feel as an object of ridicule with a whole group taking part in the fun; damn the man . . .

Head hot and throat dry, she turned the key in the lock of her front door in the corridor of her digs; surprisingly, her all-in-one bedsit, dining room and kitchen, had an air of familiarity and welcome.

Chapter Two

Am I doing the right thing? Mallory was suddenly startled by the thought.

'You say that Sara knows all about it?'

'No, sir, not yet, I can never get her on the phone. It's she who phones, she's never there. But, sir, you must please leave it to me to tell her all about it next Sunday, that's understood, I tell her first.'

'Well,' Sara's father, George Arthur Nightingale, hesitated for a bare second, then went on, 'It's now or never with me, Howard. I didn't think there was going to be all this rush. We'll have coffee here and then go on straight away to see my accountant. We see Mr Pollard at eleven-fifteen.'

'God, I'm dropping with sleep. I should be in bed!'

Sara's confession had banished sleep. He'd tossed and turned and got up and walked about his bedroom for three solid nights. 'I'm a wreck – I can't think straight.' Mallory was astonished to find himself where he was – sitting in Mr George Arthur Nightingale's stuffy little office, glass partitioned at the far end of a large warehouse, shelved from floor to ceiling and stacked with stocks of cloth – tweeds, brocades, curtain materials, lace, nets, quality materials, all the hues and colours for which Halifax and Huddersfield stocks were especially renowned. As general manager of this textile firm, owned by a London-based company, Sara's father had hugged a dream for years that one day he would be his own boss, a miraculous chance to buy his own small business, and it had miraculously fallen into his lap! He was on to it like a terrier after a ball.

'Forty thousand pounds' collateral will clinch the deal to make it comfortable. I've got the offer to buy before anyone else but there are rivals in the field. Preferential shares for you, of course. The bank has promised me a backup, and I can provide all the other capital myself, if you come in as my "sleeping 'partner". I said I'll pay twelve and a half per cent, which is better than you'd get from most other companies starting up. It's a cinch, Howard. I've got a good bit of stock up my sleeve. I've seen my solicitor, we'll see him again later.'

Mallory's brain began to reel with all this talk of finance – reserve funds, bad debts, travelling expenses, insurance, turnover – the man opposite didn't speak the same language, they scarcely occupied the same planet . . . Nightingale's fingers shot expertly through columns of figures in ledger after ledger.

Christ! The man's a fanatic! Imagine me being wildly competitive about my patients – give me a thousand tonsils and a couple of hundred adenoids, and we'll whip 'em all out in a week!

Howard knew that he was putting up a front and was throwing himself into this extraordinary situation with a curious sense of wool-gathering; the tight knot wound round his heart was slowly being wrenched apart and what he found there was pure, violent, teeth-grinding jealousy. Jealousy had reared its ugly head – a totally unknown emotion for him. Before last Sunday night his relationship with girls had been effortless, easy; but then he'd never been in love before, and these last two years Sara Nightingale had bewitched him utterly. What real hold had *he* on the affections of this green-eyed witch who these last five months had flown in from God-forsaken Ledingham, and allowed her light to flicker on him only on Sundays?

Last Sunday, as usual, late in the evening after he'd dropped her back at home after their day in the country at Wharton – his own home, his adoring parents so looked forward to their visits, and because of him they passionately loved Sara too; had she been an ugly little dwarf they would have still loved her. She was their only son's choice, they fully expected them to get married one day . . .

George Arthur, giving his daughter's suitor one for the road as he always did, the generous host informed Howard, in a quite unplanned and spontaneous burst of confidentiality, that he had been given a wonderful chance to acquire very quickly a small textile business which was right up his street. He had clinched the deal with the help of his bank, and was now looking around for a sleeping partner who would take shares in it to the tune of £40,000 which he still needed to make the finance comfortable. There the conversation on that particular subject had ended. Howard thought no more about it and, hearing Sara's and Cathy's voices as Sara entered the room to kiss her father goodbye until next Saturday, Howard and his love went hand in hand to the wide covered porch for their final passionate embrace and kisses.

Then she'd dropped her bombshell. 'Howard, darling, I think I ought to tell you before anybody else does,' she paused, hesitated, looked down on the floor then straight into his eyes, summoning the strength.

'These last months I've been out with another man – on Saturdays, not *every* Saturday. Howard, he's a councillor and sometimes he has council engagements, conferences and that sort of thing. He's Cathy's ex-fiancé, and Cathy's eleven years older than me so you can guess how old he is, he's in his mid-thirties . . .'

She stopped, his unbelieving blue eyes disturbed her but confession was in the air. 'He takes me to Manchester and we visit the art galleries and museums. He's very knowledgeable about art Howard, outside of local politics it's his hobby . . .'

'What's his name?' Howard had the rashness to ask, and scarcely recognised his own voice.

'Philip, Philip Carver. Look, Howard, you're on duty the minute you get to hospital, we'll talk about it next Sunday.' He could see that she hated upsetting him, her heart was torn as in telling him the news as he was receiving it. Sara shrank from hurting people knowingly, or she would have told him months ago. 'I love you, Howard, but you don't own me, you know.' And that was how it was left; she'd cut it short. They had a last passionate embrace and she almost ran indoors.

On duty he'd somehow kept the tumult at bay but, before he retired utterly exhausted to his room to sleep, the necessity for action was so irrefutable, so desperately urgent to do something – anything. The very next day, last Monday to be precise, a mere four days ago, he'd taken the first opportunity he could to phone her father and told him that *he* had the capital readily available for this thrilling new venture. 'So, sir, what about me as your sleeping partner?'

'I take it that you'll be seeing your own accountant or solicitor straight away?' said Sara's father, sitting opposite him now.

'No real need sir at the moment. I'll have to inform my bank, the money is on deposit there.'

'In the bank, on deposit?' Mr Nightingale mulled over the words incredulously. 'Not invested in anything? No unit trusts, or gilts, securities, shares?' He couldn't believe what he was hearing.

'Well, no, sir. I thought I'd play safe. I know nothing about financial matters.'

He checked himself from adding that he cared less. Of course, he should have sought advice years ago when he unexpectedly got the legacy. Only now, gazing at the astonished face of Sara's father, did he realise the enormity of the omission.

'I suppose it's a matter of temperament, sir. I've been on my last year doing my Practical and studying for my finals – there's been no time to think about things.'

George Arthur softened perceptibly and was prepared to digress for a second or two. 'And there's Sara, on her last lap too, m'boy.'

He had a charming smile. Howard liked the man; his iron-grey hair, short back and sides, his moustache to match, and he had a way of turning his head sideways and back again when he talked, rather like one of those Victorian-style toy models you found in amusement arcades. Howard noted it with a welcome smile in the midst of his wretchedness.

'I don't know to this day why she had to take herself off to Ledingham. I gather that she got herself a place at that tutor's studio she was so set on – she's a bit secretive, you know – didn't tell me much, she's very independent. She tells you things after she's done them.'

Yes, that's bloody well right, the young man agreed silently. 'She's been there over six months already, six months too long for me, sir,' Howard laughed feelingly. This sleeping-partner arrangement gave him a delicious idea of belonging to a family – the Nightingale family. It provided precious intimacy, goodwill.

'Well, she's outgrown her little attic studio at home – she'll have to look around and rent one or something. And how about you, Howard, now you've passed your finals. Are you staying on at the Infirmary?' Nightingale forced himself to remove his mind from being his own boss.

'I've been lucky to have been asked to stay on, they're so understaffed, but I'm looking around for a private practice. I want to set up as a GP. It's not easy to find the type I want and like everything else,' he added ruefully, 'they have to be efficiently run businesses these days.'

George Arthur laughed. 'Everything's a rat race! I like a challenge myself. I assume you have the necessary finance for that?'

Howard felt a bit nudged by the keen glance. I'm not such a dense clot as all that, he assured himself with quick inward questioning.

'Yes, I have, but that part's not difficult these days. I've taken advice.'

'Y'know, m'boy, we have to make these big decisions for ourselves all our lives, not just when we're young – look at me, I'm fifty-four!'

'I think it takes great guts to be doing what you're doing, sir.' Sara would understand when he put it to her. She loved and admired her father, and of all the family, she was her father's favourite.

'You say your uncle left you this legacy?'

'Yes, my mother's only brother. He was a mathematics master at a boarding school – a bachelor; he had his own bedroom in our house and spent all his holidays with us when he wasn't abroad somewhere. He died six years ago after suffering four years with cancer. He was in such pain even the morphine couldn't control it at the end. It was this that persuaded me to make medicine my career instead of the army in which, as you know, my father and my forebears served since time immemorial. My uncle had a cottage but he seldom used it, full of furniture, and we've still got it stored in our attic at Wharton. He left all that to my mother, but amazingly he had bundles of shares and investments stashed away and all that he left to his nephew – me! I let my bank handle the whole affair and then they put it on deposit until I knew what to do with it. Perhaps I have been negligent – I've been putting it off for ever . . .' Howard finished lamely . . .

'Well all we do now, Howard, is to see my accountant; I've made the appointment, we've just time to have coffee first.' With a bound he was at the office door, and shortly afterwards a matronly figure, one of his staff, hustled in with the brew.

'Carver, Pollard and Drake – a very established firm.'

'Carver, did you say Carver, sir?'

'Yes, why?'

'Councillor Philip Carver, by any chance?'

'The same.'

Howard breathed deeply. Coincidence? Was there such a thing, or was it a process, a pattern? he wondered, confused; instinctively he had known that the man was Sara's Councillor Carver, she hadn't told him what he did for a living, but the Councillor part had stuck . . .

'I know Philip Carver very well, m'boy – he was nearly my son-in-law. Years ago he and Cathy were engaged, but the engagement didn't last very long, though Philip courted her long enough. I don't know why it was broken off – it happened suddenly. I was very sorry, he's a nice chap. It's Stanley Pollard we'll be seeing.'

Sister Cathy's cast-off! Howard hated himself for the relish it caused him – the man must have suffered as he was abashed and suffering now. Catherine, on the very few times he'd met her on Sundays, was always sprawled on the sitting-room settee, in exotic housecoats with very deep cleavage, a drink and a box of chocolates on the table by her side. She reminded him of a beautiful leopard lying indolently in the lower branches of a tree, but if she chose to be aroused, she'd spring up and eat a man for breakfast. She had the same dark green eyes, but a sulky mouth, very unlike her younger sister Sara's. Howard wasn't in the least attracted or interested in her sultry type of beauty, although all the same he could see how men could be totally entrapped by her.

Over coffee, George Arthur allowed himself the duty to talk family to this young man, who craved intimacy with it to such an extent as to become a sleeping partner which helped enormously to raise his own ambition to become his own boss.

'Cathy's job is first-rate, you know. She's a clever buyer, though I

19

doubt she could sell so well – this designer fashion business takes her to Rome, Amsterdam and Paris and she stays in swanky hotels, no wonder she remains unmarried.' He made the same engaging movements of his head, and then looked squarely, speculatively at Howard, as though, here again, he might be gazing at a future son-in-law.

'For myself, I'm sorry that we've got an artist on our hands. Sara could have done equally as well as Cathy in business. I could have put her in the way of some excellent prospects in my field. It's not all roses bringing up a family, Howard, I assure you.'

Howard felt that, unconsciously, George Arthur was feeding on Howard's own deep desire to belong to this Nightingale family. Mr Nightingale's voice had a soft West-Country burr as he talked. He was a country lad, his parents were from farming stock, and George Arthur himself was the typical, ambitious, energetic specimen who left his roots behind, moved to London and then Manchester. He'd got himself into the best, sound quality textiles, and here, better late than never, he'd reached the pinnacle of his success. Next week he'd be his own boss; he had stock up his sleeve – it was a cinch.

Howard, bleary-eyed with deprivation of sleep on what was supposed to be his rest day, was thrilled with the concord – he clung to it like a blessed raft in a rough sea; to be closely drawn into the Nightingale circle, to be accepted as *the* man in Sara's life, apparently now against the odds, was like defiantly holding aloft the banner of Love, at whatever cost, and whatever the failure would do to his self-esteem: and why be so bloody pessimistic about his chances? Love *was* competitive, like everything else, and he would stake his bid against *Councillor* Philip Carver; inwardly he gave the word 'councillor' a particular sneer.

He remembered now with pleasure and great gratitude the party the Nightingale family had thrown for him in their home to celebrate the passing of his finals and getting his doctorate. Beautiful Mrs Nightingale, so often the 'absent mother – never there', was decidedly there on that occasion, dispensing the honours, the champagne. Sara's gang of girls, all four of them, turned up, each with her boyfriend. Cathy brought along her standby, manager of the Odeon cinema, and Howard himself brought along several colleagues – those who, with him, had triumphantly passed their finals, together with, alas, those who had not. The only absent ones were Olivia, the married sister whom Howard had never met, and her husband, both of whom were abroad on holiday.

'And now Olivia's gone and married the wrong man,' Mr Nightingale sighed heavily. 'Lester Reid, the estate agent, you know; the man had too much too soon, can't carry corn, never done a proper day's work in his life. You don't run a business from a golf course and race meetings,' he snorted, 'dressed in holiday suits and bow ties!'

The disgust with which he anathematised bow ties left Howard helpless with inner laughter; it surprised him that in the state he was he could find something to laugh at. 'How's Felix, sir?'

Felix was the absent Nightingale brother in this family of absences rather than presences. From benches as part of the audience in his younger days, Howard had several times watched Felix play a brilliant game of ice hockey in Manchester, and deeply admired him from afar. He knew that now he lived abroad somewhere, and had rather blotted his copy-book with some lively indiscretions in Chesley – fast driving, never settling down to a job for any length of time, and a few scrapes with girls . . .

'Felix – oh, he's all right, I think – on a sugar plantation in Guyana. He phoned us at Christmas – we haven't heard a word since . . .' George Arthur looked at his watch. 'We ought to be getting along now, mustn't keep Pollard waiting. Thank you for offering me a lift.'

Howard's second-hand, shabby little runabout Renault was hardly an impressive vehicle to escort the new boss to Carver, Pollard and Drake. He was lucky to park it just across the road from their prestigious offices. Unused to the interiors of business headquarters, to Howard the Reception was very impressive indeed; there was an over-large umbrella plant and a bushy bush in a tub; a bowl of fresh-cut flowers took up practically the whole of the space on the reception desk. A girl behind it explained sweetly that Mr Pollard was on the telephone, but wouldn't be long. 'Please take a seat,' she motioned to two light blue, leather-covered straight-backed chairs.

They had scarcely sat down before a tall, shirt-sleeved-and-tie man walked out of the farthest door, carrying a sheaf of papers in both hands. George Arthur jumped up at once. 'Well, Philip, nice to see you.'

Philip Carver paused in his stride, they were shaking hands. 'Let me introduce you – Howard, this is Philip – Mr Carver, senior partner here.' Howard got up smartly from his chair and found himself shaking hands with a tall man who made the necessary noises in the formality of introduction, courteously and politely, in a very cultured voice.

'Howard is to be my 'sleeping partner' in my new business,' Mr Nightingale explained, with a broad smile of triumph.

'Oh, really? Congratulations, sir, I hope you both do well.' He had shifted papers from one hand to the other to shake hands with the two clients, and now shifted them back again, smiled and nodded and headed quickly to the room having a large notice on the door notifying everybody that it belonged to Mr E Drake. Howard scarcely saw him leave . . .

My God – so that's Councillor Philip Carver! His wits plummeted and he shut out for a minute what his companion was whispering about. He's good-looking, elegant. As a doctor, Howard was trained to look at people shrewdly. It's a scholarly face, academic, good looks in the classical mould if you like that sort of type. A deep inferiority complex was overtaking him, and he did his best to squash it: I can just see him with those long hands putting his long finger tips together and sticking his chin in them, elbows on table, talking about recessions and profits and business graphs – a desk man . . .

It had always been Howard's dictum that people who look alike *are* alike basically but, although he could sum up his patients physically, he could never peer into their minds to any real effect.

The two men were quickly ushered into Mr Pollard's room and were closeted with him for nearly an hour. Documents were signed, new appointments made. They re-emerged into the blessed fresh air, the die was cast, Howard Mallory was up to his neck in it – the fully authenticated 'sleeping partner' in an ambitious man's venture into being his own boss, to the tune of £40,000 with interest accruing to Howard at regular intervals: solicitors and accountants just about tied up. He felt hopelessly out of his depth.

The street was crowded; oblivious of them, Mr Nightingale stalked along, head held high, his mane of grey hair waving in the wind. He's like Don Quixote and I'm Sancho Panza being led to dusty death! Howard mocked himself ironically, still smarting that all through the performance in Mr Pollard's office, he had been the silent one, contributing nothing, totally ignorant in such matters, cut down to size . . .

Mr Nightingale offered him lunch at the Masonic Hall restaurant – his mecca – where he could stand at the bar and converse with all the other business gents, but Howard refused, dropping him there and returning straight to the hospital, feeling so tired, worn out, scarcely able to keep his eyes open.

Parking and locking the car, as sturdy-framed as himself, the blustering wind disturbing his unruly fair locks, he made his way slowly in a confused dream towards the entrance of the Chesley Royal infirmary, its front facade still Victorian Chesley, although the inside had been fully modernised. Howard's room, particularly, up two flights of stairs if you didn't use the lift, was pleasantly situated in the new wing. In the courtyard he suddenly stopped short, and crossed his arms over his chest tightly, his two hands clutching him each side of his jacket.

Philip Carver! He had actually seen, even shaken hands with, his adversary, his antagonist. He felt so deeply hurt, wounded, that Sara should treat him in this way; allow him to go on blissfully believing that she spent her Saturdays as usual with her gang of four, her school and student girlfriends; that they met together in pubs and discos – her own stag nights as she christened them, whilst he, if he was free at all, which let's face it, wasn't often, so that he could wangle his Sundays free. As Vice-Chairman of the Rugby Supporters Club he had his own stag nights to see to; it was his duty to entertain visiting teams in the home matches, convivially round the bar; the committee meetings he organised and attended to as general dogsbody . . .

All that must end. He'd resign from active membership, he determined with the fiercest conviction. I'm not going to bloody well let her out of my sight if I can help it.

Jealousy! The strength of this new emotion utterly confounded him. He'd been easy and comfortable with the opposite sex; had never been in love before he met Sara; studying hard, keeping up with everybody, bonding with his fellow men . . . Jealousy! Nourishing continually on what it fed on; curling itself round his heart like a snake. Did Carver kiss her? Fondle her? Yet hurt and dismayed as he was, he couldn't bring himself to condemn Sara's conduct entirely out of hand: if they couldn't arrange a phone time, Sara not having a phone in her digs, he <u>could</u> have sent her notes, love letters, not throwing himself into his work so hard to speed the time until Sundays. He must forgive her. Oh God! she's all I want, she was everything – her intelligence, humour, gaity, periods of quiet and repose that relaxed him utterly, impetuous and restless as he was – always this urge to move about, get up and walk, act . . . He could see her before him now, the wide smile, the thoughtful, expressive deep green eyes.

'You don't *own* me, you know,' he heard her plaintive explanation. For Christ's sake – love should be the happiest, most joyous experience alive – not this low, burning heat of desire that choked and tightened your guts and interfered with swallowing. Doctors should be taught to treat love as a disease, he declared despairingly.

Upstairs, he walked into the doctors' communal washroom to, euphemistically, wash his hands. Three of his colleagues were already there, coming in and out of the loos and standing at washbasins and hand machines. Peter Masham was bawdily declaiming his latest experience, as he combed his hair in the mirror. 'Gee whizz. My God, I'm telling you, chaps, I've never seen such boobs. If she was farmed out she'd make a fortune.'

Old Flaherty, the psychologist, drying his hands on a paper towel, took it on himself to reprove the irreverent reprobate, 'Man, it's not the *size* that matters, it's the quality and the texture . . .' The spluttering, highly imaginative Douglas Noble chipped in. 'Lord, what d'you think? In Geriatrics, believe it or not, a frightful old woman was swearing blind to our learned Eustace Cromarty that our dashing Tim Rowe had got into bed with her. Can't you hear our Cromarty's chuckling old croak – 'Madam, surely my dear, you're not *complaining*?"

The rest of his anecdote was drowned in laughter and Howard found himself laughing with them. This was men's talk, this was normality, this was something he knew about and understood. He had his work and he loved it. His deep inner tenderness, covered up always by light-hearted exuberance, his deep desire always to prop up and sustain others – he had no need to take such a poor view of himself. George Arthur *should* be rewarded for his business acumen to the tune of £40,000 with interest accruing to himself as very much the sleeping partner. Sara *would* be pleased that he'd taken his financial affairs in hand, not that the subject had ever been discussed between them. He'd tell her all about it on Sunday. Philip Carver's relationship was nothing compared with his own induction into the Nightingale family.

'Not sleeping' was an entirely new experience for Howard; that had always been Sara's problem as long as he had known her. He tore off his clothes and made straight for his bed. Lying there, he found himself wishing passionately that Sara was there beside him, but decidedly not as a *sleeping* partner. The subject of 'women' engaged him; the eye-in-the-storm; Man's unquenchable curiosity about them, and the buried sense of loss that women bore children and they could not, and for a physician as he was, the enormous satisfaction that at least one had the means to soften Nature's all-powerful, despotic, breeding genius. He turned over, and was out like a light.

Chapter Three

'Twins?'

'Yes, identical twins. This is the problem I set you, my dear sir, identical twins have fallen in love with the same girl. What do they do?'

As usual, Sara Nightingale was in full, laughing spate, and as usual, Philip Carver was enjoying himself immensely. It had become a settled routine now to drive her to Manchester for a night on the town and sometimes, as today, Saturday, to arrive as early as possible so that they might visit an art gallery or a museum, or opt for a theatre matinée, and tonight, making their final destination, the well-known, reasonably tasteful, reasonably quiet night-club, The Bear's Paw.

'Well, what do they do? Toss up for it?'

'Oh no, sir, they are decent, ordinary, jealous, possessive, full-blooded males. In this country a woman is not allowed to marry two men at once, and neither man can bear the thought of sharing her in bed, so what do they do?'

'Doesn't *she* have a choice?'

'But, my dear sir, they are identical twins. She can't distinguish one from the other!'

She exaggerated the earnest mannerisms of a typical, learned college lecturer, leaning forward, arms on the table cloth, the meal finished, the wine half drunk, her head moving, left and right, converting the dimly lit candles on the tables and shining on the gilt chairs into an imaginary students' classroom.

'Well, sir, they cut her in half of course!' she chuckled throatily. 'Solomon's solution would be perfectly natural in the circumstances.'

'Good God, Sara,' he laughed in mock horror, 'you terrify me!'

Why had he laid siege to this clever, highly intelligent, delightful young girl barely out of her teens, when he was a confirmed bachelor already into his mid-thirties? It had been very clear from the start. Sara was the younger sister of Catherine, eleven years her senior, to whom he had been engaged to marry, and who, at the last moment had thrown him over. It was history, but he still had nightmares, spasms of bitterness about it all. On Sara's insistence, and indeed on his own, they met clandestinely, sub-rosa, and understandably she did not want any ill feeling or problems between herself and her sister. Manchester was sufficiently far away from Chesley to avoid, with luck, prying eyes and gossip.

'Mind you, sir, they wouldn't cut her in half vertically, but horizontally; then sir, the question is, which half should be given to whom. The top half to one, and the bottom half to the other, which would be the nicest?'

There was a mocking, teasing ribaldry in the proposition, but he knew that it was only words; she clung to her virginity as fiercely as her sister was outrageously promiscuous, and had been all the time of their so-called engagement, as he had so painfully discovered after all was finished between them.

'The problem, sir,' Sara smiled disarmingly, 'would have to be solved by a third party. Arbitration must be accepted at all levels. It finishes up as not a personal but a communal thing. Why, my dear sir, it may even go to The Hague, to a Court of Appeal, the European Common Market. It becomes an international problem. There's no such thing as personal choice, is there?'

'You've put your finger on it, my dear, Fate decides.'

'Fate, sir,' Sara answered firmly, 'is another name for Mother Nature, MN for short. You work it out, good sir. It all boils down to bodies and Mother Nature. That's the beginning and the end of it, the whole, monstrous tragedy of the human condition.' Dramatically, she lowered her arms, hung her head and collapsed back into the chair.

'Bats,' Philip countered, playing up to her with the lightness of heart he always experienced in the merry, gay, bantering company which often had underlying strata of seriousness. Sara asked pertinent questions of life.

'Bats?'

'Yes, bats. We should be like bats. Blind bats have a magical sonic system whereby they can fly perfectly safely and unerringly in the pitch dark, avoiding all obstacles. They know how to fly through and around all danger. Think, if we could do the same – shall we dance?'

He glided her through the sedate couples on the tiny dance floor, their images reflected in the huge floor-to-ceiling Napoleonic antique mirror in the centre of one wall, with its heavily gilded and ornamental carved frame, the huge crystal candelabra hanging from the Adams-style ceiling casting deep shadows in the dim corners whence came the sound of soft blues music. He was thrilled, more than he dared admit, by the feel of her, almost weightless, as her steps matched his; she was much more fragile than Cathy. He wondered sometimes whether the many-coursed dinner which gave him such pleasure to order for her made up for the semi-starvation he was sure she endured for Art's sake in Ledingham.

After the dance, he led her back to their small corner table and filled her glass with wine. If Sara had heartily eaten the food, he himself had drunk far more of the wine.

'I must be careful,' Philip told himself. 'Mustn't drink too much, not take any chances on that score.' The sight of her was exciting him tonight, even beyond his natural appetite for female company. The black, simply designed, low-cut semi-evening dress she wore so suited the pale skin and sparkling green eyes, and he wasn't to know that she had borrowed it for the occasion from Annette, one of her gang of girls, a regular custom between all of them. Her neck was slender and her dark hair done up high behind her ears.

Spiritedly, they began to talk about the Mondrian exhibition she had especially asked to see this afternoon at the Mountjoy Gallery.

'Frankly, Sara, Mondrian is not my cup of tea. Actually, I liked the sculpture better – I'm leaning more and more towards sculpture. I thought the Barbara Hepworth was magnificent, and I'd like to take you to Leeds some time to see the Henry Moores, they're wonderful there.'

'Sculpture as well as pictures, how old in wisdom you are, Philip!'

'I was born old, and looking at you I feel younger and younger every minute.'

Sara stared at her plate as though she was gazing into a crystal ball. 'As an accountant you *should* like Mondrian, you know,' she ruminated. 'Mondrian's a painting mathematician; he's all dots and dashes and you have to read it like a Morse code. His message is a tune, I think; put a series of five lines like a musical score right across the canvas and a treble clef on the left-hand side, and all those black blobs and grey dashes are pauses and rests, like rising and descending musical scales. You have a tune picked out like those pieces of metal sticking out of a pianola. I swear Mondrian hummed tunes and painted them as he hummed.'

'What tunes? Handel's *Messiah* or *Home Sweet Home?*' Philip rose to her bait as always. 'Those blobs are meant to be the irreducible minimum of all the shapes and colours in the world – the acme of perfect simplicity.'

'I call it paucity,' Sara replied shortly. 'There's a huge difference. Now take Paul Klee – he just takes his brush for a walk, and there's not a single repetition anywhere.'

Their views ran together as they plunged headlong into the exciting topic of art, her lively, dedicated mind and fluency of expression leading him on to an exhilaration of his own maximum. They were *en rapport* and

Philip bent himself to listen and entertain her. Sara gathered up her handbag, asked to be excused, and made her way to the Ladies, here still euphemistically called the Powder Room.

Suddenly it was upon him. Catherine! A feeling of being pulled back physically into thralldom, caught by the hairs, a vivid re-entering into the chaotic thinking which had so disastrously characterised his misspent youth – that darkest epoch. It didn't do to look back, not to one's dead self, a self never so dead that a place, an occasion, couldn't bring it all back again; he remembered with a kind of masochism that he had on one occasion brought Catherine to this very place, The Bear's Paw, not called a night-club in those days. How to pull the goose out of the bottle without hurting the goose or breaking the bottle? In your mind's eye the goose was already out, indestructibly alive; the goose never dies . . .

A vision of Catherine startlingly alive appeared before him, as tumultuously expectant, reckless in adoration, his younger self gazed at the smiling, nonchalant, incredibly beautiful young woman, Sara's age, her face hovering on the very brink of that look, the look he so patiently waited for, the look he so tremblingly craved to see, the look he'd wasted years of his youth in vain to possess; the unmistakable message that she loved him, that his passionate love was returned, that she wanted him and could no more live without him than he could without her. One radiant, precious look. He realised too late that it would never come.

Gazing silently round at the sprightly middle-aged dancers twirling each other around, and listening to the low-sounding beat of the music, he felt again the same surging emotion, the same rending disappointment of all those long-ago hopes dashed. He cursed and admonished himself, the pain was all there, leprous, as new-minted as yesterday.

He watched keenly, his eyes taking in every detail of Sara walking the short distance back towards him; so vivacious, so young, tender and gay; he realised that she was inexpressibly dear to him. and in her own right, he protested vehemently, for the right motives, if for the wrong reasons. For he knew that mixed up in these clandestine, secret meetings with the younger sister, he was exacting some sort of sweet revenge. Did he want this girl to fall in love with him, truly, wildly? Or was he using her as a kind of anodyne, a healing remedy for the raw soreness he still felt deep in his heart?

Sara sat down, looking at him quizzically. She actually asked for some wine, and holding the glass cupped in both hands, elbows on the table, she asked him casually, 'Do you know Howard Mallory by any chance?'

'Howard Mallory? Well, strangely enough, it so happens that I have met him very recently – the Mallorys of Wharton Hall?'

'Yes.'

'Why should I know him?' he asked curiously.

'Oh, no reason really. He's a doctor, you know. He's at the Chesley Royal. We meet on Sundays.'

'Oh.' he experienced a little gnawing tug at his nerves. It was just as when Cathy had told him in the same casual way that she'd been meeting other men, she had tired of him, that she didn't love him, never had and never would.

'Yes, all day Sundays, he takes me out to Wharton and we drive around and visit pubs and country houses and places, but we walk mostly – for miles. I love walking after the bad air of Ledingham. It does me the world of good.' She finished in a rush and smiled at him widely, but with a kind of wariness. As though she was deliberately disguising her own feelings in searching for his. Good God! Was the boot on the other foot? Was this her way of trying to find out whether he was falling in love with her? He collected himself quickly, searched his mind, and with some satisfaction he remembered a little nugget of information he could impart.

'Well, as a matter of fact, I was going through our mail only two or three days ago and turned up some documents I handed over straight away to one of my partners – Stanley Pollard.'

Pollard, Carver and Drake – the long-standing, well-known and very respectable firm of chartered accountants which his grandfather had founded, in which his father had practised in his turn, and in which Philip in his own turn was now senior partner, and dealt with George Arthur Nightingale's financial affairs since time immemorial. The firm did his tax returns, mortgages and what-have-you, and George Arthur had seen no reason to change because of his daughter's shameful and regrettable break with Carver. Such personal matters do not interfere with business and it was a long time ago.

Nevertheless, since the break-up he had never set foot again in the Nightingale household: Carver had tactfully passed all the interviews, and transferred all correspondence connected with them, to his good partner, Pollard.

'It was something to do with Howard Mallory, a new venture your father is engaged in. There was a document from his solicitors, I think, about the conveyancing of some premises. I only glanced at them before handing them over to Cecil – Pollard, you know. Mallory was to be a sleeping partner in the enterprise. He's put capital into it.'

'What? A sleeping partner? What are you talking about, Philip?'

'Oh dear! I don't think I'm breaching confidentiality by telling you this, after all I was just about "one of the family" at one time, wasn't I!' For a moment his expression changed, and his voice took on a note of bitter irony. He looked away to regain his composure, then turned to her with a smile and continued dryly, 'You'll be hearing about it soon enough anyway.'

'A sleeping partner – I don't understand,' Sara repeated helplessly. She sank back into her gold-painted chair, the picture of astonishment, and Carver recognised in himself a twinge of satisfaction, a nasty little sense of triumph over this younger man monopolising her on Sundays.

Howard Mallory of Wharton Hall? He knew something about the Wharton Hall Mallorys, everybody who was anybody in Chesley knew about them of course. Why, they once owned a lot of the land Chesley town was built on. All sold off at one time or another, over a century ago, when the Mallorys were the local squires; nothing left now but the woebegone old Hall itself, to pay homage to past glories.

'I can't believe it – it's not true! Neither my father nor Howard, nor anybody else has mentioned a word to me.' Her voice trailed away in puzzled amazement.

'I'm sure I'm not mistaken, Sara. Howard Mallory, a business partnership, something about new premises, an office . . .'

Her upset was palpable, and Philip's voice softened as he added soothingly, 'You'll catch up; these things take on a momentum of their own.'

She stared across at him, the expressions chasing across her face chronicling only too plainly all that she was feeling. There was a long pause between them.

'You know, Philip,' she said pensively, 'when I was very young, an infant about five years old, at Christmas time my father would entertain us with conjuring tricks. He'd get three glass tumblers and put a cloth over them, then he'd make passes over them and say a lot of rigmarole – abracadabra, abracadabra, abracadabra – then he'd dramatically swish away the cloth and the tumblers wouldn't be there, or other objects would have changed places underneath the tumblers. It made me mad that I couldn't see how it was done – I used to cry! Even now I can't bear to see these magic shows on TV, I get the same reaction. I want to *know*. It's no good just observing, if you can't see *how* a thing is accomplished.'

Philip laughed indulgently, but in spite of himself there was still this mean little triumph that he was one up on this suitor, Mallory.

'I'm sorry I can't tell you more, Sara dear – there must be a reason for the secrecy.'

'Are you a Mason, Philip?' she asked him pointedly.

'Yes, but not a very active one.'

'There you are again – secrets! And I'll bet *you* won't tell me those secrets either. When I was a schoolgirl I came across father's Masonic regalia, and a book of the rules and mysterious codes and things. I took them into my bedroom and pored for hours over them, and I couldn't make head or tail of any of it. I felt so frustrated,' she said gaily, remembering. 'And I nagged father for days to tell me the secrets. He, of course, roared with laughter and never did. Now he's up to his damned magic tricks all over again.'

Philip tried gentle humour, but she wasn't having any – it got him nowhere. Sara was very perturbed and put out. 'And I shan't be seeing father tomorrow, damn it all! I can't confront him with it as to how much of it is true. He's gone off to London for a board meeting or something. He often travels Saturdays for meetings on Mondays. I suppose he meets his pals socially . . .'

Or his mistress? Fleetingly, the thought entered Philip's mind, but he dismissed it. No, not George Arthur. He wasn't the type, any more than this one – his daughter, could be prevailed upon – or could she? He stopped short, appalled at what he was imagining. I'm a decent-living man, I hope. I don't lay siege to young virgins about sixteen years my junior . . . 'My dad always said that the next step up the greasy pole would be his becoming managing director of the whole caboosh in London, but I know that deep down, more than anything else, he wanted his very own business, be beholden to nobody but himself, be his own boss.' Upset as she was over Philip's electrifying news regarding Mallory, there was pride in her voice.

'Perhaps it was a question of now or never. That's a thought, my dear,' Philip tried to placate her.

They danced again, but the sparkle had gone out of the evening. Sara was quiet, preoccupied, away from him. It was very late and the place was quickly emptying.

'Let's go home, there's a long drive ahead of us.'

Outside, the mid-March weather was blustery and cold and both got into the car quickly, Sara wrapped up in a warm coat. They fastened their seat belts and, to ease the tension, Philip groped in his mind for something to say.

'I remember when you were a kid of about twelve, Sara, you sat beside me on the sofa in your sitting room, the artistic one, forever carting tins of varnish and turpentine up to your little studio in the attic. You used to crow over to me the names on the paint tubes, let me see, mineral violet, cyanine blue – er –'

'Terra Vere,' she helped him out sleepily. 'The names have all changed now there's the acrylics and plastics.'

'You recited them as though they were the most poetic lines from Shelley's Odes, and by heaven, couldn't you argue about Braque's 'blocks' and Seurat's 'massing' even in those days. You used to knock me out flat.'

It was all flooding back in an avalanche of memory; his own patient expounding of the Dutch School, her hot defence of the Venetian masters, the effervescent schoolgirl sitting beside him crazily eager to show him her latest copies of Greek primitives, Egyptian art, Mexican frescoes.

Philip was a man of parts, and Art was one of his many interests, as was his council work – a new, astonishingly rewarding activity and it filled up all the gaps in his familyless life.

Silence fell between them, her head was turned away from him towards her window and he thought she was asleep. For long enough on these Saturday nights he felt that he'd been acting a part, defeated by a situation he was not internally organised to withstand any more. If life existed only in straight lines, without all these Gilbertian situations and awful compromises, like meeting this young girl secretly, stealthily . . .

Life should make sense. It should be logical, rational and it was neither one nor the other. The torment of physical desire he was feeling for her, his mind swerving towards Catherine, his heart unquietly tagging after, the tenacity of feeling which still clung to her name. It was all a nonsense.

Sara on her own was one thing, but mixed up in his mind and emotions so passionately with her accursed sister, she was poison – dangerous, forbidden fruit! He checked an inadvertent sigh of what a vista of freedom, of disentanglement, of throwing off this tossing about in lustful desire which could never be satisfied, would do for him.

'I didn't know Howard had any capital. We never talked about money. He said it was vulgar. I hope he's got preferential shares. I know what that means. I haven't listened to my father all these years . . .'

She went on in astonishing detail about dividends and tax savings. Good Lord! She's got a business head as well as an artist's. Her father's daughter as well as her mother's . . .

'You're gnawing at it like a dog with a bone, Sara, my love.'

It thoroughly annoyed him that all this time, whilst he was on fire for her, her mind had been steadily fixed on Howard Mallory's money; that his invisible presence had thoroughly douched him in cold water, but did nothing to put out the flames.

She turned her head away, closed her eyes, and as the car purred on and ate up the miles, he understood, through her quiet breathing, that she'd fallen asleep.

She's got this chap she meets every Sunday; so what? His own Sundays were always the same, a round of golf with one or other of his male friends, a pleasurable lunch at the golf club, and in the evenings, a game of bridge. A most eligible bachelor, he was never short of invitations here, there and everywhere. Oh, he'd had his affairs – safe affairs with separated wives or divorcees who wanted marriage as little as he did. His affairs always ended amicably, nebulously . . .

He was given occasionally to taciturn fits of depression, moroseness, the evidence of good physical health and natural human sexual appetite, he'd find himself suddenly immersed in erotic fantasies, images, tensions, to be absolved with cynicism and turgid self-censure.

This slip of a girl asleep beside him induced a frantic fit of maudlin shame, as he struggled to get out of this dark inwardness; part of him craved to be as he'd always been; to be his age, to live every day in the present, not to suffer this tossing about with adolescent desire until he met her again. He wanted to regain his somewhat bored, jaundiced view of the world and his particular brand of negative contentment, which at least had in it no element of pain.

Sara stirred herself wide-awake and apologised for having fallen asleep.

'It must have been the wine, Philip, unaccustomed as I am . . .'

It had indeed been very potent – Laffite, the wine he liked best, even he, who drank his fair share, was feeling its effects.

'I forgive you, Sara.'

He stopped the car in the road about twenty yards away from the Nightingales' home, as he had always done. The sharp wind whipped up the unswept leaves and quick peltings of rain beat furiously on the windows. Obliquely through the driving mirror he saw her green eyes shining, her dark hair she'd undone fell across her shoulders loosely in shadows.

'It really isn't fit to leave you to walk home tonight, even this short distance.'

'Well, if you'd like to risk it – I don't think we'll see Catherine driving up the path at this time of night.'

Sara's throaty laugh disturbed him. There were little gestures, small mannerisms, which always brought her sister back into the picture. It was not possible for Sara herself to understand how much the past, knocking at his heart with so much insistence, was intruding into this moment. To give way to it was tantamount to an extreme act of masochism.

The familiar cannonballs on the wooden gate posts came out of the night as a darker blackness; the trees, rocking wildly, bent their branches in low salute as they passed the laurel drive, carefully stopping short of the large brick porch with its three steps up, appearing to yawn indifferently and indiscriminately, not caring who entered its portals.

His arm came into contact with her coat, sending a deep shaft of exasperation through him. Quickly, he sought inside for her body warmth, his mind focusing slowly on the head cradled against him. Pulling her face into his line of vision with his own, he took her mouth, infinitely desirable, and the opiate of past dreaming finding some reality at last, his nerve-endings split into proliferating heat, the blood thickened, the fire licked inside of him.

Oh, my God! It needs cold-blooded guts to ask a girl to be your mistress! Always before it had been the women who'd done the asking – how do I ask? I'm not capable – I'm simply past the stage of necking and she can take gallons of it.'

'Philip.'

Her smothered whisper added dangerous fuel to his fevered imagination.

'Philip – you've not seen any of my pictures for years. You know my garden studio is only ten yards behind these bushes.'

She released an arm clasped tightly round his neck and pointed in the dark towards a thick clump of bushes and tall, jumbled stalks of dead climbing flowers.

'Would you like to see them?'

Strategy! He felt his whole mind and body stiffening. What next? In a quick, transient clearing of the dark he thought he caught her worshipping look of love, just for a second, at once concealed, or had he imagined it? Never once had she spoken of love, not in words, but sometimes . . .

He would adore her to love him; to give it to him as a gift, asking nothing from him, and obscurely he felt great satisfaction from his own seeming inability to truly love any woman in return. Love had become for him the enemy, the trickster. He had to put up a high, strong fence between himself and love. Love's ravages were too great; he had to pay it homage from a safe distance. He'd *had* love.

'You said only last week you'd *like* to see them,' she reminded him, her tone cool as though she herself would be unworried whether he saw them or not.

'Why, yes, I did.'

Why this strange hesitancy to accept? Derisively he lashed himself. He was distrustful of women.

I ought to be shot. I'm like a dog on heat and she shames me.

Penitently he smiled down at her and acquiesced. 'Come on, then – a walk in the rain will do me good.' Clear my head, he added silently.

Huddled together they made a dash across the lawn and down through the bushes along the rockery path.

'Oh, good,' Sara exclaimed laughingly, 'my old oil stove's burning. Sometimes the draughts blow it out.'

A dim light could be seen shining palely and secretly through a pane of glass. Good Lord! Then she'd intended this all along?

'Been keeping it warm for me?' He made no attempt to soften the sarcasm and was staggered and quite unprepared for the sudden furious turning on him, stopping in her tracks as though for two pins she wouldn't go on.

'What do you take me for? It burns night and day for my pictures. My mother sees to it when I'm away.'

'Sorry, Sara,' he apologised brusquely.

She led him into the thick shadows of the old wooden summerhouse, sodden in the rain with unkempt grasses and the briars of old roses getting in the way. But it struck him with a pang that in broad daylight on a bright summer's day it would be a pretty Hansel and Gretel-ish sort of place, a trysting ground for young lovers, and again he found himself torn between acting the Don Juan, a burning desire to ask her to come away with him, and at all costs to keep his collected pose of urbanity, elegance and slight langour. How so ludicrously different, the image and the man!

Inside, she fumbled for and found two stumps of candles and Philip took a lighter from his pocket and lit them.

'There they are.' Sara pointed without preamble to a row of six or seven paintings propped on a shelf and, turning sideways, carefully skirting the paint table, raising the candles high in each hand, Philip gave them knowledgeable attention. One, terrifying in its ugliness, a bitter landscape of abandoned, worked-out earthmines, a veritable Slough of Despond; another, a huge black whale-like cloud spuming behind it a slipstream of vapour, a vast, black demon – that's how she'll see Nature, he guessed, anthropomorphic, alive and threatening.

'Heavens, Sara, these knock me sideways!' He studied the row of paintings one by one, appalled by the grimness of their subjects; slimy canals, grimy old men – masculine, cruel paintings! They had a corrosive, ruthless quality which stupefied him; where were the lyrical, soft type of pictures he remembered her showing him years ago?

'Over there – that's to go for the scholarship,' she said. 'The model – she's crazy over Falkland, and she detests me for some reason.'

She seated herself into an old easy chair she'd cajoled her mother into giving her; that, a small table and a kitchen chair, furnished the hut. Sara's voice came across to him slowly, lazily, narrowing the distance between them. Obediently, Philip turned to the wall farthest away and gazed with mounting amazement at the olive-skinned, raven-haired naked beauty who stared back at him. Thickly layered paint on a rough surface, carnal, infinitely lush, the great eyes half-closed, the mouth slackly open, ferociously demanding, the head slightly lolled to one side, the whole picture breathed obscenely stark, annihilating, sex.

My God, *she* paints *this*! How do I equate that with this figure innocently sprawled in the chair? He felt hollow, sick, whacked; swinging round on her, excitement was running through him like a knife. It was Catherine! Catherine he saw sprawled in that chair! Moral scruples were melting as quickly as the candles in his hands; he looked down on them, the hot was running through his fingers, the flames gutting and frantically burning. In sudden, crazy haste he blew them out. He was across to her, pouring out words, somebody he didn't know was pouring out mad, scandalous words, and he and Sara were a mixed-up heap on the floor. She was fighting to push him off, his legs banged painfully against the paint table which spread-eagled drunkenly against the wall. The crazy fumbling under the clothes, pulling at her dress, pushing back her hair, tearing at buttons . . .

Ridiculously he was raising himself to his knees and suffering a choking, regurgitating taste in his mouth. He got up and stood away from her. In the pitch dark he adjusted his clothing and Sara adjusted hers. He could not have felt deeper horror had he committed murder.

From that moment he knew the whole depth, range and gamut of terror, lived through aeons of torment, rivers of anguish. Rape! I tried to rape her! His very soul was singed. He felt himself cringing away from any possible contact from touching her as she slowly got up off the floor and she stooped, tremblingly putting the table to rights. His blurred vision caught sight of her aghast, frightened, astonished face.

'Sara – I forgot myself . . .'

His thick voice was foreign, not his own. Utterly distraught, he went to the door and opened it wide, the stove popping and blowing crazily at the fierce rush of air. He stepped out, his footsteps on the damp lawn inaudible, as noiseless as if he had gone into thin air, as if he'd walked off the face of the earth.

He wrenched open the car door, threw himself inside, put in the clutch and turned the car round. Through his glazed eyes he thought he saw the ectoplasmic ghost of Catherine walking up those three steps of the porch; how many times, stricken and lovelorn, had he watched Catherine dissolve into the darkness of that porch!

He heard a faint cry, like the disembodied voice of Catherine, responsible for a thousand mischiefs. It was the voice of Sara crying out to him through the rain and drizzle.

'We need to be like bats, Philip – remember? Like bats . . .'

It would be madness to see her ever again. He accelerated and raced away as though from the scene of a crime.

Chapter Four

Cogito ergo sum; I think, therefore I am. That concept didn't help.
'I can't think, I can't think at all . . . therefore I am not . . . thinking, feeling, sensing, intuiting . . . I'm an introvert/extrovert.'
All seemed irrelevant. She was still fuming with rage; these bouts of anger and frustration had turned Sara inside out during the whole of the last three weeks, on and off; she and Howard had had their first flaming row, and on the telephone, too; it was the landing telephone, shared with two chorus girls who continually peeped out from their respective front doors anxiously waiting for her to finish. There was a musical on at the theatre just now – *Half a Sixpence.*
Their first real row was left in the air . . . To think that he could do such a mad, crazy thing, both of them, Howard *and* her father! Howard becoming a sleeping partner in a new business, and daring to do it without once consulting her until the deed was done! When Philip told her the news on that fatal Saturday night three weeks ago, the next Sunday morning she'd phoned the hospital and left a message with the Reception to be passed on to Howard that, owing to some quite unforeseen news concerning her father, she was taking the first train back to Ledingham.
Arriving at her digs, she at once sat down and wrote a furious letter to each of them, posting them first class.
The replies had arrived first class also, begging her to come home to Chesley next weekend, when all would be explained.
Oh, Howard – I know why you did it – it was his reaction to her confession about Philip! He's not up-to-date with the information, she informed herself bitterly . . .
It was a tactical move on Howard's part; he was fighting back like playing rugby union – hugging the ball, out-manoeuvring his rivals, hurling himself bodily out on the touchline, then the one, frenzied, streaming with sweat as he placed the ball for a triumphant try . . .
Sara's brain couldn't accept what he'd done. Forty thousand pounds – a legacy in the hands of somebody as close to her as her father, decent and hard-working and ambitious as her father was – it was a gamble; small

businesses were going bankrupt right, left and centre – the guilt *she'd* feel if Howard lost it all – neither of them had considered failure for one minute. She couldn't trust herself to go home at the weekends. I simply can't cope with a grand passion right now, my painting is going to pot. Time was getting too short for her diploma and hoped-for scholarship. Her mind was adamant, but something in her heart couldn't help but admire Howard's recklessness, and be flattered by it.

But Philip. Oh God, Philip! The dreadful finality of that running away in the dark, the sound of his car reversing and dashing down the drive. He'd done a bolt, terrified at what he'd tried to do. Sara knew, she'd been told often enough, that men were programmed to seek sex partners, but never once had she felt anything but safe with Howard, and surely Philip had behaved out of character? Underneath it all there was bitterness about women, and Cathy was the cause. She was sure her instinct was right.

I'm not going to breathe a word of what happened, not to anybody, not to anybody, she repeated. It was to be her secret – and Philip's, if ever she saw him again. If she went home to Chesley she might even be tempted to telephone him. No! Pride would at least prevent that. She was twenty-two and still quite happy in her virginity. I suppose at my age I'm the last virgin in the whole world! Her smile returned; resilience, optimism, can't be put down for ever . . .

Thank God for Jennifer, she always does me good. She'd had a very busy and interesting day out from the interview room at the Community Care Child Welfare Clinic where she put in daily part-time work for a minimum wage. She was to accompany tall, slender, hard-to-know-her-age Miss Jennifer Whittaker, on her rounds through some of the poorest streets in Ledingham, abutting the greasy, slimy Ledingham canal.

'There's not much on my list today, cross fingers. It's been pretty hectic lately. Bad cases come in spurts, don't you notice? It's as though some ogre has been let loose.'

'Like Goya's picture of Saturn eating his own children,' Sara ventured, laughing.

They got on well together. The thick plait wound round Jennifer's head flashed pale in the meagre sunlight; it was always the same when she was disturbed and unhappy, Sara longed to the depths of her being to be like Jennifer Whittaker, to have golden hair, to be serene and cool: to understand that however it appeared to the contrary, life was good . . .

They quickly found themselves in the maze of high-rise flats, knocking firmly on doors, laying trails of clinical appointments, informing a widow, who looked highly relieved that she was one, about the Care Advisory

Service and who to see about a widow's pension. A thief had stolen somebody's bicycle; a child was taken into care – it was a mental problem and so far nobody in the community could solve it.

Sara had particular interest in the case of the young mother Tania Tennant, because very unexpectedly she was in at the birth of Tania's baby, and Tania was all of fourteen years of age. Sara found herself helping the midwife when the ambulance failed to arrive in time to take her to the hospital. The scene scorched an indelible mark on Sara's memory; the screams of pain, the agonising cries, legs sprawled apart, that black cavern in between; and the vomiting and sickness in the poor girl's pregnancy.

Tania lived with her mother and brothers and sisters; the sixteen-year-old father of the child had long since disappeared. She and Jennifer calling now, found the baby crawling on the floor, clad only in a half-sized vest – it was easier that way . . .

'How quickly he grows up,' Jennifer said encouragingly to the sulky young mother.

'I've brought you your ginger biscuits,' Sara told her in her turn, and gave her a little present of gingernut biscuits. It was a joke between them, and it coaxed a smile out of Tania: ginger biscuits had been what she'd longed for insatiably, all through the pregnancy.

Outside, afterwards, walking side by side and pushing their way through the crowded streets, Sara said gloomily, 'Well here it's scarcely an Engagement Market, or even a Marriage Market, it's just a Sex Market – Mother Nature just wants to breed, that's what women are here for, a woman has a womb. I hate being a woman!'

'It has its trials,' Jennifer laughed affably, 'periods, abortions – would you have preferred to be a man?'

Sara blinked at the question and was thoughtful for a moment. 'No,' she answered, her mind shying away from Howard and Philip. 'They seem an utterly different species to me, one thinks one understands them, but you don't. We are supposed to have souls floating about either inside us or out, and souls I think are sexless.'

'That's a relief anyway,' Jennifer replied merrily, never ever having had the joys and sorrows of sex in all her life, and seeming quite happy without them. Jennifer was religious, and went to church on Sundays; it seemed a good antidote.

'I know,' Sara mulled the thought, her green eyes flashing, 'men are so amazingly inventive, why can't they take out our wombs, encase them in plastic so that we can hang them on the sitting-room wall; there could be little windows we could see through to know exactly what was going on, and we'd have typed instructions to tell us how to give it regular feeds.' She enthused on the theme, 'Aldous Huxley's *Brave New World*, I'm all for it!'

They'd reached the heavily polluted canal bank, on their way to the familiar landscape of the next block of flats.

'I understand that the hospital is starting up a fertility clinic,' Jennifer informed the young apprentice to Child Welfare, 'I must say that I dislike the language of eggs when it comes to women – putting frozen eggs inside us – it makes me feel like an unfeathered fowl!'

'I'm putting all my eggs in one basket!' Sara sang joyously. 'What would you call them instead – chocolates? A little nest of chocolates inside us.'

'Oh, they would melt in the warmth . . .' They couldn't pursue the matter further; they'd arrived at the ground-floor flat of Grandma Quinn, avoiding the pestilential flies round the row of dustbins, superlatively healthy specimens which hurled around them in a mad game, hitting them with the velocity of grapeshot.

They moved further along the street.

'Ello, cum in, luvvies.'

Jennifer was Mrs Quinn's 'little ray of sunshine'; she'd helped her considerably with her varicose veins, getting her, from her own pocket, surgical stockings for her badly swollen legs. Mrs Quinn had brought fourteen children into the world. There was a large, toothless gap in her mouth.

She gave Sara a sweet smile. 'Ah wanna show yer summat.'

She led them to what appeared to be an old wooden beer barrel that she'd lined with a bin liner, and diving down to its bottom-most depths, her scrawny arms extracted from it the largest cake Sara had ever seen.

'There's twelve eggs innit, luvvies,' Mrs Quinn said proudly. 'It's for me 'usband's birthday.'

'Twelve eggs?' Sara gave a rush of irrepressible laughter – three cheers for all the Mrs Quinns of the world – in spite of her lost battle with Mother Nature, MN for short!

What felicity! She'd baked for all her tribe of children and grand-children and great-grandchildren and Sara guessed that many would have brought an egg or some fruit, or some ingredient to put into it – a Community Cake! Purely tribal, the extended family, the unemployed and unemployable, cash benefits on Fridays, dead broke by the following Tuesday, a heady mix of religion, race and culture, and with it all, these little examples of family happiness. It belied Sara's pessimism, gave her optimism that one day – aeons hence, as the sacred martyr, Saint Catherine, had cried out before being broken on the wheel and crushed to death – 'All will be well, all will be very well.'

Back in her digs, Sara lit the gas fire. It had all been rather small beer today.

The bedsit that Sara had found for herself, reasonably large, was blessed with one unlikely and original feature: two washed-out-looking beach deck chairs were placed one each side of the aged gas fire, a meter beside it for the money; there was a small table and one upright kitchen chair next to it for meals. An ancient oak wardrobe, a battered chest of drawers, a sink with a draining board and, next to that, against the wall, Sara had herself provided a yard-long table to take her paints and brushes. She had taken down the pictures of a charging elephant and another of a landscape that had a wintry tree painted in the foreground and, on the strict understanding that she would leave them there when she left, Sara had nailed on three walls some of her own pictures, including a small framed scene of Wharton Manor, Howard's beloved home, with the soft landscape of the garden in front and the tumbling brook to the side.

Over the bed, opposite the fireplace, with laughter in her eyes, and a chuckle in her throat, Sara had reframed and put back again a lavishly embroidered sampler with the words 'Lead, kindly light' spaced out in dazzling gold letters.

The bedsit was very cheap to rent. Her mother had expressed no curiosity or wish to come over to Ledingham to see for herself where her daughter was living, so near the stone walls of the filthy canal twenty yards away. Her parents had trusted her implicitly when she made up the story about the recommended lodgings lovingly presided over by the spinsters Polly and May.

Sitting now in her deck chair, Sara placed her sketchbook on the floor beside her, which was covered by a threadbare carpet of indistinguishable colour.

Stiff upper lip, she told herself grimly. She prayed for fresh air in that stuffy room and found herself longing for a glimpse of home. Oh, hell! I feel I'm living on two planes, flies and butterflies, after today's jaunt through Ledingham's back streets. And what will Wolfe Falkland have in store for me?

She was due to have her first half-hour private tutorial with him tonight. He had suggested it, as he often did for pupils he thought were lagging behind. She knew that in the last three weeks her usual brilliant way with paint and canvas had deserted her. She couldn't concentrate. Howard, her father and Philip all jostled for room, demanding attention, and this minute, stirring herself to get ready her meagre evening meal, there was another rush of emotion, overwhelming her yet again.

On the floor! Not on the bloody floor, for God's sake! Details swept into her vision. The struggling and rolling on the floor of the summerhouse hut in her mother's garden; she could hear Philip's snarling voice when he got up in the dark – he *snarled* at me! Something about women . . . women were all the same . . .

'You know, Philip, if only you'd tried leading me up the garden path, and me with my mind fully awake to it all. If you'd talked me into it, and you'd taken me for a weekend to a beautiful mullion-windowed hotel in the Lake District, an hotel, oak-panelled with huge antlers on the walls and blazing log fires, and feeding the deer in the park outside.' She could see it all. I can't be taken by storm – I can't! Am I never going to see him again – never? The thought was unbearable.

Then, feverishly, her thoughts switched to Howard, taking her through fields of corn at Wharton, opening and shutting farm gates, Howard singing his bawdy rugby songs and making her laugh, flinging his arms round her in sheer animal joy, lifting her off her feet and hugging her . . .

The next three weeks I'm going to give myself up entirely to the pictures I've still to get done for my diploma; I shall stick it out and paint through the weekends. I will not go home to Chesley, I will not be distracted. What Howard and her father had done was done . . .

Efficiently washing up the debris after her hurried meal, she took a fresh towel and distastefully took herself to the shared bathroom; the lavatory was at least separate, thank God! She was never at all sure that Mrs Fish's ubiquitous cleaning lady ever cleaned the bath thoroughly and Sara was meticulous about such matters. She decided on a quick shower.

Back in her room she dressed with careful thought, zipping herself into a tight, maroon-coloured skirt and a starchy white blouse with a stiff upright collar behind the neck and added a wide, glossy, black belt at the waist. She held back her glorious dark hair with an artless, shining blue bow, and completed the outfit with black, twenty-denier tights, as the weather was atrocious, and flat-heeled black shoes.

Primness and purity was always the order of the day when she attended Wolfe Falkland's classes. She was ready for anything at this first private tutorial. No inner nervousness, no appeasement, no placating. Peace at any price. She was detached, independent, aloof from the chaos of life all around her. Let others get on with their lives and she'd get on with hers.

Finally, Sara quickly donned herself in the two-sizes-too-large black mackintosh which Cathy had handed on to her ages ago. It reached down almost to her shoes, covering her like a large overcoat.

There was a timid knock on the door just as she was on the point of leaving and old Joe, the bow-legged little man who always clutched his loose trousers as though they might fall down at any moment, was there in the corridor. How he times it so accurately is a complete mystery to me! Sara gave him her wide smile. He must be clairvoyant or something . . .

'Hello, Joe, yes, come in and keep my fire going for me, it's freezing tonight.'

Joe's bedsit was on its own in the attic – a cold, tiny room with two gasrings, a chair, a bed and a table. Hooks on the wall took his few clothes. He seemed to have no other worldly possessions.

Joe was an awful scrounger. The other residents, the generous, roaming actors and actresses, less impecunious and hard drinking than himself, gave him the little food he wanted, and Sara greatly saved his gas bill by allowing him to sit by her fire all the evenings she spent at the studio and, with an eye to her own pennies, he sat for her as her unpaid model. She drew marvellously and with understanding that unconscious pose, the chest like an accordion under its ancient pullover, and those upturned Charlie Chaplin old boots from which, after taking them off and toasting his toes before her fire, there emitted an odour so rich, so humming, it could have knocked a strong man down. Joe's socks sang to high heaven and the first thing Sara did on returning home was to open her window as wide as it would go.

'Don't forget to turn the fire down before you go to bed. Good night, Joe,' and she ran downstairs and into the dark to catch her bus.

Since that dreadful first interview eight months ago when her heart had been so high and confident and she had been brought so low by the rough treatment she'd received from that raucous bunch of students and the tutor looking on ironically and grinning, positively encouraging it, she had worked out a strategy.

She was extremely polite, good-mannered, stand-offish, correct. 'Yes, Mr Falkland, no, Mr Falkland.' She never called him 'Wolfe' as the others did. It was hard to maintain, but she could play a part – her mother's daughter – very successfully, if she was so inclined; it was as different from her normal, vivacious, good-humoured, buoyant self as could be. It was not easy to keep up, but her ability to shut out and give massive concentration on her work in hand made her the best pupil in the class. She knew that she puzzled Falkland, he didn't know what to make of her and it amused her greatly . . .

The massive figure was standing alone at the far end, his back to the permanent wall screen, there for his slides. 'Five minutes late, Miss Nightingale.' He took his cue from her – she was Miss Nightingale, never Sara.

'I'm *so* sorry, Mr Falkland,' she answered with exaggerated concern and a bright smile. 'You must blame the bus, it was late.' If she appeared hostile he'd know how to deal with her, but already his challenging effect on her made it difficult not to show it.

He sauntered towards her, making for her easel and her latest work, up for inspection. 'You look like a witch with that long black thing on – you only need your broomstick!'

'Oh, God, he's being personal!' This was entirely unexpected. She flounced into the cloakroom and hastily divested herself of the offending article and returned carrying her overall and walking towards the easel in her turn.

'Now you look like a schoolgirl!' he said, his voice soft and gentle, the white teeth through the beard flashing in a smile. He turned to the easel and she put her overall on the chair next to it.

'Now then, this picture of yours – think of the maxim, 'I am, I can, I ought, I will'.'

'Oh,' she said, smarting that he'd called her a witch and a schoolgirl practically in the same breath. She found herself replying testily, 'I'm not, I can't, I shouldn't and I won't is an equally positive philosophy to live by,' she snapped back.

'So I should imagine,' he answered drily, 'judging by this latest effort of yours. Christ, woman – look at that fluffed line!' He stretched out a finger and insultingly rubbed it from top to bottom all the way down her latest picture.

'Oh, that? Er, yes.' Looking at it, she panicked. 'Oh, God, it's ghastly!'

'Do, do tell me, do you mind? I only want to know. What do you aim at in your work? What are you driving at with pish like this. What are you *after*? I mean,' he goaded her, 'it would be intensely interesting to know, Miss Nightingale.'

So this was his mood! She tensed herself to meet it. 'Oh, that's easy,' she did not suppress an indiscreet smile. 'I want to square the curves of the Renoir, knock out the Cubists' cubes, tear through the stops and starts of the Pontillists, and then go my own way, found my own School.'

'Oh, indeed? God Almighty! So that's it! She wants to start her own School! Pioneer! What glory! What splendour!'

'Nothing if not modest, Mr Falkland,' she said derisively. She suddenly altered her tactics, ready to arch her back, bracing herself to cock a snook which really would get under his skin. Her blood was up. The front she'd always put on for his benefit fell apart.

'But will you, I beg of you, Miss Nightingale, will you *please* condescend to pasture your genius in the greatness of others for a *little* longer, just a *little* longer, before you start your own School? And you can make a start right now. Please wash out completely this blotched bit and do it again. In fact, you're having to wash out so much of your pictures lately, I want you to take my short cleaning course. I've spoken of this before. It might end up that picture-cleaning is all you're fit for.'

Oh, Lord, I must scotch this, for goodness' sake! I'm only just out of debt. I'm not taking on any more!

What a crass optimist she'd been. I'm too big for my shoes, her thoughts raced on in their customary anxiety. 'I'm sorry, Mr Falkland, I . . . I couldn't take the cleaning course.'

'Indeed, why not, pray?'

'I can't afford the extra fees,' she said, stiffly and self-consciously.

'Who mentioned fees?' The cocked eyebrow matched the supercilious grin, but the eyes had become more gentle.

'Of course you want a fee. Your studio is a private one. Aren't fees the filthy lucre wot we lives by?' she retorted brightly. Now he'd go on probing and she'd never confided in *anyone* just how hard it had been, what an uphill fight it was.

Reluctantly, she decided to be more explicit. 'The bounteous Voluntary Ledingham Clinic doesn't pay me a salary which keeps me living here, if you must know,' she said off-handedly, 'I'm only a sort of ranger scout. I've had to beg an allowance from my father.' She stopped. Hell! How to explain her father to this man – that in his late middle age he was starting a new business, and her boyfriend was closely involved. Suddenly, she would have liked a shoulder to cry on.

'Really, Mr Falkland,' she stared at him coolly. 'I'll take the cleaning course if that's what you want, and I'll pay you your fee, Mr Falkland, if only in instalments.'

She saw the deepened irony in his eye. She began to hunt uneasily the flitting thoughts in her mind. A full minute beat by, and in the second that intuition warned her something tremendous was afoot, his arms were round her, a huge hand slipped down to her diaphragm and in one deft movement she was hoisted on high on the flat of his palm, a fish on a slab, a pimple on a totem pole, legs together as though she were about to perform a perfect swallow dive.

Oh God, oh God, what's he doing? What's he doing?

'What are you doing? How dare you, Mr Falkland, Mr Falkland!' His voice completely drowned her panic cries.

'Sara Nightingale,' it rang out in tempestuous exaltation, 'I draw your face from memory. I know every line, every changing expression in it. For God's sake, girl, listen to me. Give up the blasted clinic and come and work for me. Do you think I want to charge *you* fees? Shut up, you thin little guttersnipe. What chance are you giving yourself messing about all day in a godforsaken clinic? You're taking longer and longer to do less and less. Keep still or I'll drop you. You're eaten up with technicalities, don't you know that? I'm not sure even of your scholarship if you go on like this.'

Staring down in startled amazement, she met full on so great an intensity of chagrin, longing and desire, her wits scattered to the air.

'I'm giddy, I'm giddy –'

'Stop wriggling or you're up there for good.' He marched her all round the room, perched above him on one huge hand, like the strong man in a circus-performing act. He roared with laughter. Suddenly, she was shot down into his arms like an expended bullet and the warm springy growth of beard was pressing on her throat, her neck, her mouth, and a huge chemical reaction leapt into the pit of her stomach. She was swept by the colossal magnetism of that crushing embrace and, oh God, hair! It was stifling her; electric tendrils springing out of human bodies, black, blonde, the colour of wine, spidery symbols of strength, of fertility!

As if fighting for her life she pushed him violently away. His arms dropped instantly, and as he stood away from her, the shape of some huge volcanic mountain, and still intensely affected by that tensile embrace, she felt the depth of tumult streaming out of him. She glimpsed his eyes, intent, derisive, and in a kind of panic-flutter, she attempted conciliation.

'It's the beard,' she said lamely. 'I – I don't like them, so close.' Cowardly appeasement! Why did she have to add 'so close', hinting that without his beard she might have enjoyed his iniquitous conduct?

But it worked. 'Ahaaa! So that's it! Too great a sign of my strapping virility, is that it? Don't worry, my child, I don't want to make love to you – yet.' He did not take his gleaming eyes off her as she swung away, reaching wildly for her ghastly failure of a picture.

'Do you think I'd ever be bothered with women assistants?' The mockery was back in full force. 'Think of the chance I'm giving you! Some women 'ud be on their knees. Now, my little one, you can tell Miss Gordon tomorrow you're giving up the clinic. There's a hundred and one things you can do here. It'll give me more drinking time, that's important.'

Men! She was only just beginning to take their measure. They were unpredictable; Philip, Howard, her father, now this . . .

The door banged and rattled loudly, relief, normality, swam back as blood-cooling as a shower. The first two students stamped in, Wolfe fumbled for a cigarette and turned towards them, indifferently tossing a greeting. The studio filled quickly, the young disciples banging and slapping their thighs to revive circulation, caterwauling their opinions of the weather, as friendly as playful bears.

Sara had an honoured place in Wolfe Falkland's studio now. She dressed differently, her manners were different, compared with most of them, her moral standards were utterly plebeian, but she was their most brilliant student. *They* knew it, and this was all.

It was Studies in the Nude this evening. She began her painting of Lottie Carmichael, the model, with the deepest realism, under-shadowing the pear-shaped breasts which must have suckled a school of young, she told herself privately. Lottie Carmichael was supposed to be one of the city tarts and this was her weekly 'evening of rest'. Nonchalantly, Sara sketched in her thick thighs, the beefy forearms, noted the stoical way she sat on a stool, gazing to space like a sensuous, thousand-year-old sphinx. Under the special angle of green light there was pathos, Sara thought, a certain dignity of form even, in this breakdown of lines. But gradually the evening proceeded as dreamily as a play, the sense of which was galloping ahead of her ability to grasp it.

After the class was over, for the first time she joined the other students in the Ring o' Bells. She took her glass of wine to the farthest corner of the bar, the watchful deep green eyes taking it all in. As she'd imagined, that hugely tall figure up at the bar was surrounded thickly by his student acolytes and when he bent down to them, the globe-shaped bar lights picking out the dark bronze in the black hair, black-shirted, with a thick, dark red tie, she noted the gold ring on his finger. When he laughed his eyebrows shot up and wrinkled his forehead.

Strain and tautness slowly dissolved out of her body, and a merciful veil spread over that hidden part of her brain which, however hard she tried to banish it, engrossed, preoccupied her day and night. Philip. Howard. That strange phenomenon so easily observed by outsiders, yet remaining shrouded in mystery for those actually going through it. The inevitable pattern of inner tumult, uncertainty, insecurity and nerves seemingly inseparable from being in love, or in love with love itself.

She had a sense that Fate was taking a hand; that Wolfe Falkland had stepped firmly into her life, to act as a third in some sort of harmonic triangle. Things began to fall into place; the times he had her scuttling all over the studio like a scalded cat, searching for his best brushes to *give* to her, she now realised, because he always made excuses not to take them back. The railway tickets he produced from some fund nobody knew anything about, so that with one or two other students, she could take a day jaunt up to London now and then to visit the Tate and the National Gallery, or the Courtauld. She was always one of the party. Yet, as with all the other students, but at her particularly, he snapped, barked and bit one minute, cooed like a dove the next, his hot and cold tactics seemed to get the very best out of them. Sara particularly was a sitting duck for his caustic wit; he'd tried everything in the book, but never once had he got any change out of her.

He walked across to her, his pint of beer in his hand, and sat down beside her, leaving them all at the bar. 'You'll inform Miss Gordon tomorrow, won't you? I'll phone her to forgive you working your notice. I know her, I'm sure she will. You'll miss the inner city, dogs, bugs, knives, heavy food, strong laxatives and illicit loves.' He seemed to know all about it.

Sara laughed gaily, she could be her true self at last.

'I'm a parasite,' and there was a strong feeling of deep emotion as she told him. 'They have to live their lives there. I stand apart and sketch them.'

'You honour them by sketching them, Sara. You'll never make a social worker. They're born, not made. You are an artist.'

He talked to her companiably and intelligibly, speaking softly, listening to what she had to say, making her feel surer, bigger in herself. It bore upon her what an immense gift her tutor had given her. Free tuition, no more clinics, no more division of labour. Gradually, she came to full flower of vivid awareness. Wolfe Falkland was desperately keen that she should win her scholarship. Incredibly mixed feelings flooded her. Gratitude, lofty acknowledgement, and remembering what had taken place in the studio – tickled amusement! I'll phone Hillary . . .

'Well, Wolfe, I'd better be off,' she smiled at him. She'd actually used his name, crossed the barrier, no more the stilted 'Mr Falkland'. Furtively, as she put on her witch's cloak, she took in this great form sitting quietly beside her, the edges of him blurred in the hazy dark.

Outside, she began to shiver in the night's cold air. Then his enormous height was beside her, a large comforting shield between herself and the weather. He saw her to the bus stop and watched her get safely onto the bus, back to her dingy studio bedroom by the banks of the canal, back to Joe and his mucky socks, back to the itinerant 'birds on the wing', bottom of the bill actors with their corrugated faces, lounging in their comfortable, sleazy bohemian rooms on the first floor – jugglers, flat top-note sopranos, hard-working chorus types, sending most of their money home for husbands, wives and kids – their gaiety, their moroseness, their indigestible suppers of winkles, pickles, sausages and boiled onions which kept body and soul together; back to Mrs Fish, her homemade slippers the colour of two dead mice.

Chapter Five

Mallory was lost. On impulse, he'd got into his car and belted it sixty miles. He was in Ledingham. Much to his parents' sorrow, he'd cut his rest-day visit short. He'd been so morose this last month, preoccupied, uncommunicative.

Damn fool! The address of Sara's digs was in his address book at the hospital; it's Acacia something, I'm sure of it. Acacia Street? Acacia Place?

Grey outlines of ant-like men and women moved along the pavements. He was in the centre of the town and it was 8.15 pm. He directed his gaze as much as he dared at the side window, searching for a car space; suddenly he braked so violently, the car behind him braked to turn within a foot of him and the driver furiously hooted his horn.

The Palladium! Sara had said something about a theatre, the Palladium; he saw the large black letters shining out on brightly lit glass as his brain frantically tried to recall long-forgotten pieces of information. Theatrical digs? That was it; it's worth a try, try anything. He found a parking space and locked the car door.

Time was becoming a huge lump on his back; urgency and high nervous tension carried him through; he found himself politely questioning the receptionist behind the ticket booth, clearing up for the night. He explained his predicament to the young girl; designer glasses perched well down on her nose, she appeared sympathetic to his plight. She was cashing up, couldn't leave the box office. She pointed to a door. Somebody, anybody! Desperately, he began opening and shutting doors, to find only small, dim, empty rooms. The play had started, nobody about . . . Ah, at last, a bit of luck, an electrician, fiddling with wires and switches. Mallory could put on a great air of authority. The scion of generations of army colonels, it was in his blood, and the man obediently left his switches and came across.

'Can you tell me where the stage manager's office is, by any chance?'

'Certainly, sir,' and the man took him to the bottom of a small flight of stairs. 'Second right along the passage. It's a maze of passages, don't get lost,' he called.

Nice lot, these Ledinghamites, so far . . .

The stage manager, behind his desk, looked up inquiringly in response to Mallory's unceremonious entry. For the third time, he explained that he was trying to trace a patient who lived in some theatrical digs in the town, could he . . . 'I'm a doctor, off-duty, but it's urgent, it's a matter of life and death,' he lied in his teeth. Why is it a matter of life and death? he asked himself stupidly. He only knew that it was.

'Oh, I see. I don't know if I can help.'

Mallory thrust a hand through his wayward hair and reached in his pocket for a cigarette. He smoked only in times of crisis and, oh, Jesus Christ, this was one of them.

'Elaine,' the stage manager called out to the young assistant stage manager, sitting in a tiny cubby hole adjoining his room. 'Will you show Dr Mallory to Archie's room, dear?' He turned to Mallory. 'If Archie can't help I don't think anybody else can.'

Mallory looked at his watch, 8.45. Oh hell, if Archie can't help I'll kill him.

Little cell-like dressing rooms, one after the other. Elaine poked her head through the door of each one of them. 'I've forgotten which is Archie's,' she said nonchalantly.

Newspapers, cracked mirrors, grease paint, the intruder felt as much out of his element as would the ex-king of Adjabadan; this back-stage labyrinth of an aged theatre and its riot of doors gave him a sickening sense of claustrophobia. 'Archie might be on stage. He's an actor, you know.' Elaine smilingly enlightened him as though he had all the time in the world.

I won't give up now, not if it means stalking on stage and holding up the bloody show! I'm going to see every damned one of them.

They found Archie. 'Mrs Fish? Oh yes, I'm staying there; yes, I know the girl, green eyes, lovely figure.' He looked Mallory up and down enviously.

'The remarkable Mrs Fish,' he continued amicably. 'She looks like one, smells like one, and drinks like one; unfortunately, my particular circumstances make it imperative that I stay in such a place for a wee while . . .' He dabbed a large powder puff into a bowl of powder, retouched up his face, then properly turned round on his chair and seriously considered the matter. Mallory did his utmost to hide his fuming anxiety.

'Eighty-four Acacia Place; it's a bit difficult to find.' He went into a long, detailed rigmarole which seemed to Mallory's fevered imagination to take half an hour to explain. Then Archie brightened. 'If I were you, I'd try the pub in Acacia Place first, the Fox and Hounds. Our Mrs Fish is sure to be there.' He sniggered, then turned round once more on his chair and continued unconcernedly to refresh his make-up.

Mallory went back to his car and crept it into the main street, wonderfully buoyed up that he'd got this far, and luridly cursing that it had taken so long. Ledingham was as strange as any lost city of the Andes. If only to God I had a street map; I'm a louse, but all the damned shops are closed. Crowds had melted away, people were warmly entrenched behind their doors, inside little houses, watching television, eating their suppers. Mallory was feeling light-headed. But it was staggering how all exhaustion, all weariness fled, when he saw in faded letters, high up on the wall on the first house of a row of similar houses, old, dilapidated, Victorian, once obviously very respectable, now very downmarket and seedy. Number eighty-four was apparently two houses converted into one in the centre of the row.

'Almighty God, what a muck hole; the girl I love lives here?'

Archie's words came back to him. 'Try the pub down the road – Mrs Fish is bound to be there.'

He found it and tried it – the Fox and Hounds.

And glory be to God, within two minutes, a distraught young man, in blue denims and the brightest Joseph's technicolour zip-up jacket, was standing at the low, dark table of the little crepe-faced woman by the name of Mrs Fish, in whose direction the landlord had obligingly directed him. He felt all the triumph of the dogged Detective Sergeant in a TV serial who'd followed an obtuse set of clues to pin down the murderer.

'She'll be at the studio, dearie, she's never anywhere else. Parade Street, off Fenshaw Street, opposite the Ring o' Bells.'

More pubs, rotting theatres, back-street dingy digs, alcoholic ladies!

He drove beyond the bridge of the darkly gleaming, slimy looking canal and it took him another twenty minutes of roaming around, his hands on the wheel slippery with sweat. He parked the car and was actually, miraculously, inside Wolfe Falkland's studio. It was 9.30 pm.

Not one of the students working there looked up, and with a piteous sinking of the heart, he saw that Sara was not there. Something inside of him, a stratum of pride, made it agony for him to ask her whereabouts. White-faced, he inquired.

'Oh, she's somewhere around,' a cool young man informed him. 'We've finished class tonight, you know.'

'But you're here, aren't you?' He was amazed at his own aggressive snarl.

Another student laughed. 'Oh, we're spent up. True artists, we can't keep away.'

A man tipped his head at a canvas lying awry on an easel. 'Her picture's very wet, she'll be across, I think.'

55

With glowering obstinacy, Mallory walked up to the painting and glared at it and, with deadly shock, he realised that apart from her sketches this was the very first of Sara's paintings he'd ever seen.

A man lying propped up in bed, yellow-skinned, goitre-necked, eyes bulging like a buffalo's, swollen eyelids barely slit open, utterly repellent, it epitomised suffering, drink and lean sickness; a poor drudge; glad even to be a drudge, the mentality of a walking age not one foot removed from the grave. He had seldom seen such in Chesley Royal Infirmary.

'Is it good?' he asked.

The man nodded. 'Very. Poor old Bradley, our ex-caretaker, cancer; she visits him regularly.'

Mallory felt body-warmth oozing out of him. So this was the ceaseless activity which made part of her character as incomprehensible as a closed book! He was baffled, off-guard and smarting. Why didn't she *talk* about it? Just mere hints now and then which I was never asked to take seriously. Exasperation hurt him, there should be confidence between us . . .

He could see that this wasn't just a job she'd taken on in this one-eyed city of Ledingham. These students, unconcernedly wiping their brushes, staring at their pictures, they were band of knights searching for something, some Holy Grail, and all were in deadly earnest to find it. The whole set-up was frightening; he stared at them in deepest trepidation. This was something he had to battle with. What do I really know about her after all? I want to know everything – share *everything*. She was as mysterious as a harem woman hidden away in some eastern bazaar.

He stood before her in the Ring o' Bells. She was violently startled.

'Good heavens, Howard, you make yourself invisible and you're *there*! It's incredible.' Her expression was one of admiring agitation.

Patience, exhaustion, triumph, were stamped on him; he smiled, and grimly he saw her reaction.

'God, you look absolutely drained.'

'I've been some time finding you.'

His face, the whole of his inside, were winding down at once as he drank her in, so relieved was he that he'd found her, and from henceforth he could put her in this setting.

She tried to ease the situation by introducing him to a great big man-eating gorilla, Falkland. Mallory felt suspicion welling up in him on sight. The insolent way he looks *me* up and down! The gorilla was hostile and dangerous. There was great power in the gorilla, you could sense it a mile away and, by God, Sara was far from immune, you could sense that, too. Oh, for God's sake, driving himself silly over Philip Carver, just to find things monstrously going on here? His complacency had been absolutely monolithic as to what was happening in Ledingham. He'd behaved as though Chesley was the centre and core of her life, as it was his own.

Revolt swept over him in turbulent waves; he felt like a helpless David without sling, stone or pebble, weaponless against this Goliath with the unclean, bloodshot eyes, red veins in his cheeks, large hands and paint in the fingernails. The man's raised, supercilious eyebrows incensed him. He felt wildly disorientated.

Sara gazed at him in mounting alarm. 'I'll get a drink for you,' and she stood up.

'An empty stomach, I think, Sara. Take your friend round the corner and give him some food,' the gorilla said quietly. The power of the man did not diminish when he opened his mouth and Mallory felt his jealousy freeze him, stiff and awkward.

Sara dragged him along to a small students' cafe in the back street behind the studio. It was warm inside and both took off their jackets. He forced himself to eat the ham and eggs she ordered for him. His head became a little lighter, he began to lose the griping pain inside of him.

'I don't very much like where you live,' he said, proprietorially.

'Oh, it was fine when I was working in the clinic. The inner-city is just the other side of the canal and it was very convenient to get home. I'll be searching around for something more upmarket when I can find the time.'

From Howard's point of view, she was far safer in the clinic than in the dangerous climate surrounding Wolfe Falkland . . . 'Wasn't the clinic congenial at all – don't you miss it?'

'I certainly saw Mother Nature working on all four cylinders at once. I think I myself must have been born in an absent-minded moment on Mother's part – she doesn't like babies all that much.'

Howard's eyes creased smiling.

'Well, when I'm a GP I'll be delivering 'em, won't I, if need be.'

'I've seen an abortion gone wrong and I've seen a live birth, Howard. I'll never forget them.' Her voice took on a passionate intensity. 'The mothers in both cases didn't want a baby and wouldn't have loved it. It was like being forced screaming and kicking on to a labour table by Mother Nature willy-nilly.'

'Life is a gift, Sara,' Howard rejoined quietly.

'And so is death. Look at poor old Bradley, our ex-caretaker. He can't die quietly, or quickly enough.'

'I saw your picture of him. Did you sit on the end of his bed to sketch him?'

'Not quite. Wolfe said I honour him by that picture.'

It was borne on him how much Sara saw the tragic side of life whereas he had great faith, expected the best, was sure that one day a cure could be found for everything. Seeing the sombre, sad expression in those deep green eyes, it took him all his time not to stand up, go round the table and hug her and whisper in her ear, 'I'm here, darling, trust me.'

Instead, he talked quietly as a doctor might. Those unwanted babies, *their* lives would have been precious to *them* whatever their circumstances, it always is. It seemed unanswerable, and both of them looked down sombrely at the empty plates. Sara decided to smile and he felt the atmosphere changing. 'We're the sport of the gods, three cheers for Mother Nature!'

'MN for short.' Both said it in unison and they laughed together as they so often did.

Now was the moment, the time to tell her about her father. Very skilfully, he thought, he gave her all the details about their meeting and seeing her father's old warehouse and comparing it with the new one, and how proud George Arthur was to be his own boss, and how his own capital was lying around, doing nothing . . .

She cut him short. 'Howard, you can charm the birds off the trees, but the fact remains – *I* was not consulted, kept in the dark, it was a *fait accompli*; I still can't think straight about it. I know my father. You've been brainwashed by his enthusiasm and his account books and whatever; you've been blinded with science. Supposing you lost all your money, how d'you think I would feel? I could never live down the guilt of it, it would haunt me for evermore. Don't misunderstand me, Howard. I love my father, I'm supposed to be his favourite child. I just let him talk about his dream and I listen. He never came with mother to our school speech days and prize givings when all the other girls' fathers did. But I understand better now, all the business frustrations. I feel trapped – you've trapped me.'

'*You* trapped!' Howard laughed outright. 'As if anyone could trap you, Sara. It just so happened that it was *your* father. I knew I had to do something with the money sometime, and the pressure of my finals was over. I like your father immensely, I'm glad to be in a position to help him, but it could have been anyone else.'

Was it true? Looking to the floor, Howard questioned his own subconscious motives; what it came up with startled him in its clarity. No, it wasn't her father, it was Carver, Philip Carver, who'd put the match to the flame . . .

'You're trouble, Howard, if you don't mind me saying so. You were born with a silver spoon in your mouth; my father wasn't. He's had to make his own way up the greasy pole. I care about money. Until a few days ago I've had to watch every penny I've spent.'

'It's a cinch, it's up my sleeve!' Howard coaxingly lightened the atmosphere, trying to get her into a better mood, breaching the barricades and, in spite of herself, Sara laughingly responded, pushing the fringe away from her eyes . . .

They addressed themselves to their supper, which was getting cold, then Sara, moving her plate away, had obviously something more to say, and didn't know how to proceed. Howard held back his news with an effort.

'As a matter of fact, my dear one, you did *me* a good turn by investing your money in father's business.'

'Oh – did I – that's marvellous, how come?'

'Well – er – all this time I've been living under false pretences, as it were, in Ledingham; both Mum and Dad thought I'd found myself some very superior digs, which would have cost far more than I was actually paying for a bedsit by the canal. I lied to them because I had to find more than half the amount extra to pay my tutor his fees; then there was all the paints and brushes and canvases. I was getting no grants – I'm out of the catchment area.' She stopped and started again. 'When I wrote to father telling him very bluntly how furious I was that you'd been dragged into family affairs, I thought the time was ripe to let him know my true financial position and suggested that in the circumstances, perhaps he could see his way to increasing my allowance, which he did by return of post. He nearly doubled it – he could scarcely do otherwise, could he?' She adjusted her face solemnly, but with a laughing gleam in her eye. 'It's original sin!' she said.

This took his breath away – the sheer blatant opportunism! It didn't seem to go with the self-forgetting dreamy-eyed artist he knew, and this eye-for-the-main-chance, sharp business woman – it's like Jekyll and Hyde – they don't blend; so starkly different, not so much black versus white, more like a gold and silver necklace wound round her neck, adorning her personality with new dimensions, and worn with such gaiety and verve – one with the other – one day it would choke her – he was thinking with a doctor's eye.

'Couldn't I have helped?' he asked very gently.

'You, Howard? Good heavens! What do you take me for – asking my boyfriend for *money*! Of the two options I'd rather lie to my parents than take advantage of your generosity – and loyalty,' she said, looking at him fondly and directly.

But how far had he got in her affections? Carver – he was like an itching bug. 'If a house was on fire, I couldn't be sure what you'd do, Sara, my love,' he said lightly. 'You'd either charge right in – do-it-yourself rescue attempt, or as an artist, you'd be standing aside – sketching it! I don't think it would enter your mind to call the fire brigade.'

Sara digested this and laughed gaily, finished her coffee, and counter-attacked. 'No, darling, I am the 'forethought' person – I think and plan, and have all the worries and anxieties beforehand – so things go as I want them to – in a straight line; one has all the worries and anxieties in one's mind to begin with, but the plan is carried out and that finishes it. You, on the other hand, darling, you are an 'afterthought' type, you rush into the house on fire regardless. You wouldn't be thinking at all, you'd burn yourself to death, so somebody would have to rush in and rescue *you*!'

Each was teasing the other, good humour was fully restored, and Howard loved her more than ever. He was possessed by her.

'That leaves hope. One couldn't rush into a house on fire in the first place unless there's hope for a good outcome –'.

'I like the little fairy called Hope – found skulking at the bottom of Pandora's box after the box had been turned upside down, pouring out all the dirt and ills of the world! I will say this for you lot – you're better at dealing with surprises than we are – we don't like surprises upsetting our plans, but I must say, father doubling my allowance *was* a nice surprise.'

'Out of Evil cometh Good,' Howard quipped.

Now was the moment! He grasped it with heart and brain. At all costs the issues had to be kept separate – her father on the one hand and Philip Carver on the other. He pushed back his hair, stiffened his shoulders and said casually, off-hand, 'By the way, I've met your Saturday-night escort, Councillor Philip Carver.' He derisively emphasised *Councillor*. 'Your father took me to his posh, very upmarket office to sign the documents. We were interviewed by one of the partners, a Mr Stanley Pollard, but I had the exquisite pleasure of meeting Councillor Carver and being introduced to him, on the way . . .'

The change in Sara's face was dramatic, the startled eyes glazed over, the smile vanished, the silence between them was electric . . .

'If you want to know, Philip Carver is not my escort anymore.'

'Oh, how come?' Bitterly, he was not going to let her get away with it as easily as that, even though she looked the epitome of tragedy and unshed tears. She drew meaningless scribbles on the tablecloth.

'That's my business, I'm not going to tell you.'

Howard spilled over into explosive satire, and she was his captive audience. 'You've quarrelled?' Not yet made it up? But how can that be? He's so good-looking, Sara. That classical profile, very comely I'm sure, polished, extremely presentable, a lady-killer forsooth, elegant, an enchanter, Lothario, Adonis, Apollo, *and* a councillor to boot.'

He rubbed it in with the greatest levity and she could not help but respond.

'Anything more – surely you've not finished . . .'

'Oxford or Cambridge obviously.' He sought for and easily found more words. 'Genteel, a man of taste, a connoisseur of pictures, a *cognoscente* . . . ,' he slowed down.

'If you've finished I'll add to your list: on the surface he is cool, collected, reticent, all the things that you are not, Howard.'

'That's nice, nothing like a change from Saturday to Sunday.'

'I think I was always just Cathy's younger sister. I think Cathy broke his heart when it comes to women . . .'

What had happened? The question nagged his own deep hurt, but instinct told him to lay off and he changed the subject quickly.

'Well, Sara my love, your art course here is nearly up, you'll soon be back at home for good. Then we'll –'

Quickly she interrupted him. 'Oh no, Howard, I can't set up a studio and look round for commissions in Chesley for a long time. If I get my scholarship, and Wolfe thinks I stand a very good chance, then I'll be off to Rome and Paris and Florence and Vienna. I might even get to New York, who knows? And as Wolfe's assistant, full-time, I'm learning so much, all day and every day, it's wonderful.'

Her eyes fled inwards, dreamlike into space, and Mallory's hopes dwindled to zero at the same time that pleasure and reason made him glad and proud. She deserved every honour that the powers-that-be could bestow.

'If I may be so bold as to ask – what does being Falkland's assistant entail exactly?'

'Oh, er, they're very light, really. Ned, our new caretaker, moves the heavy easels about, I see that the students behave themselves and keep their brushes clean, and I look after Wolfe's precious slides and see that they are in correct order and that the machine for them is working properly. I see that the cloakroom is tidy . . .' She trailed off.

Underneath his assumed flippancy, the optimism and cherished harbouring of castles in spain, Mallory was aware of a shrinking diffidence within himself. Had he been living in blind imbecility this last year? He'd seen Carver off only to find her firmly entwined in intimate daily contact with that larger-than-life, bushy-bearded artist, whilst he himself was sixty miles away in Chesley. The truth confused and encumbered his senses. He'd been so utterly positive that his own impetuous wooing of her would in time be bound to succeed.

'Do I come anywhere in your scheme of things?' His voice sounded choked and rough.

'Howard, my darling, of course you do.' She was visibly moved, and stretched out her hand to his and squeezed it hard. 'Just don't try to box me in a corner. I don't – I'm not –' She left it unsaid, then went on, 'You're still trying to get experience and I'm training to be an artist. We've got to get first things first, haven't we?'

'You *are* my first thing first,' he answered quietly. How could he concentrate on his work when she was talking into his ears every minute of the day?

'Do you believe in euthanasia?' She looked up from her plate and asked him directly, as a doctor.

'Euthanasia? Well – er – from a patient's point of view perhaps,' he replied guardedly, 'but from a professional point of view, candidly I don't know.'

'Our old caretaker, Bradley, is longing to die, but they won't let him,' she explained, impatience in her voice against authority.

'Doctors feel cheated and betrayed by death – it's their failure.'

'They don't think of it as a religious question, Death as a great adventure to the next stage – becoming an angel or something?' she asked, serious but with amused eyes.

Howard responded, smiling and beginning to feel much more relaxed. 'Very few of us are angels here, do we change all at once, or all that much? The Infirmary's got two AIDS patients at the moment, one is resigned to his fate, the other will suffer anything, but *anything*, if we could keep him alive.' His own inner concerns were very much engaged with these two patients, they were young, in their prime of life, and he knew that the thought of an overdose of morphine had crossed the minds of several fellow members of the staff.

Sara brightened and sloughed away the frown that creased his forehead.

'Holland leads the way, and others will follow,' she prophesied lightly. 'One day, in the dim and distant future, little rooms will be dotted about in every town centre, where those who are old and tired of life can shut themselves in, in comfortable surroundings with lovely pictures on the walls, a nice settee where they can lie down, press the button conveniently next to them, and swoon to death peacefully by means of a beautifully perfumed gas; what could be more civilised? A new adventure has begun, without fuss.'

'There's the funeral expenses don't forget,' Howard chuckled, his easy nature asserting itself rapidly.

'Oh yes, that's a problem; they'd have to post their insurance policies into the door's letterbox, and the door wouldn't open until they'd done that chore; oh dear, it would have to register itself, officialdom would have a beano – nothing's simple . . .'

Their conversation took on a bizarre ribaldry, Howard's face glowing with devoted love, so palpably relieved that so much of their intimacy had been recovered.

'It's awfully late, Howard.' They got up hastily from their chairs and put on their jackets, her expression telling him all the things she couldn't say in words. Mechanically, Howard paid the bill and they walked outside to his car, and it was only then that the full import of her future plans struck him as hard as a physical blow; she would not soon be safely back in Chesley! The crazy dream that had winged him along this evening to this god-forsaken Ledingham, had been thoroughly stamped on. God help me, he thought ruefully, I'd actually planned to ask her to marry me tonight! He'd flown into cloud-cuckoo land, not giving a damn to where it would lead him . . .

Sara flatly refused to allow him to drive her home to her dingy, murky 'digs'. 'No, Howard, I'll catch my bus as usual – you've a long drive ahead of you.'

They stood together, holding each other, and she was as emotional as he was. Impetuously she flung her arms around his neck and kissed him as she'd never kissed him before. Her kisses promised all the sensual pleasures he so longed for, but he felt he'd never be in any position to demand. She gave him succour, but she did not give him hope.

Sitting in his car and seeing her standing outside in the lighted dark, then waving him 'goodbye', for the first time the blackening doubt entered the depths of his soul to such an extent he felt numb; the deadly fear that Sara Nightingale was never, ever, going to be his wife.

Chapter Six

'Yes, Blanche, I do believe I've finished, at last.'

'Ee, luv – it's marvellous. Do I really look like that – my face, I mean?'

'Your natural expression is peaceful, when you get the chance.'

Sara was very glad to press a good fee into her model's long, fine fingers. She could afford it now – not having to ask Joe to pose any more, poor Joe; of course, she still allowed him the use of her gas fire nightly, and still had to open her window wide to diffuse the smell of his stinking hot feet – magnanimity was a good gift to possess.

She let Blanche out of the studio door and, thoroughly back into the world after her trance-like concentration whilst painting, she moved to the long table for the tedious business of cleaning her palette and washing her brushes. She hadn't slept well the last two nights, her brain was always so damned active . . .

'I'm the father and mother of grief to Howard, I know.'

She cursed her inability to be strong in the face of his anguish of love; her thoughts flew to the Ring o' Bells, jigging arms and bellowing bursts of laughter, smoke as thick as tissue paper, and Howard suddenly here, the feverish, glittering blue-eyed Ariel, apparently arriving without foot on solid ground. Wolfe knew at once what was going on, the back of his head had an alertness, a stretched, listening look. Howard clicked his heels and bowed like an over-polite Japanese, Wolfe sardonic, insultingly amused. Ordinarily, Howard had that rare combination of laughing optimism and kind thoughtfulness – it so soothed her between her dreaminess, and sudden bursts of great practicality . . .

For weeks now – and no weekends for breaks at home in Chesley – the purpose and meaning of her life wholly given over to her art course in Ledingham and the vital need to bid for a scholarship, she'd been trying to blot out Philip's evident abandonment of her. Sadness was a precious raw material to rub and stipple into canvas – she'd utterly forsaken the glowing colours that she'd used when she first came to Ledingham, making good in her spare time the notes and sketches of the landscape she'd seen so happily, tramping through the woods round Wharton with Howard on those carefree weekends.

Philip is a monogamist at heart. Cathy soured him for ever! If I went home and did contact him, how would he react? She knew that if she'd forgiven him, he'd never forgive himself; no, it was finished, all ended between them.

The sickening whine of the rusty-hinged studio door startled her mind with a heart-thumping jolt. Her tutor was inside and was as startled as she was to see her there.

'Good Lord, Sara, can't you keep away even on Saturdays? You're overdoing it, girl, you'll get stale. I've come to collect some slides I want for Monday's class.' He had no need to explain, it was his studio, after all.

'I was wondering if it was good enough to enter for the practical, or whether I should send something else?'

'Let's see.'

She had always deliberately covered this picture up with a heavy cloth and hidden it in an obscure corner, not drawing attention to it in any way. It had been easily missed amongst all the other pictures and canvases piled against the walls.

'She's Blanche, a new model. She's only in her late twenties and this is her sixth pregnancy – she's got five kids already!'

Wolfe was staring at it as though he hadn't heard a word. He bent his head and appeared to be cogitating an answer to the conundrum. Looking up at the high glass ceiling then staring at the picture, so deep in thought was he, she might not have been there.

At last he turned to her.

'But by heaven, girl! D'you know what you've done? This is an icon! You have constructed and painted an icon!'

'An icon?' she repeated stupidly, she had never seriously studied icons . . .

'It's there – you've painted it; an icon hits on the truth of things beyond the language of painting. If you were blind in a small room you'd have done this just so. It owes very little to your tutor, madam . . .'

But this was ridiculous, putting herself on a par with him! Pupil teaches tutor – this was triumph indeed.

'Don't be silly, Wolfe, you're having me on.' It was a typical form of mockery, but his face showed more incredulity than mockery. What was the mood of this man stumbling across her alone like this – Sara was diverted, intrigued, prepared to go along with it.

'You see, Sara, you've not merely painted a woman, you've painted full-blown *womanhood* – a principle; it has all the symbolism of an icon.'

She could not see it with new eyes; to her this was a young woman in the ardent grip of Mother Nature. Blanche had told her that after her first birth, five stitches were needed to repair her torn vagina. How could she tell this man that? You could easily speak of it to Howard, he was a doctor. She was far too shy, wary, still deep-down scared underneath, that this man had the power to reduce her to insignificance, inferiority, with a word. Why was he making such a mystery about this stark, truthful, what she'd seen before her eye, portrait of Blanche?

'We've forgotten, Sara, that two thousand years ago Christianity was the most dangerous religion to belong to – it went completely underground for two, three hundred years – the earliest icons were portraits of St Peter, St Matthew, all the Apostles; the originals are hidden away even now in monasteries and convents, Mount Sinai, obscure, impossible places – the Tomb paintings were found buried in the catacombs in Rome, and don't forget, those primitives knew about naturalism and perspectives . . .'

Her tutor was in full, enthusiastic spate, and in this he had her greatest respect and admiration. He was a superb teacher.

'Now look what you've painted.' Brimming over with excitement, Falkland explained it all to her. 'Blanche has taken on the role of a sainted icon. You find her leaning backwards, loose drapes, painted white, always very large eyes gazing into the distance, introspective, seeing into eternity; the feet rest on a stool, symbolising that spiritually speaking they are not on this earth – the feet mustn't touch the ground; there are no shadows. The sky is either a square of blue or plain yellow, no clouds, nothing foggy. They are embraced by Heaven itself. Hell is always depicted by black paint on the ground or a hole or a small passage leading underground. Do you see that you have painted your Blanche in exactly the same way? The same colours? Her eyes look into everlastingness, you've kept the background the palest gold, you've clothed her in a white shift, her legs sliding off the bench and on to a small footstool, the floor is black, it's all there!'

Astounded as she was, Sara's great sense of practicality did not desert her now. 'Well,' she laughed, 'if the model was in eternity, this artist who painted her certainly wasn't. I was trying to show brown skin through the flimsiest network of the finest threads of white paint. Rembrandt as my guide, mentor and friend, via you, my tutor,' she found herself saying.

They were talking artist to artist, his deep bass voice half-hypnotising her as he told her, 'Both Plato and Socrates were given the accolade of saints in the icons artists painted of them, and Orpheus too when he tamed the animals with his music; the subconscious of Christians is just the same as the subconscious of pagans,' he added satirically.

'When you get your scholarship, my dear, be sure to go to St

Petersburg. They've got a fine collection of icons. The Russian Orthodox and the Greek Orthodox churches have always used them for ritual worship in their Masses. There's one drawback. Where you get laws, which make for permanency, they also get fossilised; then you get a succession of styles which get stiffer and stiffer until they become mere cardboard figures; the earliest icons are not like that.'

'Then what *are* the rules?' Sara asked innocently. *Her* subconscious mind had understood the rules all right, but consciously she was painting that huge pregnant bulge, with pity for womanhood, and Mother Nature's disregard of sagging breasts, scarred and battered stomachs . . .

Wolfe regarded her quizzically and deliberately from head to foot. 'It's one o'clock and I'm going to the match! If you've nothing else on – you've finished your picture – why not come with me? You look washed-out, tired, if I may say so.'

'I haven't slept, I'm a poor sleeper,' she told him, abashed and upset that it was showing in her appearance.

'It's Rugby Union, of course, Ledingham versus Middlesborough. It ought to be good.'

Rugby Union! The joy of Howard's life! Yet never once had she ever gone with him to a rugby match. Howard, still loyally supporting Chesley Town as a non-player, blissfully imagining that these last many Saturdays she was gaily spending the time with her gang-of-four girls when she was surreptitiously enjoying herself – in Manchester, with Philip Carver. A deep twinge of guilt prompted her not to refuse but to accept this man's suggestion, so topsy-turvy were the emotional undertones mixed up in her heart.

'All right, Wolfe. Nice of you to ask me.'

'Right.' His flashing teeth grinned through his beard. 'We've just time to get a sandwich and a drink across the road,' and Sara, to her great surprise, found herself escorted to the Ring o' Bells.

It was forcibly borne in on her that this commanding, massive maestro might be a lonely man at the weekends, his flock deserting him for pastures new, going their own ways, left him high and dry, mooching about, talking to nobody. An incredible thought. It melted her defensiveness. Wolfe phoned for a taxi.

The unpretentious ground where the match was played was barely a couple of miles away from the city centre and Wolfe amiably led her to a seat under the covered pavilion.

'I usually stand with the hoi polloi, the language is saltier,' he laughed, his manner, like hers, thoroughly relaxed.

Sara found herself greatly enjoying this foreign game. Soon, she took out her sketchbook which she always kept in her shoulder bag and busied herself putting a pattern of lines and curves on paper. The flying figures, the dancing, clever footwork, the tumbling heaps of mixed-up bodies on the touchline, fascinated her.

Wolfe let himself go like a boisterous schoolboy, his booming voice adding to the roar of the crowd. 'Get on with it!' He turned to Sara and slapped her knee with gusto, Sara hastily pulling away her short, short skirt, and holding it there firmly with her handbag.

After the match he took her to an old-fashioned brasserie where he seemed to be known, and Sara obediently allowed herself to be persuaded to try a pizza dish, full of exotic bits and pieces, which she ate with relish, and she sipped the half bottle of wine he had bought for her whilst Wolfe indulged himself in an enormous glass of real ale.

After the meal they moved across to sit in the tub chairs placed on their own before the shooting six-inch flames of the mock gas fire, licking purple shadows under the heavy oaken mantelpiece. He sat there viewing his young assistant with such an avuncular expression, glinting deep eyes smiling, contented chin sunk down into the black-throated bushy beard, for two pins Sara felt that if he'd patted his knee for her to go and sit on it she'd have happily obeyed and curled up on his lap like a purring green-eyed cat, her head cradled on his chest.

Eventually, they were outside on the pavement.

'Before you go home, I'll take you back to *my* studio, Sara, for a final cup of coffee,' and before she could consent, he'd hailed a passing taxi and they were in it.

The studio in which he made his real money, kept to accommodate rich clients — architects, lawyers, presentation portraits of company chairmen and county aristocracy, well-heeled establishment folk that even Ledingham possessed — was strikingly different from his teaching studio across the road; that one, so messy with rackety chairs and sprawling easels. This one was order par excellence, and order in a chaotic world pleased Sara very much.

The whole room was painted in neutral beige, divided into panels by means of beautiful soft-coloured Persian rugs hanging from ceiling to floor, and each blank space in between containing the type of chair in which a model would be required to sit: Tudor, Jacobean, wing chair, modern.

Sara had visited this studio only once before when he took her over to lend her a beautiful leather gold-lettered book which was on a bookcase in the far corner. Books were evidently Wolfe's hobby and only luxury, and on that occasion he'd shown her proudly some extremely expensive first editions.

Sara peeled off her coat and he motioned her to sit down on a hard-backed plain chair next to a small oak table for two, Wolfe evidently intending to sit opposite her in a similar chair.

'You know, Sara,' he said as he ambled over to the neatly partitioned-off sink, draining board, cupboard to hold a quantity of crockery, and an electric kettle sitting on the shelf against the wall . . . He quickly made coffee, brought the two mugs to the table and sat down opposite her, his eyes having an inward-dwelling gaze. 'When I started my studio I had the old, simple Renaissance idea of gathering round me a few pupils, apprentices is a better word, young men and women who'd mix my paints and do the repetitive stuff, fill in some of my mural background. They'd call me 'maestro' and pick up by learning as they went along; a few chosen spirits, a select, choice band with fire in their bellies, those who knew there's more to life than the mere earning of money with nothing left over of themselves to spend it on. So long as they had promise, they could be as penniless as I was when I began.'

The brilliant teacher took over, he couldn't help himself. Spreading out his hands expressively, tearing off into a fascinating spate of anecdotes on Blake and Palmer and other artists who'd starved themselves to fame; making her feel part of it all, an infinitesimal scrap but still a part of the wonderful mosaic which made up the fabulous, stupendous art of painting, a feeling that she herself bathed in the self-same sea.

'A painter always needs to have a sense of longing in his heart, it's what he brushes into his canvas. Before I knew where I was, the Ledingham Education Department had got their hooks into me, offering me grants, equipment, my teaching studio at a reasonable rent, every kind of inducement. I tell you, Sara, in a few years those tentacles of a partnership with Ledingham Council was stretched so completely round my neck, I found myself set up with the whole paraphernalia of a teaching school, the whole bloody lot! It's the death knell of an artist.' A hard facetiousness was spreading thickly in his tone. 'I've got this,' he gestured round his small studio, his private bolt-hole. 'I make ends meet. I haven't quite sold my soul to the devil.'

Sara felt uneasy and at the same time highly flattered that he'd lifted such a large corner for her to see into his private heart; that their relationship had moved from the imperious hectoring interspersed with the tender, patient, responsive style he had always used with her after she'd become his assistant. Never once since that occasion when he'd hugged her and kissed her, had there been any question of his repeating the liberty.

He got up, took the two mugs and hunched over and put them on the draining board. Then he moved to the far window, outside now black with night. He stood there for what seemed like ages, staring into the dark.

Sara's artist eyes took him in from head to foot, the six foot five inch height, the Roman head and splendidly modelled nose.

She found herself wondering what he'd look like shorn of that face and throat-covering; as he walked slowly towards his chair, it struck her that without that full-blooded beard he'd seem imperilled, exposed to danger, stripped of his wolfishness, his jaw vulnerable. She had never seen properly those beautifully mobile lips which could speak words that could trip her up mercilessly, his hardness prodding down on her mind's softness. Without his beard he'd look all too human, a man as well as a ruthless painter.

She looked at her watch. 'Good heavens, Wolfe! It's nearly midnight! Thank you very much for the coffee, and for the very nice day,' she added appreciatively with her broad smile and unconsciously provocative, artistic sizing-him-up glance. 'I'll get a taxi home if you don't mind calling one for me.' It was wonderful to be able to afford it, to spend this amount of largesse on herself.

'Oh, the night is young, I'll come along with you.' He came forward.

'D'you know, Wolfe, that'll be our fourth taxi. One to the football ground, another back again, another to get here, and now one to take me home! I don't wonder why you don't buy yourself a car!'

It was an innocent remark, but with her over-sensitive antennae on the alert she'd seen at once that she'd said something contentious; his face darkened and he sat down heavily again in his chair.

'Sit down,' he commanded her and automatically she obeyed. 'You want to know why I don't drive a car? Well, I'll tell you.' The black eyes took on a terrifyingly ferocious expression, the silence between them electrifying in its intensity. 'I had a wife once. I killed her.'

Sara's heart raced within her as he shattered the silence with this stricken announcement.

'She had a car and I drove it backwards straight over her and killed her.'

'Oh, I –' Sara was lost. She could think of nothing to help him.

'I'm sorry,' was all she could stammer out.

'Sorry!' He laughed at the inadequacy of it, but was ready to explain.

'It was in Vienna, we were both twenty years old. It was her car, her parents had just given it to her and bought a new one for themselves; Maria had taken on a penniless artist, earning a meagre living and learning his trade – thumbing pure gold leaf into the cracks and crevasses of half the church altars in Vienna. It teaches you how to use your fingers when you paint, Sara,' he said sardonically. He breathed deeply, then carried on calmly, placing a hand over his eyes for a moment. 'The inquest verdict was 'an accident', defective brakes. Her parents had told Maria, but she had forgotten to tell me. We'd only had the car a couple of hours . . .'

There was acid in the way he uttered the words; the lid of his secret tragedy was taken off and laid at Sara's feet; his guard was torn off and the girl opposite him saw a tragic and bitter man.

'The head of the household, the provider, the protector, the responsible male — that was everything in Vienna in those days, and I was none of those things.'

He began slowly to pace the room, deeply absorbed. After a minute or two he stood towering over her across the table, eyebrows lifted, eyes keenly scrutinising.

'Have you ever seen a dead body?' he asked dramatically, shooting the question like a squirt of ice-cold water directly into Sara's face.

With a supreme effort she returned his gaze.

'No, I — no, Wolfe, I have never seen a dead body.'

'A somewhat mangled body — I went over it twice.'

Oh my God! It bore upon her how sheltered her own life had been; events that had seemed so big, so important — how would she have coped in this man's place?

'I've seen near-death,' she countered desperately. 'Bradley — our old caretaker — his portrait, remember?'

'Oh, that!' He smiled indulgently and sat down heavily into the straight-backed, Tudor-style chair opposite her own.

'Penance, my dear, you never get rid of penance. It makes you go on doing things you wouldn't go on doing otherwise.' He sighed deeply. Sara had always felt that there was a born actor lurking somewhere in the inner workings of this brilliant tutor of hers. His swaggering walk, his eloquence and mocking laughter, a larger than life character, but now she was all at sea; his deep distress, the wound that would never heal . . . and they'd arrived here after a good day's entertainment, she carefree and confident.

He seemed to make up his mind about something. He reached across the table and swallowed her two hands in his own large, tight grasp — a repetition of what she and Howard had done only two days before!

'Listen, Sara,' he began, 'you're very young in the ways of the world outside of your painting. It's a great phenomenon to be sure, since you've little judgement about anything else . . .'

Well, here he was, gloriously right back to the man she knew, as if her access to this private studio and the confession of his tragic past had never taken place.

'You don't *speak* venomously – you're too good-mannered, but venom can reveal itself in your portraits all right. You can give a nasty leer to your models, as well as Blanche's saintly look.' His voice descended to depths of urgency.

'Sara, one day you'll get caught up with someone like that hot-eyed rugby player who came to see you, dying of love; you won't stand a chance.' He paused, and before she could even shape a venomous thought, he went on hurriedly, 'Art is an act of worship. Only artists know, there's nothing outside of art for the likes of you and me. Sara – marry me. Marry me, Sara!'

He stopped and smiled sheepishly at her startled, incredulous, open-mouthed gasp.

'Marry me for five years! It'll keep you safe and give you time. Time to develop and time to change; you can go off to the Continent, do what lies in that stupid head of yours to do, work hard and you'll be a fine painter one day – the world will be at your feet – think of it.'

Marry me! The words buzzed and echoed in her brain. *Marry* him? She hadn't heard aright, it wasn't possible, everything was blurred . . .

He continued in full, lyrical allurement, dazzling her with wonderful vistas.

The full import of what he was saying dawned on her slowly. Her time in Ledingham was coming to an end and he wanted to keep her there at all costs! The truth of it pole-axed her in spite of all her experience to the contrary. In fights she held her own, she had power over this man – he wanted to marry her, he loved her!

'Of course, if after five years you find you can do without my loving care, don't hesitate to discard me.' The gleaming black eyes were gentle, his heart wide open to her, wariness and suspicion vanished. It may have been the unaccustomed quantity of wine she'd consumed at the brasserie but impulsively she lifted her hand and gave his beard a timid affectionate tweak. Nothing could have told her why she did it, he knew she didn't like beards and she saw him scanning her expression with a quick flash of startled receptivity.

'I said I'd teach you to like it,' he laughed softly. 'I'm still willing if I've a willing pupil.' His rich, hypnotic voice goaded her in derision. There was not a word about accepting his amazing bizarre proposal of marriage, the little tweak to his beard he knew was a small conciliatory gesture.

'How do you know I'm not a willing pupil, you haven't tried,' she heard her voice, the tone of it utterly strange to her ears, registering the fact that she'd given him an open invitation, and having made it instinctively she stood up and put a distance between them. This was appalling, he'd baited her to recklessness.

Now that she had made it she received not one jot of pleasure. I'm as blatant as Cathy, there's nothing to choose between us!

It was the leap of the wolf that sees the speckled doe! Too fast and furious for her to gather what was happening, he was up and his arms were flung around her.

'How long have I waited for this?' he crowed. 'You don't understand the role of a woman in a man's life, Sara. Women are trees and men want to nest in 'em! But you're not a tree, you're no more than a little sapling. You haven't enough leaves on you to cover even yourself, my little Nightingale, so stop thinking you're a tree and try wrapping yourself round this warm body for a change.' He began pouring wild, extravagant strings of words into her hair. He was tempestuously pleading, 'Come to bed with me now, Sara, come home with me now, it's no distance.'

She was drowning in the depths of that impassioned voice. She found herself being led through a maze of typical Ledingham back streets, through a cobbled courtyard as black as night.

But Wolfe, the vociferous Wolfe, was strangely silent, and now it was she who was doing the talking. It was Sara who breathlessly did the covering up for them both. They stopped before a wooden door sandwiched between large shadowy buildings on either side.

'It's a mill next door,' he told her, breaking the silence. 'It once housed the live-in caretaker. It hadn't a bathroom and I had to put one in.' He had to bend his great frame to get under the door lintel; he switched the light on and a large collie dog sprang from the hearth, wagging its behind off in welcome.

'Hey, man, be polite,' Wolfe ordered him down, affectionately digging his finger into his ruff and perhaps at the same time wrestling with his own emotions.

Sara's trained eye took in at a quick glance this sitting room which must once have been a kitchen. The walls were whitewashed and a few of his pictures, neatly framed, hung on them. The solid oak furniture seemed Tudor-bare in its spotless austerity; books everywhere, on the window shelves, on the floor – he must live on a diet of books! The old black iron kitchen range had been left there as it always had been, a dark brass fender surrounding it and giving light to the plain dark red carpet. But incredibly, scarcely to be believed, before the fender there was a large, real, at least fifty-year-old rag rug such as she'd seen elsewhere in Ledingham, made up from cuttings of old clothes and red petticoats, anything the families cared to possess, stitched through a sturdy backing of brown sack or canvas.

Oh, Mother of God – it belonged to his mother, I'll bet it did! It brought Sara reeling to her senses. Where was she, what was she doing? Where was she going?

His hand was firmly on the small of her back as Wolfe guided her up a very narrow, boxed-in wooden staircase and, staring down at her from the wall of the barely yard-wide top landing, hung a large portrait of an old lady; deep, dark eyes with hooded eyelids, a strong jaw, broad forehead, and a thick rope of shining white luxurious hair. Wolfe's mother! She was sure of it.

Standing trembling next to her, Sara could almost see the old lady's face creased into a thousand laughter lines, splitting her sides in mirth at the spectacle of this great progeny of hers leading this scared virgin into the bedroom – sacrifice of the lamb to the slaughter.

'This is the spare room,' he informed her quietly.

He switched on a faded bedside lamp, then he left her.

The pink light shone palely over the nondescript commonplace furniture. Wolfe had probably bought it, thrown in with the cottage. The large double bed, a chest of drawers, the wardrobe, incongruously, one jungle-hot picture, obviously an early vintage Falkland, made a glorious splash of colour on the wall.

She stood by the bed in a kind of green-eyed watchfulness. Already she felt she was making a pitiful job of this first irretrievable fall from grace. She was in no-man's land; she could make neither a sin of virtue nor a virtue of sin. She was merely conscious of a querulous frame of mind.

Dear God, why not? What's the point of being a stuffy virgin? Catherine had years ago stolen all her fruits of joy. Philip could never forget Cathy; virginity was at a discount. She was whimpering and wailing like a badly played pibroch screwing her to higher and higher pitch, as though her central nervous system was some kind of tuning fork.

Oh, where *is* he?

Her pride was convulsed that now conquest was in sight he was taking his time! She lost all knowledge that this same man loved her, that he was her friend and protector, that he had tremendous faith in her as an artist and would stake his all to prove it.

He grew in her senses as a frightening tower of super masculinity. In burning imagination she felt his chest pressed like a mattress on her cowering flesh. Her throat was too paralysed to cry out when she saw him at the door. He came slowly forward to the bed, looking down at this whey-faced girl under the rigid drawn-up sheet, her taut length stiff as concrete. The soundlessness was electrifying. It could be heard. The large double bed seemed to be swelling bigger and bigger and she was shrinking down smaller and smaller to the puny size of a wooden doll.

In a horrifying portent of menace the stillness exploded in a roar. 'Good God! She's a virgin! In this day and age! Virgo intacta, aren't you? What do you take me for? Don't worry, I'm no plunderer pioneering ice-bound territories. It's not to my taste. I'd rather a brothel, I'd rather a prostitute any time – you know where you are with a prostitute.'

His rip-roaring voice pounded on with the fury of a battering ram.

He flung her clothes on the bed. 'Get them on.'

He stood there at the end of the bed, arms folded, fists tightly knotted, head thrust forward, eyes satyr-like, and he watched her. He *watched* her naked body get out of bed, feverishly put on her clothes, her hair a tumbled mass about her shoulders.

But this wasn't true! It was a nightmare dream. Her brain was too paralysed to know where dream ended and truth began. There were no tears, her own glaring green eyes met his with infinite scorn; tremblingly, she took control of herself and with consummate acting, she managed like a chameleon to change her stance into the coolest exterior. Not for worlds would she let him see the humiliation, her bitter pride, the lost sense of the right fitness of things. She turned her straight, deeply hurt back on him, stumbled down the stairs and out of the house. He was a yard behind her all the way – a huge invisibility. In the main street he took her shoulder and guided her to the nearest taxi rank. 'Peter,' he said familiarly, 'take this dear young lady home.' Thrusting money into the taxi man's hand, he bowed her into it and slammed the door.

She did not turn to see the look of utter dismay and shame and deepest mortification which lingered after.

Yet another bloody taxi, but, oh, she was glad of it, to sit in the dark depths of the back seat, close her eyes, and try and bring her scattered wits to some sort of normality. To think that one small, harmless remark about taxis could propel such a chain of events culminating in her sitting here. Another leap of memory that had set the tone for so long – the very first time she'd set foot in his studio and the absolute riot he'd calmly allowed to go on, a fiendish grin on his face.

Once in her room, she took off her coat, made herself a cup of tea and sat with it in her deckchair.

Oh God! What a hash she'd made of it all, her self-esteem was in tatters; to have let herself get into that fix in the first place, it was madness. And to find herself competing with prostitutes and brothels – what a let down! Did

Howard and Philip go to brothels? she wondered. No, of course they didn't, she was certain of that — and I'm not a one-night stander either . . . She flung back her head and began to see the tragi-comic side of it all, and didn't know whether to laugh or to cry. Wolfe had been prepared to show her all the diamonds and rubies of the sexual calendar, and she hadn't even made room for him in that big bed, but had placed herself squarely in the middle . . .

I can't be taken by storm, I damn well can't be taken by storm, she repeated with huge vehemence, even though, she reflected pensively, he asked me to marry him — for at least five years! she smiled wanly — well that was something . . . In a vivid leap of memory there flashed into her mind the full details of a brilliant picture she had once seen in a public gallery somewhere, when she was a kid — she couldn't remember where, was it a Poussin or a Caravaggio? A wonderful, most powerful picture of Pyramus and Thisbe, that priceless legend of a handsome young man and a beautiful young girl, staring at each other through a chink in the garden wall that separated them. Their parents had refused their consent for the couple to marry, so Pyramus and Thisbe arranged to meet secretly beside a rippling spring, outside the city gates: here a lioness appeared, straight from the kill and all blooded, to quench her thirst in the spring water; a tragic, devastating misunderstanding arose, and the couple killed themselves in horror and panic . . . How that lioness symbolised Mother Nature in all her predatory boundlessness to sexually keep apart or bind together! Does the male and female of our human species see each other no more clearly than through a chink in a wall? Sara asked herself dully . . .

She gazed around her with a sudden loathing of her surroundings: this bedsit; the smell that Joe had left in the room; the sloppy, tipsy Mrs Fish, and that itinerant bunch of the acting fraternity who always bagged the telephone; she hated the lot of them . . .

Oh my God — how am I going to face that devil incarnate on Monday? What invective would he contrive to throw at her? Perhaps for once the scales had tipped towards her, to balance a little, the humiliation *she* had suffered in their very first encounter, almost a year ago . . .

Well, at least I've got my diploma; she had passed her final exams brilliantly, and with the portrait of Blanche now finished, her quota was complete and ready for her scholarship bid.

Howard's hastily scribbled love letters, so ardent, so loving, sent to her by every other post, forced themselves into her consciousness like a soothing shower; she hadn't answered all of them, she hadn't *time* for love; love had to be kept on ice, it demanded too much, and it was too much in the coil of that damned sexual mistress – MN for short, she warned herself.

Smarting, tearful and laughing in turn over the outcome of the day's events, her mind strayed wistfully to the lovely emerald-green strapless evening dress she'd bought in a very rare fit of extravagance, and never once worn. Of course! Of course! I'll damn well write a letter to that devil Wolfe Falkland, tomorrow, tonight – get it posted to reach him on Monday, and I won't be going to the studio: I'm going to have a holiday, I'm going to take a whole week off . . .

She was losing touch with her college friends – her 'gang of four', and there was no extended family in the Nightingale clan – no uncles, no aunts, no nearby cousins her own age, George Arthur and her mother had long ago abandoned any idea of accommodating and entertaining distant relatives . . . It suddenly struck Sara very forcibly that one could feel *too* free, *too* independent: Howard and Wharton seemed a long way away . . . This virgin was going home, Chesley itself was Paradise.

Chapter Seven

'We have a saying in our country. 'Stand up, sit down, eat your food, move your bowels, and when you're tired, go to bed!'

Dr Hamid Azim's handsome Indian face was wreathed in smiles. Four doctors had drifted into this communal washroom in the new wing, obeying the calls of nature and freshening up, either going on duty or going off it, and always there was ribaldry.

'Well, that's pretty basic, anyway,' laughed Dougie Blamey, turning his head from the washbasin and washing his hands.

'*But*,' Hamid emphasised portentously, 'all the time you're walking two inches above the ground.'

'Two inches above the ground?' Tom Wilding repeated, raising his voice above the sound of the hand-drying machine. 'That's proof that one is in love!'

'Bodily elevation, that's rich!' Cecil Haycroft came out of the loo, zipping up his trousers, and looking tired and ready for bed. 'I'm sick of bodies!' But, the genial atmosphere quickly reviving him, he struck a comic pose and went on, 'Oh, wicked intoxicating two-legged monster, what would we doctors do without you? I wish to God we could stuff you into the nearest wardrobe in sight.'

Howard Mallory, standing apart, now joined in.

'Ears bunged up with wax, creaking joints, bad breath, fallen arches, going bald, and do they go quietly? Not on your life! The body is like a fox at the throat of a chicken right up to the tolling of the bells when we all get down on our wobbly knees and reverently kiss it goodbye. That's Mother Nature for you.'

Laughingly facetiously, he was echoing one of Sara's favourite themes – the imperfections of the human body as she saw and sketched them in the slums of Ledingham.

Sara, Sara, Sara, Sara Nightingale! He sang the name to himself over and over, and, suddenly sobering, he left his colleagues with the urgent desire to escape.

I must get out of this place. He desperately wanted time to himself –

three hours off duty – to leave the hospital confines and try and sort out problems that were pressing so sorely on his heart and mind.

He had in his care his first AIDS patients, two of them; two bewildered dying young men in their prime of youth. As a physician he had no drugs that could do any good, he could only alleviate their suffering a little. Prolonging the agony, he told himself bitterly. It all seemed pointless.

In his room he quickly divested himself of his white coat and donned a brightly coloured lightweight outdoor jacket, zipping it up warmly – springtime could be cold in the North.

There must always have been pockets of AIDS somewhere on this planet, but what in hell had triggered it off to become a plague like this? Such questions worried him intensely. He cared about his profession and felt deep pangs of helplessness and pity for those two particular patients.

Out of the hospital and walking quickly, but with no set purpose, into the town centre, Mallory felt that above all else he wanted a quiet, happy, secure emotional life. He needed to love and to be loved and not at the age of twenty-seven feel all the turmoil of an adolescent schoolboy. My God, how he'd missed Sara's company yesterday – their precious Sunday together. His parents were on holiday, there'd been no real need for him to go to Wharton and mooch about the house, not feeling sociable enough to trail into the village and socialise, talking pleasantries to the villagers, sticking the ready smile on the face . . .

Sara kissed him very reassuringly when they parted after his impetuous attempt to bring the sleeping partner business out into the open during his frantic visit to Ledingham. What had it really achieved?

Sara, Howard was certain, was as much out of her depth in this love situation as he was. Try building up a picture with love and sex as the ingredients and heaven have mercy on you: she can use the wrong paints, she doesn't know the technique. She can smudge the canvas and let the colours run wildly into each other; he felt as though he was looking deeply into her heart; there was this incessant, ever-present desire to hold her, to touch her – she can't sweep love under the carpet and out of her life for ever . . .

There was a hell of a lot of traffic and people about, even by Chesley standards as he made his way to the park. Oh, of course! Of course! In front of the ornate wrought-iron, wide-open gates was the explanation – a huge notice advertising the Chesley Horticultural Society 50th Anniversary.

Before he knew where he was he had joined the queue, paid his money into the merrily circling turnstiles – it was going to be a record day. He found himself in the first of the enormous marquees stretching to the farthest end of this justly famous Chesley beauty spot.

He felt keenly the atmosphere around him. It was wonderful to be at one with this shoulder-to-shoulder crowd, all so at peace with their world of flowers, spreading themselves along the trestle tables, admiring the exhibits, buying the seed catalogues and the healthy-looking alpine plants; dozens of nursery firms competing with each other for the handsome trophies in this highly competitive business.

The tap on his shoulder was a timid one as if the person doing it was not sure of himself, and when he turned around it was herself. A very attractive female, he noticed at once. She had dark, liquid bottle-green eyes, there was something slightly familiar about her . . .

'Dr Mallory, I presume – I do hope I'm not mistaken?'

'It is indeed, my fair lady.' He felt that it was more like the sort of reply Philip Carver might have made. It was out of his character. Philip Carver was never far from his mind.

'I'm Olivia, Sara's sister – I've seen snapshots of you.'

'Oh, of course, I see the likeness now. Very nice of you to introduce yourself,' he said more formally.

The likeness was indeed there in the same dark bottle-green eyes and thick dark lashes, but this one had the brightest of auburn hair. Evidently the Nightingale females had a penchant for new hair fashions. Sara had changed the style of her dark wavy hair every time he saw her and Cathy favoured a pigeon-wing on her forehead. Even the beautiful Mrs Nightingale, when they met, had blue-rinsed streaks in the glossy silver-grey . . .

He and Olivia moved along between the stalls, prize daffodils, masses of specimen tulips, aubrietias, pansies, little pools and tiny waterfalls tumbling along, made by means of cleverly hidden hose-pipes – all was much-needed balm to Mallory's troubled spirit.

They were standing now in the flower arrangement marquee, gazing with admiration at the winning arrangement, titled 'Adam and Eve in the Garden'. A large, proud, matronly figure guarded the gold medal at her little table next to it.

Lovely leaves of palest green clearly outlined the female shape of Eve and larger dark brown leaves the taller and firmer shape of Adam – each moulded around a thick centre pole and rib-like intertwining of branches. The outstretched leafy arm of the temptress held out a rosy apple and Adam's long arm with skilful twiggy fingers was within an inch of grasping it. Bright cherry-like pebbles provided the nipples and little grey stones the navels. The lower parts were decently covered by square aprons of white marguerites, strings of them reaching round the waists. Olivia laughed.

'I see that Adam's apron is twice as large as Eve's – I wonder why?'
'Rather more to hide!'

'And up or down would make a difference,' Olivia rejoined with a sideways glamour glance and suggestive giggle. She pointed to the painted cherry stones. 'I've often wondered why men have nipples. Nobody asks what they're supposed to be for – they don't help to feed the baby.'

'Mere ornaments, dear. Leftovers from our peculiar androgynous pre-birth state when we were both male *and* female. It might have saved a lot of bother had we remained so,' he murmured quietly almost to himself. This interlocution was dangerously paralleling the washroom conversation in the Chesley Royal, and in this first acquaintance with Sara's sister he didn't want to go too far.

They found a coffee bar in another marquee and were thankful that here at least there was room to breathe.

'You may know I've got a son – Bobbie?' she inquired of Howard, her face smiling and softening perceptibly.

'Yes, I've heard of Bobbie.'

'He's just started at Mount Croft prep, we've got his name down for three public schools, including Shrewsbury. We'll have to start saving up. Lester's a spendthrift,' she said airily, as if the matter didn't bother her unduly. She might be the same herself.

'His heart's not in the business, he's better at other things.'

'Like gardening, getting inside the bonnet of a car?' Howard suggested helpfully.

'Oh no! Like being in bed!'

Olivia flirted outrageously with this unexpected male companion, eyes fluttering, getting more and more coquettish as time went on.

My goodness! If she's like this with coffee, what's she like with a few drinks inside her? Howard wondered, greatly amused by the differences between the two sisters. Sara, happy-go-lucky she might be, but she was much cleverer than this flighty one. Sara, though dreamy, had very practical goals: Sara was an enigma, her sister could easily be categorised as a type.

'I'd like four kids – but we can scarcely afford one . . .'

'You'll know Philip Carver – Councillor Carver?' he asked casually.

'Philip? Oh yes, not seen him for years though; he was engaged to Cathy at one time, you know. Cathy used to say that sex for Philip was like an itch he couldn't get at to scratch! Cathy broke it off. He's quite a well-known figure in the town now, isn't he? These things have their effects,' she finished philosophically.

So that's it? Howard had an agonising glimpse of Sara's flushed face when she told him in Ledingham that the affair had ended. Given the chance, she'd be very happy if it started all over again; the creepy thought fidgeted him away from this over-frank sister, mouthing intimate relationships so heartlessly. Carver was, after all, an urbane thoroughbred, his own sense of fairness had to admit . . .

'You are Dad's sleeping partner in his new business, I understand?'

She'd come to it at last. Howard had been patiently waiting for Olivia to make the first opening.

'Yes. Let sleeping dogs lie – let sleeping partners sleep! I'm very asleep in the business – I just get the interest on my capital every so often.'

'Lucky you have that amount of capital,' Olivia said complacently.

'Sara tells me that I was born with a silver spoon in my mouth; actually, Olivia, I have an awful guilt feeling about legacies – what have we done to deserve them?'

'Oh, it's luck – we should never decry a bit of luck. We all deserve that; it's like winning a lottery ticket!'

'Well, looked at that way, I *am* lucky. I'm half a textile merchant, and a sound asleep one.'

'Father has always worked too hard. He's been away from home such a lot – that's been mother's problem. They now lead separate lives. I'm glad Lester's not like that, though we keep poor. We like a bubble existence – parties!' She raised her eyebrows archly and looked down on the floor, reminiscing about parties. 'Anyway, Howard, it makes you almost a member of the family, doesn't it? I do wish you luck!' She finished and stood up, ready to leave, wiping her mouth on a minute handkerchief.

'Thank you, Olivia.' For an instant, Howard had the delightful uplifting sensation that she was treating him as her future brother-in-law. It gave him an enormous uplift. They strolled towards an exit.

'You know, Howard, there's a big gap of years between Sara and Cathy and me. Sara's the artistic one and nothing is going to stop her. Let's hope she wins that scholarship she's so set on . . .'

At once, the girl he so passionately loved was back here in the room of his mind, that elusive figure that even in his dreams – as soon as he thought she was his, his body and soul would tantalisingly fade away – the eternally vanishing Euridice disappearing into her underground cave. He mocked himself savagely. Only I'm not her Orpheus, my personality is not playing the right tune. The gold medal Adam and Eve was heavily symbolic.

Strolling through the Garden Tools section, they stopped now and then to admire the latest design in wheelbarrows, the painted green and red electric mowers, hedge-cutting shears, spades for giants down to those for toddlers walking in daddy's wake, the smell of peat and flowers mingling like incense within the grey light of these huge, against-all-weather marquees.

They parted outside the wrought-iron gates, a peaceful feeling of quiet contented leisure among the people thronging around. Making straight back for the hospital, Mallory felt that the fog had gone out of his mind, if not his heart. He strode quickly through the street with lighter step. Scarcely had he got inside the large, wide foyer-like entrance to the hospital, high ceilinged, typical Chesley Edwardian, when he heard a frantic voice from the reception counter calling his name.

'Dr Mallory! Dr Mallory! We've been calling you on the tannoy for the last two hours; there's been an accident. Will you speak to Dr Wilding immediately? You can speak from here.' She handed him the phone.

'What the hell?' Mallory's heart was pounding like pistons as his mind raced for an explanation; it came at once -

'It's Sara, I'm afraid, your girlfriend – thank God I've got you at last!' Tom's voice gave a palpable sigh of relief and he lowered his tone quietly as he broke the news.

'Now don't panic, she's had an accident. It's all now under control, she's under sedation . . .'

Howard's bowels went like water, he didn't wait for more. 'Right, I'm coming,' he managed to reply, already struggling out of his coat and flinging it on the counter. 'Take care of this, will you?' he heard himself automatically saying . . .

En route to Tom Wilding, Mark, a male nurse, with difficulty caught up with him as he raced for dear life along the miles of corridors; the grapevine had told him that the likeable Dr Mallory was intimately involved.

'It's legs, sir, mostly – the railway station – she fell headlong down those iron stairs over the bridge. They're steep, you know, frightfully dangerous. They should do something about it. Apparently she was overloaded, carrying rolled pictures, couldn't save herself, so the ambulancemen said.' His hoarse voice took on that slight smugness which the imparting of bad news often conveys – the something which *he* knew and Mallory didn't.

Tom had informed him in his quick, firm, professional manner, that Mr Cryer would operate in two hours' time.

Afterwards, thinking about it, Howard couldn't recall how he'd got himself into the famous consultant's room so quickly, although he did remember exclaiming to Tom, 'Cryer? I'll see him!' And thanking heaven's mercy that it *was* Cryer and not Mr Davidson. He had no confidence in Davidson . . .

Mr Cryer was a chunky, bald-headed monk of a man; there were no flowers or family photographs in Cryer's cell of a room. Howard, tightly controlled, petitioned to be in on the operation, explaining his relationship with the patient in short decisive sentences, holding his breath, his heart pounding.

Mr Cryer hesitated for a moment, glancing down on a list of his forthcoming team of helpers. Ruthlessly efficient, the famed specialist disliked sentiment above all else, but even he was moved by the pleading eyes of this tense figure standing the other side of his large and heavy leather-topped desk.

'All right, young man,' he assented quietly. 'It does a physician good to see the final destination of his magical potions,' his own eyes glinting at this sly effort at humour.

'Like to see the X-rays?' he added. 'They've just come in.' Mr Cryer drew a bundle towards him and Mallory came round and looked over the great man's shoulder.

'Multiple fractures,' the surgeon explained, 'leg bone very ragged – crushed tendons in the right foot.' He held up the photo for Mallory to see, then one after the other the films showed the grim evidence of a bad accident – shoulder blade, collar bone. 'Oh, my God!' It was a catalogue of injuries; Mallory's expressive face showed plainly his agony and Cryer took pity on him.

'My dear fellow, she's young, she's pliant, she'll survive.' Cryer was the man all right. Mallory fervently thanked him, still keeping a tight lid on the bulging core of deepest alarm and dismay.

Surgeons are like greyhounds, Howard informed himself outside of Cryer's room; you backed your fancy and cursed the rest.

Although he had little time to wait, it was pure torment to be sitting in his room, physically still, upright and stiff, and with tense, wrought nerves. He died a thousand deaths. He tried to make of himself a kind of passionate wishing machine, a perpetual turning over-and-over prayer-wheel, like those used by Tibetan monks, so that when she awakened all the screaming shock and pain of it could be transferred to himself. Such a miracle *could* happen – somehow but no, of course not . . .

After aeons of time the longed-for, dreaded moment arrived and Mallory took his place beside the scrubbed-up and silent Mr Cryer which was all that he was allowed to do as part of the team – Tom Wilding, Jones the dresser, the two anaesthetists, and Sister O'Hennessy and Nurse Birch.

When the patient was wheeled in and placed gently on the operating table, although his face was stretched hard and the hair of his head stood on end, Mallory's eyes were calm; no panic, everything under control.

Then, as though mind and spirit were caught in mid-air, throbbing, heart-stopping, impossible-to-fathom emotions swamped over him as the sister expertly rolled up the long vest-like shirt that clothed the unconscious body and there for a moment, exposed beneath him, lay all of his heart's longing, the very ultimate of desire. He sensed the quick masculine consciousness of Wilding in the glimpse of this otherness, smothered as quickly as perceived and, indeed, only come about at all because he knew of her as a special patient – as Mallory's girl.

Not in ten lifetimes would he forget his rapt pride. No battering, no gashing wounds and purple flesh could hide that glorious symmetry of waist to thigh, to knee to foot, *this* was his reality and nothing would alter it, nothing. He who had seen and joked bawdily over dozens of such sights, caught his breath tremblingly over the one.

His wavering uncertainty finally fixed itself awe-struck on the surgeon's hands. Soon, he got the detached view of the operation itself.

Cryer's glasses gleamed, as with colossal concentration his skilful fingers explored and probed, his minions held in rapt attention the carving out of living bone into the most delicate of little ratchets like a many-toothed comb so that when nature took over each little piece would fit into the next as neatly as fingers in a glove. Cryer was a king among men! He was stupendous, unbeatable!

It was late evening when the operation finished. After a moment's thought, Mr Cryer straightened up and wasted no more time. 'Another transfusion at once, I think. She lost gallons, didn't she – enough to sink a battleship!' His tone unusually jocular, was solely, Mallory thought, for his benefit, and he tried to keep his expressive face composed and calm. He heard himself saying crisply and matter-of-factly:

'What about mine, sir? What about mine? If it's the right group, sir. Of course, there's just a chance we've got some in store.'

It was the custom for the hospital staff, and most adhered to it, to donate their blood, to have it docketed, recorded, grouped and banked. The mere words of Howard's request belied the aggressive, determined thrust of jaw, daring Mr Cryer to refuse him. Mr Cryer knew that there was a battle on his hands, that the deeply troubled young doctor in front of him, who was blatantly raising the emotional temperature, would even argue the point and fight grimly and for ever to have his request at least tested.

'I don't see why not, if it's the right group. I can't see anything against it – get on with it, Mallory – see to it, Nurse.' He turned to Sister O'Hennessy, gave his wintry smile, and was gone.

Sara was wheeled into a room close to the theatre, the male part of the team dispersed, Howard's precious bottle of blood quickly arrived, and the two nurses brought the apparatus into life-giving effect over the still, deadly pale, embattled figure under its plethora of blankets.

The result of the blood test proved positive.

'I believe in prayer, doctor,' said Sister O'Hennessy, beaming, her face as triumphant as his own. Nurse Birch joined in. 'You're a lucky man, Dr Mallory. It was a lovely thought, it was –'

Both nurses were Irish to the core; more than half of the Chesley Royal staff was made up of that ubiquitous race. It seemed that necessity plus natural bent could suck healing out of the air in that land of emerald grass, of dark bogs and mountain mists.

'I knew it! I *knew* it!' Howard laughed outright and hugged himself. He could hardly refrain from hugging Sister O'Hennessy and Nurse Birch as well. He had the certainty that Fate had taken a hand – it had been ordained from the beginning.

He sat beside Sara's bed and watched his own rich, ruby-red, beyond-all-price blood seeping into the veins of this motionless body, so close to him and yet so far away. Wouldn't he have given her every drop of blood he possessed?

Just as he was on the point of leaving the forlorn, prone, beloved girl, the transfusion over and finished, Mallory had a huge bonus. Sara opened her eyes, saw him and recognised him, her mind drifting into consciousness for a moment or two.

Exultant at the service he'd been able to give her, the love and tenderness in his own eyes, patent for the two nurses to see and smile at, he bent down and kissed her bruised and bandaged face, full on the mouth.

Almost dead on his feet with sudden fatigue, he staggered to his own room and fell fully clothed on to his bed. He felt that from this day on everything for him would be divided into two. Everything that had happened between him and his heart's love was but a prelude to the long, uphill struggle ahead of them both, to repair and make good again that youthful wreck.

He had an exhilarating sense of power – his very blood was inside Sara and ran with hers. It was a bond that could never be broken; in his imagination he was already married to Sara Nightingale . . .

Chapter Eight

Muriel – Muriel Kennedy – leaned forward in her chair as far as she could go, hands gripping each other tightly on her lap.

'I think Walter is a homosexual!' she said.

'Really? How can you tell?' Sara asked innocently.

'Their voices.' Muriel was staring at Walter; he was walking along the ward with a bedpan and her eyes were following him almost as though she was willing them to leave their sockets and accompany him round the corner to the mysterious sanctuary where all the unmentionables were deposited.

'Their voices,' Muriel continued with utter conviction.

'You can tell even over the telephone, even when you've never seen them!'

Muriel was full of opinions, opinion about this, that and the other, some wise, some ironic, bitter. She could express an opinion at the drop of a hat, any time. Fifty odd years old, a divorcee and grandmother, and when she was not incarcerated in hospital with a broken leg she was a highly qualified teacher at an independent school.

'I like homosexuals,' came the soft, piping voice of Ethel, octaves higher that Muriel's. She sat primly, wrapped up in her chair on the other side of Sara's bed, curtains well drawn back between the three cubicles. It was rest time after the early mid-day meal, before visitors began to arrive.

'They're always so nice to we oldies.'

Ethel was prepared to stoutly defend homosexuals, and Sara was reminded whenever Walter approached Ethel, his manner invariably took on an old-world courtesy.

Ethel Lilley-Watts, aged over ninety and as sprightly in spirit as a hopping little sparrow; she suffered badly from osteoporosis and broke bones so often that her sojourns in the Chesley Royal Infirmary were on a par with annual holidays to Bournemouth, no worries, everything laid on to make her comfortable.

'It's blockage, you know, emotional blockage. I see a lot of it in school. Older boys falling in love with younger ones – it's just an ordinary stage in the mating game, but there's a blockage somewhere. They can't progress to the next stage – to the sex interchange; homosexuals are stuck,' she said firmly, 'like wasps in a spider's web.' Her mouth shut hard in a disapproving line.

Walter reappeared with the bedpan and took it to a row of sinks stretched along the centre of the ward where he made some apathetic remark to Maurice, the co-male nurse in this sea of feminity.

Sara's green observant eyes watched them together sympathetically. 'Have you noticed,' she ventured, 'that the female nurses, not the older ones, have the greatest pleasure in taking the mickey out of them two boys? The girls will *bring* the bedpan, but they always order one or other of the boys to go and fetch them.'

This embarrassed Sara beyond belief. She'd do anything to attract the attention of a more compliant, older nurse but this was the order of the hospital routine and this was the part of it she loathed. 'But, you know,' she added with sudden insight, 'when the female nurses get into the men's wards, the male nurses will be bossing the females around, making them do the dirty work in their turn, or perhaps there's a hierarchy, even in the matter of bed-pans.'

Muriel nodded knowingly, 'That'll be it.'

For many weeks now, Sara had been transferred to this huge orthopaedic ward, the upper reaches of which were out of her sight. It seemed as endless in length as the new Chesley supermarket. The ward was freshly painted in grey and the enormous lights, hanging one after the other in long strips from the ceiling, were always full on all day. They bothered Sara's sensitive eyesight excruciatingly, but she bore it all with commendable stoicism.

Now she could watch, sketching in her mind the comings and going of the nurses; white blouses, black skirts, short, tall, fat, thin, sweet, sour – her curiosity was insatiable. She had a special eye for Sister Roberts, boss of the ward. Flaunting her sexy walk up and down, apparently doing nothing until the two doctors arrived together, white coats contrasting with dark faces; then the whole of the staff seemed to take on an extra vitality – alert, on their toes, this was what the hospital was all about.

'I do like the orderliness of it all.' It appealed to Sara greatly, trying to make order out of the perpetual chaos she was constantly trying to fathom in this strange world. The prompt arrival of the cleaners, appearing when the patients were only half-awake, sweeping up expertly, cheerful middle-aged mums one and all; then the auxiliaries, trudging into each cubicle with basin and hot water, washing their backs, expressionless, saying scarcely a word; next the dinner ladies, trailing along the huge steel trolleys, having ascertained beforehand your preferred dish of the day, which duly came, piping hot and appetising, and that extra mug of tea smilingly ferreted out of the urn for Sara, whose mouth in this place was always dry.

The arrival of Cyril three times a week from the physiotherapy department, bringing with him his rubber boot and a small bucket and a hand pump, was an event. He filled the bucket with hot water and pulling the boot onto Sara's raised foot, he filled the lining of the boot with boiling water; it was amazing how quickly either the water cooled, or the circulation in the crushed tendons of her broken ankle warmed and responded. Soon, the blackened flesh had almost returned to normal. Now Cyril had finished with the boot and had got on to the massage stage. Sara scarcely looked at him. He came and he went.

Seemingly every half hour, the nurses reached for their chairs round the trestle table in the centre of the ward outside Sara's cubicle. They huddled over their files and records, endlessly comparing notes, writing earnestly, until as if by an inaudible signal, they all jumped up and with one accord dispersed, one nurse or other detaching herself and insisting on taking Sara's temperature, although it had already been recorded at least three times.

'Mysterious indeed are the ways of God,' Muriel opinioned irreverently.

The broken pelvis, fastened together with an intricate arrangement of steel pins and clips, the silver struts skewering her leg in three places, all had in their turn been removed and now after nearly four months Sara had progressed to the exceedingly painful and frustrating business of trying to wield a heavy steel zimmer-frame to support a few a painful, dragging steps a yard or two up and down the ward.

'Oh dear,' cried Ethel, an amusing thought smoothed the old face. 'I remember when I first came here years ago, I hadn't a clue why they were so continually giving empty wheelchairs their exercise up and down the ward, then I discovered that they were disguised commodes! I was too shy and constipated to ask!'

Muriel threw back her head and laughed heartily.

All three chuckled together in this cosy, aimless chatter.

Sara eyed the dinner ladies, stolidly performing the irksome task of packing up the dirty dishes, piling them high on the trolleys, and felt enormous sympathy for all this lowly industry which they themselves seemed to positively enjoy. 'Think of it,' she said thoughtfully, 'the rice fields, all those people knee-deep for hours in muddy water, just so that you and I can eat our rice puddings.'

Their imagination soared. 'Young boys shinning up coconut trees and banging down the coconuts for us!'

'Women endlessly picking leaves off bushes and carrying enormous baskets on their heads so that you and I can have our cup of tea,' said Ethel.

'All that bending and stooping and grubbing,' said Muriel.

'Fighting rain, snow, drought –' said Sara.

'Breeding animals, milking cows, cutting up meat, carting it about,' said Ethel.

'Merely to stuff it all into our peculiar tube-like arrangement known by the unlovely name of stomach,' said Sara.

'All of which requires an unpleasant, intricate plumbing system to dispose of what it doesn't want.'

'This spectacle business,' said Ethel, adjusting hers on her nose.

'Hearing aids,' said Muriel.

'Varicose veins,' said Sara.

'Pimples, boils, carbuncles, blisters, warts,' said Muriel.

'One toe out of ten screaming blue murder because there's a corn on it.'

'One aching tooth out of thirty-three and your life's a misery.'

'Chiropodists, clipping and clopping.'

'One eyelash in the eye, or one speck of dust and it's hell.'

'Sore throats, coughing and sneezing.'

They piled on the agony hilariously, like the flying ding-dong of ping-pong balls in a frantic game of table tennis.

They smiled indulgently when a small, immensely pot-bellied old man in the baggiest of trousers waddled into the ward carrying a large bunch of flowers which he laid tenderly on the bed of his very plain wife, patting tenderly the wispy bunch of screwed-up hair on the top of their head and greeting her as though she was the Queen of Araby.

The first visitor had arrived.

A well-upholstered nurse made her way to Ethel, who was suddenly extremely tired. Her little body in the chair, knees curled up for warmth under a thick rug, appeared to shrivel down to nothing.

'Now, Ethel dear, ready for your nap?' nurse asked as though she was addressing a thumb-sucking two year old, kindly, patronising. Ethel was favoured with a special rubber mattress and the nurse went up the ward to fetch it.

'One thing I never get used to,' Ethel remarked, 'and that's calling us all by our Christian names. It takes away our dignity,' she finished primly. 'I don't like it.'

'Mrs Lilley-Watts is a bit of a mouthful, dear,' Sara countered genially.

'It's supposed to make us all feel friendly-like,' explained Muriel. 'Nobody is more equal that others – imagine my pupils calling me Muriel' Muriel's forehead wrinkled up high at the very thought.

In less time than it takes to count one, as Sara put it, Ethel was lying on her back on the special mattress, the little bag of bones fast asleep and snoring her head off.

'Ninety-three,' Muriel pondered, speaking in a low voice. 'Do you want to live that long?'

Sara, who in her young life had never even attended a funeral, gave the matter her serious thought.

'We haven't much option, have we? Mother Nature fights for herself. She lets go as reluctantly as a bull terrier tears the pants off a postman.'

Oh, she could sum MN all right, that multi-breasted goddess, all powerful, ruthlessly in charge of the human race, fighting for it to the last painful breath at one end and breed, breed, breed at the other . . .

'You're very young to talk like that,' Muriel looked at her askance.

'I worked it all out in the slums of Ledingham,' Sara explained, her feelings of horror and of admiration of what she had seen there were deeply stirred. In a hospital one had time to think.

Muriel nodded. 'A sorry end to a sorry drama.' A note of bitterness crept into her voice. Evidently harking back to a failed marriage, Sara guessed.

'It needs gallantry to be old, in fact it needs gallantry to be a human being at all!' she added on a youthful rebound. She had to hand it to MN. Her own body had received such a battering. MN had indeed put up a tremendous fight for Sara's life and she had won; all still very painful, but this child of nature was slowly on the mend.

It was inevitable but a crying shame that all this bonhomie had to end. This life-saving had been especially valuable, an eye-opener for Sara, to find herself on such good terms with two intelligent, quick-witted women so much older than she was. Good-natured, uncomplainingly, she watched and listened to them and learnt a great deal; and had learnt also a great deal about herself in one way and another.

But end it did. In the twinkling of an eye, as Muriel put it.

The quiet questioning as to their circumstances, the inaudible conversations between sister and the doctors in the doorway, brought it all about with extraordinary swift effect, like the sudden vanishing of two or three bodies all at once in the TV murder thriller on a Saturday night viewing.

One morning, Muriel Kennedy and Ethel Lilley-Watts were both whisked away, Muriel into the care of her married daughter and Ethel into the tender care of a convalescent home.

Sara's bed, with Sara in it, was forthwith wheeled along and transplanted in the one special Amenity Room abutting the ward at the same time as an empty bed was wheeled out of it.

Obviously it was intended as a great favour, Sara suspected, not quite so much on her account, but in deference to the very popular, indeed the beloved Dr Howard Mallory. Howard himself denied absolutely having anything to do with it. No, Sara Nightingale was Dr Mallory's girlfriend whom he obviously worshipped.

It had been the talk of the ward and the envy of the young nurses for long enough. The powers that be in the form of sister had kindly decided that Howard was worthy of a little privacy during the few minutes he could snatch away from his work – before or after his exhausting shifts or during his meal times, whenever he could possibly manage. it.

Sara loved it; this pleasant, quite large room which actually had four walls and a door. The thick glass of one well shut out the excessive, glaring lights of the ward and two large windows let in natural light from a greening garden outside, just turning into autumn. Sara could hop painfully on her frame and stare down enviously. A washbasin in the corner provided oceans of hot and cold water and Sara could perform her own ablutions, which was sheer bliss.

For a few days, the Amenity Room was heaven on earth, then a conversion set in. Quite frankly, she was bored to tears. Nothing was happening. She was not as self-sufficient as she thought she was. Oh, how she missed Muriel and Ethel and the hustle and bustle and dedicated activity and hurrying about in that huge orthopaedic ward; the get-togetherness of the nurses round the trestle table, their constant confabulations, the smiles and walks and her mental sketching of the visitors.

One breakfast lady, one dinner lady or the odd nurse brought Sara her meals, and that was that.

She had finished the book her mother had brought her. Sara saw her mother now in her mind, making her spectacular entry, pausing at the doorway of the ward, sailing forth, all eyes on her, following the lure of this beautiful lady, hair just so, flashing green eyes under dark lashes which all of her brood had inherited, gliding along as though she was playing a part on a theatrical stage, a big fish in a small pond.

Sara did her best not to be uncomfortably critical, loving thoughts vying with a sense of guilt, inferiority, insecurity, the feeling of never being fully at ease with her mother.

Father Nightingale came in the evening when he could, which wasn't often. He was away on business so much; he would glance fearfully about him at the patients in their cubicles, curtains drawn back, his mouth slightly open, out of his element entirely. She encouraged him to talk about the warehouse, since these days he had no vocabulary to talk about anything else and, by mutual agreement, Howard's vital part in the venture was never mentioned.

Sara realised with sad regret – her hospital sojourn had brought it home to her – that mentally and spiritually, she had left the up-and-down vagaries of the family home long ago.

Wolfe, her tutor, to Sara's immense satisfaction, considering the circumstances in which she left Ledingham, telephoned the hospital frequently. After being told the news, on her behalf he gave notice to her landlady, Mrs Fish, to terminate her tenancy and arranged for her luggage and art paraphernalia to be returned to her parent's home.

The girls, her gang of four came regularly to begin with but now, after so many months, they were all so busy either tying the knot or refraining from doing so, merely moving in with their partners, that their visits tailed off, they popped in and popped out again pretty quickly . . .

'Oh, my heavens, Howard! What would I have done without *you*!' The very thought was unbearable, unspeakable. Sara wrapped herself in the oh-so-comforting reflection that for some reason Howard was besotted by her; then came the sobering thought that she didn't deserve such devotion. A slightly puritan streak lurked in her somewhere. She ought to have done something special to merit a man's total love for a woman.

An opinion of Muriel's came to mind. 'Your Howard,' she said, 'is like a camp fire in a dark wood. He's breezy and quick and alive and there's a deep warm glow in his heart and people can warm themselves there, out of the cold.'

'God, how much longer am I to stay here?' Lying painfully in bed on her back, Sara took refuge, as she often did, wandering slowly through the galleries of her vivid imagination. Staring round the softly lit walls she saw there, the masterpieces she pored over in her art books and Wolfe's slides she'd looked after so lovingly: Raphael's *Virgin and Child,* the exquisite, fluid brush strokes; and there were the famous Leonardo pictures; the softness of form and effortless harmony; Claude's landscapes, the incomparable Poussin; and here was Cézanne. You could look all round his figures, all the angles at once. And there again in the next gallery the ineffable French painter, the romantic Watteau, dying of consumption at the age of twenty-seven. Sara gazed and took in the minute details of his famous *La Mezzanine.* Watteau, the painter of gay fêtes and gallantries. And here was Fragonard and Boucher. She idolised them all; what a rich store she could call upon.

Some time must have elapsed. She found herself pathetically back on earth – in the Amenity Room of the Chesley Royal Infirmary, between the sheets . . .

She did not hear the door opening, there was someone in the room; then there was the banging-to of the door by some outside agency which brought her sleepily to her senses.

'Oh – it's you, Cyril.' Oh, hell – oh damn, Cyril was the last person she wanted to have to talk to just now, still suffused as she was with the wonderment of her dream state.

Cyril, a man of few words, greeted her shortly and sat down on the low easy chair beside her, ready to do his stint of massaging the damaged muscles of her badly broken but now mending leg. She closed her eyes again and felt his expert hands squeezing and letting go, rubbing, smoothing and manipulating her calf muscles. Dutifully, she replied 'yes' and 'no' to the questions he asked of her.

Cyril, in his late twenties, was infinitely forgettable in appearance apart from some rather special spectacle frames which may have expressed another side to his character, some hidden depths which were decidedly not on the surface. He had a small, petulant, pouty mouth and receding hair which, even at his age, showed signs that he would go bald very quickly.

It all happened so suddenly. It was over in seconds. It was so utterly unreal – a nightmare! Horror! Sara found herself with her nightdress up to her neck and the sheet and blanket that had covered all but her right leg was a tangled mass as he desperately clutched her left breast. Little noises were erupting from his choking throat like a hissing hosepipe, his lips wet with saliva, a growling animal at bay.

Before she knew where she was Sara's two arms had thrust him off her with a mighty heave, knocking him back onto the chair and giving him an almighty slap on the way there, which left him with a bright red mark on his ashen face. With glasses askew and staggering up, he steadied himself against the wall a yard away. His mouth was dribbling sounds of utter contrition and remorse; it was evident that Cyril was as astonished at what had happened as she was.

'I'm sorry, I'm sorry, I'm sorry, I'm sorry.' He kept on repeating it like a wailing dirge over and over again until it was an echoing sound in the dark part of Sara's mind. Her heart was palpitating, her eyes had stinging tears as she fought for control but, presence of mind rapidly returning, she found herself sending up a prayer of thanksgiving that she hadn't shouted or screamed blue murder, which would have brought all the nurses running.

This had to be kept secret, an insufferable, dreadful, private episode between them: shocking, odious, never to be spoken of. Sara felt her own breathing calming down and in rage and fury such as she'd never known in her whole life before, she sought for words.

'You bastard Cyril, you devil!'

'I'm sorry, Sara, I – I'm so sorry.'

'Sorry? For God's sake, is that all you've got to say?'

This had been sexual harassment with a vengeance; indecent assault and all he could find to say was 'Sorry!'

'I suppose it was the door being closed,' she said.

Somebody outside had shut it. It was an unwritten law that the door was left slightly ajar, unless a patient specifically asked for it to be closed. Here she was, even in this situation, trying to pour oil, to find excuses for him! Fury was foreign to her nature, it wasn't right . . .

'I've fantasised about you, Sara.'

'Fantasised? About me?'

This was unthinkable, surreal. How could he possible fantasise about me in the black and blue state I've been in, and me completely unnoticing?

Cyril took his glasses off and put them on again, turning his shamed face away from her, not daring to look squarely.

'You despicable, odious – wretch!'

She finished, unable to find the proper words to express her horror at what had happened.

'Be your age, man. Why couldn't you be your age?'

This was an inspiration. She remembered how once the girls had talked about sexual harassment. Several of them had encountered it in one form of another, even if in her case 'assault' was a better description. Telling a man to 'be his age' was a dreadful put-down. Cyril under her steady gaze seeming to dwindle to the size of a naughty boy caught in an act which had got him expelled from school.

A minute of excruciating silence fell between them, each waiting for the other to speak. This was too ridiculous for words. It added insult to injury that she had to say something and it couldn't be done gracefully.

'Get out of my sight, and don't you dare come anywhere near me again.'

She felt like a new-age warrior Boadicea, contemptuously dismissing him from her presence.

Cyril slowly gathered up his bagful of oils and ointments; with tail between legs, and still blindly confused and utterly undone, he made for the door.

'And arrange for somebody else to take your place,' she hurled after him, putting as much threat and menace into the words as she could. Even now, she felt that such a tone of voice was utterly foreign to her nature. She didn't know she had it in her . . .

She fell back into her pillows, exhausted.

Ah, but she could congratulate herself. She'd been in splendid control of the situation, in terrific form; far from she herself being put down, she found a paradoxical renewal of self-respect, a sense of her own worth in this astonishing brief encounter.

What an idiot! Beds! A bed was a most dangerous article of furniture; a scene – a tiny vignette of a large bed in Wolfe's unromantic spare bedroom.

Another of Muriel's 'opinions' impressed itself: 'Sex for men is an appetite. They want to *eat* you – swallow you whole. It's *food*.'

'Like a lamb chop for breakfast?' Sara had trailed on, laughing.

'Any time, and they like the mint sauce with it, but the lamb chop is essential.'

Those spectacle frames, those fantasies! Perhaps Cyril is a flasher in the dark, when he goes out at night – a groper . . .

Her own imagination was getting the better of her and she switched off into helpless, silent laughter, her mind worrying her into trying to find a solution, a practical answer, a quick cure that could stop the Cyrils of this world in their tracks from making such fools of themselves.

Jellybabies, that's it, that's what they need! Some immediate food a man can grab out of his trousers pocket and pop into his mouth every time an inappropriate stirring of desire got hold of him! A jelly-baby impregnated with a harmless anti-desire drug. After all, men are so clever, they can fly to the moon, surely they can come up with something so simple? There's something in men that cannot be named.

Then there emerged into full vision, from the deep, hidden, clamped-down corner in her memory, a tall, elegant, immaculately dressed figure – Philip. Philip Carver, her first love, the man who left her, literally ran away from her in the dark outside a small hut in her mother's garden. And close on his heels appeared that gigantic Titan of a man, that mighty Samson who *she* had scuttled away from like a frightened rabbit down a dimly lit enclosed wooden staircase, as fast as she could go. Memories, these she had to erase quickly back where it came from; memory was dangerous dynamite to play about with. I must put Cyril behind me, forget about it. It was a stupid tragi-comedy. No big deal.

A comfortable quotation came to her, a text she had heard somewhere: 'A man on his journey does not turn round to swat every fly that bothers him.' Cyril was more than a fly. He was a rotten monstrous clawing beetle on her, but it helped to put this prurient episode into perspective. She had changed, she'd grown up these last four months; she wasn't the same girl who left Ledingham in such a hurry and she knew in her heart that whatever might happen in her relationship with her tutor, she had shaken the dust of Ledingham behind her for ever.

Against all odds, she had returned home still a virgin and she pondered the question further. It's so out of fashion. What's the matter with me? She remembered that she'd read somewhere that it was a common custom for a fierce desert warrior, splendid in flowing robe and turban, having first impregnated his virgin bride in the secrecy of his tent, greeted the waiting crowd of expectant fellow tribesmen outside astride their frisky Arab steeds, impatient for the breathless moment when he ran out, gesticulating and leaping on the back of his own horse, wildly waving aloft with fully outstretched arm a piece of white cloth; there was a deep red stain of blood on it, the hallmark of an unsullied virgin. A mighty cheer went up . . . And what about the men virgins? There'd be a howl of shame, I suppose! Sara argued the point crossly and felt the hours dragging by, her Cyril encounter rubbing up hard against the emotional rebellion as to where she was and what she, or rather what she was not, doing with her time.

It was close on midnight when Howard appeared at the door, a white-coated figure straight from Intensive Care. When he saw that she was awake tiredness seemed to vanish from his face like a mirror wiped clean by a fine silk cloth. He came towards her, blessing the privacy of this Amenity Room, and the pale, dim light shining through the glass partition from the ward outside. If truth be known, the last months in many ways had been pure bliss for Dr Howard Mallory, having had the enormous privilege of being able to use his knowledge and skills, stage after stage, leading her out of mortal danger, watching her battered body being slowly healed, actually having her living in the same building, under the same roof, being *there*.

Now he was lying beside her, squeezing himself full-length on the bed and passionately, hungrily, kissing her cheek, her neck, her hair, her mouth, Sara basking in the low murmurings of that male voice into her ears.

What would he make of Cyril if she dared to tell him?

He'd castrate him – that's what he'd do, he'd castrate him! Sara told herself with triumph but she knew she would not deliberately create a scene if she could side-step it with wariness . . .

Now her own passion spilled out in a cry of anguish and despair, like a hurricane gust out of the wind. 'For God's sake get me out of here,

Howard – it's killing me! I want to put up my easel and canvas and paint, Howard. I want a brush in my hand. I want life to be simple. I want solitude, but not this solitude. I feel that I'm weighted down in a lead box – the same routine day after day,' her voice chocked and she held back tears and stopped, gropping for more words.

The suddenness of the outburst startled Howard to such an extent that he could only disbelievingly get himself into her bedside chair and stare at her keenly, taking on consciously the persona of a concerned doctor to calm her down, scanning her face with great gentleness and alert blueness of eye.

'But Sara, my darling,' he said, the lover taking the place of the doctor as he thought out the implications.

'I don't think *I* can do anything sweetheart, you've still a long way to go.'

'That's the point, I'm held back, it'll be years before I can walk in this hospital!'

Oh, this love of men for women! She knew that part of the young man gazing at her very intently, would be loathe to see her go, and her growing response to this love was jostling and adding to her confusion. She tried to clarify her own mind: *my* love affair is between me and my painting – my portraits, to get my scholarship, to travel and see the originals. Oh for heaven's sake, she'd had a wretched day . . .

Howard put it to her plainly. 'What, crawling on your hands and knees up the stairs to your attic studio in your parent's home, or thumping up on your zimmer-frame?' From his tone of voice she knew that he didn't approve, but the loving smile belied it. 'We'll think of something' my darling,' he promised.

He tucked the sheets around her and kissed her. 'Goodnight my darling . . .'

It was indeed a worried and distracted doctor who strode out of her room that night.

PART TWO

Chapter Nine

Philip rang the bell and Stefania opened the door. Obviously Stefania had fallen flat on her face for this handsome gentleman with the sad eyes and his look of distinction as though he ought to be a Member of Parliament or something. Her eyes goggled, rounded and black, her upper lip swathed in fine dark hair. Philip thought her unusual and he smiled benevolently. She ushered him to a chair in the drawing room, dusting it before he sat down.

'Dr Mallory doesn't like eet zur – he hates it! Coming home and expecting to sit on his favourite chair and finding eet gorn! Zere's anozzer one een its plaze.'

'Mmmmmm.' Philip made a small, judicious noise and, encouraged, Stefania blurted on, her dark foreign face eager with gossip.

'An jess when you aar geteen used to the Jacobean, you start all over again weeth zee –'

'Sheraton?' Carver suggested helpfully.

'Yes, zur.'

'Thank you, Stefania.' Philip nodded a courteous gesture of dismissal and reluctantly she took the hint and departed. He settled himself more comfortably in the fine antique wing chair which he had not seen before, and gazed around for anything else that was new.

'Oh yes, that very nice pie-crust up-ended table in the corner, useful as well as ornamental.'

It was the invitation to the wedding that re-started the relationship with the Mallorys on a social basis. The horror of Sara's accident which he'd heard about months later, and Sara's convalescence at Wharton Manor, had spurred him to send her an enormous bunch of flowers, and an explanatory note that he'd only just most belatedly heard about it, and wishing her a very speedy recovery. When the invitation to the wedding arrived, if only as the business accountant for the whole of the Nightingale family, it would have been churlish to say the least not to have accepted, and presented a nice wedding gift.

Now, with four years gone by, he loved the regular sharing of a meal with them in the intimacy of their own home.

The front door opening and shutting and vigorous wiping of feet on the doormat brought his reverie to an end. Howard strode quickly into the room. Time had consolidated a firm friendship between the two men. Rather surprisingly, they found that they had much in common. Both had the same taste in classical music, and more particularly, both hated Chesley Town bending over backwards, or rather forwards, to get on to the twentieth-century band-wagon; to put a new commercial face on itself regardless of effect, so that one had the ludicrous spectacle of pieces of avant-garde sculpture, weirdly contorted, and practically leaning on a life-sized statue of Queen Victoria flanked by two fat nymphs.

It was Sara, the ever-curious, inquisitive, practical one who had come across this solidly built 1890 stone-faced house, so conveniently near to the town centre, which they had made into their home on a rather too large mortgage. Philip had allowed his professional brains to be thoroughly picked over and then, to his embarrassment, she had insisted on paying topmost fees; typical of her, he smiled.

The one advantage, the fact that clinched it, was the good-sized double garage adjoining the house which Sara had made into a studio, and which would be really excellent once they could afford to enlarge it further. Space was made for Sara's Fiesta and Howard cheerfully left his Volvo out in the cold.

The two men 'Hello-d' and 'Ole-manned' each other warmly.

'A drink, Philip?'

'Thanks, Howard.'

'Where's my wife?' Howard asked abruptly.

'Not back yet.' Philip deliberately made his voice as mild as possible, Howard quickly mixing him a drink.

'Where the hell is she?' his host muttered as though talking to himself. He handed Philip his glass and, excusing himself and holding his own, he strode back into the hall.

'Stefania –'

'Yes, Doctor?' Stefania's voice came brightly from the dining room where she was polishing the glasses.

'Has Mrs MacAlister phoned?' He was looking at a page in an open book on the hall table. 'There's no message here.'

'No telephone calls since I arrived, sur.'

'I thought it was arranged that if my wife wasn't here, you would be?'

'I'm only here to help with the meal tonight, Doctor, nothing was said about this afternoon.' She retired again with hurt dignity into the dining room.

'Damn and blast it!' The exasperated expletive was uttered loud and clear and Howard returned to the sitting room.

'Sorry, Philip,' he apologised, his manner concerned and upset.

'That patient of mine is bedridden. I'd especially arranged for somebody to phone here on her behalf. These calls can't all be taken in surgery time.' The tone was ominous.

Philip noted the grim set of Howard's jaw. 'It's not all milk and honey here,' he cogitated, as he languidly reclined in his early nineteenth-century chair and sipped his drink.

Talking fast, Howard switched on the radio from his chair and tuned into a concert. No sooner had he got it to his liking than he began to revolve the knobs on and off to something else, fidgeting restlessly, looking for something better and better still.

Good Lord, the man's a bundle of nerves. It's worse than I thought.

'It's that damned gallery, Philip.' Howard switched off the radio with a loud buzzing snap. It was in his mood to have a confidential talk, and evidently he wanted to get it in before Sara arrived.

'I know it's been a bit of a struggle working the practice up. My predecessor allowed things to slip badly but my two partners are fine. Everything is much better and since both my parents have died – you know the story – and the bankruptcy of the estate, or rather non-estate, is settled,' he laughed shortly, 'don't you agree there's absolutely no reason to keep the bloody antique gallery going?'

Philip chose his words carefully. 'Well, I gather Mr Nightingale's not doing too well. It was a very tricky business . . .'

'No, he's not; he's under-capitalised; and if I withdrew my capital now it would go badly for him. He hasn't paid me any dividends in the last three years. He needs time. Sara's got the frantic idea that I might lose my money, and she's determined to go on selling antiques until she's bought me out.'

The devastating news of his father's fatal heart attack, which cut short their honeymoon, the absolute bolt from the blue discovery that the family estate, such as it was, was bankrupt – and Sara, wading in, working like a fiend and inimitably full of ideas, to save some treasures from the wreck for Howard's mother's sake. Then, only a year later, determined from the very start to slip off her widow's veil and keep it off, Mrs Mallory herself had just faded away and died.

To take over a going-downhill furniture gallery, stock it with the Mallory antiques and some valuable pictures, bumming up the creditors that they'd clear the debts and get better prices that way – holding them all at bay, this needed guts and courage.

Bits of land and a few more assets were sold off, and it pleased Philip to think that he himself had something to do with the easy terms arranged, thus earning Howard's everlasting gratitude and friendship . . .

The Chesley Art Gallery was the richer by two of the best Mallory pictures, an early Frith and a Francis Coates, and a small Cotman Philip had bought for himself.

'Sara's discovered she's got a flair for making money,' Philip demurred. 'One can understand her not wanting to . . .'

'That's not the real reason. It's because she couldn't take up her scholarship — the accident — one doesn't have to be a psychoanalyst to know that. Then having to rush back from our honeymoon without going anywhere near the galleries in Rome and Florence and Munich and Vienna — all those places we'd planned to visit. Now, it'll have to come later. But it isn't necessary, Philip. All this frantic work to make *my* position safe. I'm not dependent on my capital. Why can't she be getting on with her painting? That's what she *should* be doing.'

'Has she really let it all go?'

'Not entirely. She paints abstracts, and Stefania and Mrs Waite. She can't paint *me* — says I'm unpaintable!'

He tried to laugh it off but it was plain that he was hurt.

Of course he's right. Philip agreed. Neither Howard, himself, or anybody else could make it up to her. The agony of having so brilliantly won her scholarship and the grants that went with it, only to have to relinquish it all because of a time-limit rule which couldn't be breached.

'It's such a complicated schedule here,' Howard explained. 'When Stefania's not here, if Sara was doing her painting in the studio, we could have a telephone there . . .' His voice trailed off indecisively as he ran his hand through his recalcitrant fair hair.

'It isn't as if she doesn't do wonders to help in other ways. She runs this place, pays all the household bills, rates and what-have-you. Why must she go on running the blasted antique gallery as well?'

Philip had been sitting on the fence, so to speak, but after an eloquent silence, and concentrating on it as a problem which required an urgent solution, he came down firmly on Howard's side.

'A doctor's *is* a bit different, Howard, and if there's no need — it's a tragedy if she lets her painting slide.'

Howard straightened up eagerly, gulped down his whisky, and at once refilled his glass and topped up Philip's.

'If you agree, then couldn't you?'

Philip understood. They began to speak a language of eyes, Philip showing deep sympathy and looking away, embarrassed because of Howard's open acknowledgement that perhaps he had more influence over Sara than had Howard himself; as though the husband was beginning to resign responsibility for what was happening between himself and his wife. Soberly, Philip promised to do what he could.

'Don't suppose it will be much,' he warned.

He knew that Howard wanted to say more; he was all pent-up to say more, a great deal of his heart's soreness was about to be laid bare, but movement outside indicated that Sara had arrived and swiftly she was in the room.

'Oh dear, sorry I'm late – hello, both! No, don't get up. How are you, Philip?'

Gaily, she kissed them both, making no distinction between the two and, walking quickly into the dining room and into the kitchen, they heard her confident voice giving precise instructions for the meal.

Good meals were important to Philip and dinner was simple but delicious. At least Howard's no cause to grumble here, he thought indulgently. He applied himself to satisfy their conversational needs.

He's a good chap. He looked at them both with compassion, because Life was pushing them around. All the same, *she* seems to enjoy it – the way she plays it . . .

She was all grace and charm, faultlessly supervising the meal with Stefania, regaling her guest and husband, laughingly informing them about how the tops of the Egyptian pyramids had mysterious holes in them which focussed the sun's green rays directly onto the bodies of the mummies buried inside them.

Perhaps she ought to be a 'mummy' of a different kind, Philip thought silently, with a strange pang of heart.

She seemed not to have a care in the world . . .

Howard suddenly collected himself and looked at his watch.

'I'm on duty tonight. Sorry, Philip, it's my turn on the rota for our evening calls. I had a stillborn baby case this morning – very sad.'

Philip had never heard him talk shop at the dinner table before and his host was looking down at his plate pensively.

'That's *very* sad.' Sara turned full on to her husband, her memories at once flying off to Ledingham, flooding her . . .

'A priest was called,' Howard told them. 'That was a blessing, anyway.'

'As many blessings to accommodate as many angels as can stand on the head of a pin?' Philip suggested sceptically.

'One angel on the head of a pin. Blessings should be counted one by

107

one,' Sara countered, soberly. 'The child, even a stillborn one, has a soul.'
'The soul falls back into limbo,' Philip replied mildly.
'I suppose limbo is a sort of oversoul,' Howard put in, thoughtfully.
'To be recycled?' Sara's green eyes widened. 'I believe that Mother Nature is utterly soulless. Animals don't have souls; life – Mother Nature, – is purely shape and body. She's too cruel to have a soul.'
'Well,' Howard laughed, 'I'm here to nurture the body and one can't have a soul on this earth without a body to go with it, that's for sure. My body does its best for me so I must do my best for it.'
The meal over, Sara got up and headed for the kitchen to speak to Stefania and see about coffee.
The two men sipped their wine from their fine crystal goblets, the table centred by a flower arrangement of what appeared to be a new brand variety of chrysanthemums which did not look like chrysanthemums at all. Philip knew something about flowers and regretted that he now lived in a flat and hadn't a garden he could call his own.
Howard lifted up his right arm with the goblet in his hand towards the delicious small chandelier above them hanging from the ceiling and long since modernised by electric bulbs inserted into their original pale amber glass shades, the whole antique fitment delicately poised by means of three golden chains.
'Look ye well at ye goblets,' Howard laughed wryly. 'Ye may never see them again. They may be gone by next week, and perhaps the chandelier as well!'
Howard's words were facetious but his face had little mirth and he sighed; Philip could see that he hated these constant changes.
Before he could express more of his heart, Sara's cheerful voice was heard calling them into the drawing room for coffee and shortly afterwards Howard announced that he had to leave, as he had done on other occasions when a doctor's duties called him away.
'But I shan't be long,' he promised as he bent and kissed his wife – full on the mouth, Philip noted with an astonishing jolt of his own senses, but before he quickly left the room, Philip caught the appeal from Howard's very blue eyes looking straight into his own. 'Now's your chance. Talk to her, for God's sake,' was the unspoken entreaty.
Philip found himself profoundly disliking the idea of trying to influence this iniquitous wife to give up the gallery, to stay at home more, stop using the house as a storeroom, and to concentrate her mind on her neglected artistic career; it was a tall order . . .
Discreetly, under the cover of preliminary light talk, he drank her in.

He'd never seen her look better. If the curves of her body had filled out a little in the past four years, he'd never seen a woman's skin more finely textured, a mouth and a smile more good-tempered. There was a new 'something' about her, a kind of blithe assurance of one used to having her own way; mixing with the art dealers and businessmen and wealthy clients, and contending with profit and loss accounts as she did.

Sara drew up a table and they began to play a desultory game of chess. Waiting for his next move, Philip's eyes focused on the mantelpiece and his mind swerved to the extraordinary scene at the wedding ceremony. Sara's own eyes lifted to the picture blazing down challengingly on both of them. Tauntingly, in the highly coloured brush strokes, there appeared to be a swimming mermaid caught in the branches of an underwater tree, struggling frantically to get her tail disentangled.

'Has it any esoteric meaning, I wonder?' Philip asked laughingly.

'Well, yes. I think it's meant to be the Tree of Life, or the Tree of Self-Knowledge. The comedy at the wedding was a particular tête-a-tête between Wolfe and me. I might have known he'd turn up half seas over – I was crackers to have invited him! I haven't really an eye-for-an-eye disposition,' she excused herself smilingly. 'It was a replay of something that happened at my very first meeting with him in Ledingham; I can see the funny side now – I couldn't then.'

Philip chuckled as, using her hands expressively, Sara's description became lurid. 'He must have hired the whole get-up from some theatrical agency: satin-lined opera cloak, crimson cummerbund, Spanish hat, patent pumps and, of course, his own beard in all its glory.'

Philip's mind harked back to the scene of the marriage. Who would ever forget that voice booming out as loud as a compere's to all four corners of the reception room, making sure that every guest would hear. 'Dush this footballer know he's got an artist on his hands, or i'sh painging a ni-sh lil' hobby for S-Sunday afternoons?'

By heaven, Philip recalled with sudden joy, if Colonel Mallory had worn a sword, his hand would have flown to it.

'Sara, lil' hoity-toity puss, why . . . are you marrying? I'll tell . . . I'll tell you why.' Conspiratorially, he lifted a finger to stroke the side of his nose.

'Couldn't stay in hospital for ever, crutches, mummy's summer house n'good any more, Mrs Fishhhh gone. Falkland's shtudio, ah Falkland's shtudio too hot to hold her, so le'sh,' he raised an arm in dramatic salute, 'lesh go t'th'ancestral home of the Mallorys. Oh, we're privileged to *clean* the Mallory Collection aren't we? Good way t'shpend the time. Sara, y'like a cat lookin' f' somewhere to lay the kittens!'

109

'Four years my lil' Nightingale.' his voice rose to the pitch of the seventh tidal wave, his hands raised above him and pronouncing doom like a thunderous biblical prophet.

'Four years, then no marriage and, by God, no pictures either. And nobody'll care a tinker's cuss.'

Thunderstruck, all stood gaping as they listened to that prime bull's roar pulverising the Mallorys, the whole assembly absolutely rooted and transfixed.

Howard's colts were moving in but it was Sara, Sara the bride who stopped them; one moment of gasping silence, then she turned to the groom, grasped Howard's hands and pushed them up to his shoulders and, with an idiot laughing sing-song, she began pat-a-cakeing his hands with her own, calling under her breath to Hilary, the matron of honour, who, quick as lightening, as though she knew the drill, followed suit with *her* husband. Lester, the best man, waded in, magnificently beating time, the whole company taking it up. 'Woof, woof,' they sang, the colts wolf-whistling it, bawling it, enormous hilarity, dancing it, the too-formal occasion bursting at the seams to let go; total good humour, uproarious goodwill . . .

Falkland stood in all his glory at the huge gilded door of the reception room and looked for a moment utterly nonplussed. Then his eyes gazed directly into the bride's and hers into his – hers in triumph. In understanding he knew, and she knew that he knew, what the rhythmic clapping and uproar was all about. A secret message passed between them. Time rolled back to their very first encounter in his studio – the ragging, she an object of ridicule. Now they were even, she was quit of something.

But, contrarywise, Falkland was thoroughly enjoying himself. Playing his part to the end, face wreathed in a sardonic grin, he bent his huge frame, top hat in hand, and swept it almost to the floor in the widest possible bow, restoring it to his head at the most rakish angle, turning abruptly, marching through the large ornate door and shutting it behind him with the largest possible bang.

Sitting opposite her now, contemplating Sara settled in her own home, Philip envied Falkland. The man had made a gesture, extremely vulgar it was true; he felt himself stupidly ineffectual compared with such a man.

'How do I get down to the gallery – what do I say?'

He stretched out his hand and moved a bishop on the board. Only the smallest part of his mind was engaged, the rest gave itself up to enchantment – the quick movement of her head, the soft expression in the dark green eyes, the colour of her voice.

Well, here goes . . . I don't relish it. How *does* Howard cope, a doctor married to an antique gallery owner and an artist to her finger tips?

'Are you in touch with Falkland?'

'Oh, yes. He telephones me quite a lot – about art catalogues and exhibitions I don't go to, alas.'

'You haven't laid many kittens lately, have you, Sara.' Both laughed, remembering Falkland's vivid description of her predicament.

'Good Lord, kittens can't compete with antiques, moneywise, Philip,' was her light explanation. 'I've rigged up a tiny studio in a spare attic in the gallery. I keep my hand in with the sketches and abstracts. I can't do portraits there, of course, and I've very little spare time.'

'Portraits were your speciality – you were going to make your name with portraits, Sara.'

'Well, call it hubris, if you like. That's Howard's name for it, but he can't escape the fact that I owe everything to the Mallorys. It was at Wharton that I convalesced. Howard's parents took me in. I wasn't even engaged to Howard or anything. It's an awful thing to say, Philip, but I think I'd have died if I'd gone to my own home. You know how my parents bite and scratch each other whenever they're together. They are lovely parents – apart.'

'I understand.' Philip was easing himself, feeling his way towards Howard's urgent appeal to use what influence he had . . .

'You know, Philip, the bankruptcy was dreadful. Terrifying to think that Howard's inheritance went to help *my* father instead of *his* mother! One thing, at any rate, as Wolfe, blast his eyes, so explicitly stated, at least I could *clean* the Mallory pictures and pay for my keep.'

Philip smiled. Pay for her keep! As if the idea could possibly enter the Mallory calculations! He admired her fierce independence, it was the core and marrow of her being.

'Your father's business,' he asked cautiously. 'Howard isn't dependent on it for his bread and butter, you know. It shouldn't give you nightmares.'

All the pawns had gone and two knights faced each other as the next possible move in a tricky pattern.

'Nobody has asked you to take the burdens of the world on your young shoulders, Sara, least of all Howard, *or* your father, for that matter.'

'Howard has no business sense whatever, you know that,' she spoke crossly. 'It's the way he was brought up. It amazed me, the state of things at Wharton and, what I found more strange still, their cheerful acceptance of it. You should have heard old Papa Mallory laughing about it all!

'"It's all falling to pieces, Sara, the ceiling floats on nothing! We've a wonderful collection of pistols, Sara, but they're rusted to death!"

'"We've some rare books in the library," Mrs Mallory would chime in, and then she'd light-heartedly show me their ghastly condition. 'Oh, and the gorgeous Dresden gold-pendant clocks, only none of them *worked*.' Sara's expression was comical in exasperation.

'The old dears rattled off their sins of omission absolutely without guilt; why didn't they *do* something? No, they'll draw in their horns, send away the servants, live on their ancestors' investments, do anything rather than go into the world and make fortunes themselves.'

'And what would our go-getter have done?' Philip quizzed her.

'Replanted the forest,' she said promptly, 'converted the Manor into four good flats, lived in one of them and sold or got rent from the others, even if it meant selling a lot of their treasures to do it. The stables could have been taken over by a riding school. I tell you Philip, they simply can't *concern* themselves with money.'

Philip felt extremely diffident, beginning to hate the examination. 'Every time I visit you, you've rearranged the furniture. I never know where I am! Can Howard find his way about?' His tone was light, his eyebrows quizzically raised in mild inquiry.

Sara eyed him in surprise, then laughed heartily. 'Heavens above, I think Howard's been getting at you. Well – er, yes; the showroom overflows sometimes after I've been scrounging round the auction rooms. You'll appreciate that I don't want the expense of hiring another storeroom when there's a rush on. The gallery is short of space, and so it goes on.'

'And so it goes on,' Philip repeated meaningfully.

He tried another tack. 'How about starting a family, Sara?'

He knew he'd made a mistake as soon as he'd asked it, and could have bitten his tongue for asking; who was he – a bachelor – to inquire so bluntly about such an intimate matter?

But she took it lightly. 'What? Babies? Crawling among the paintpots and wetting all the antiques in the gallery? Not all hens lay eggs!' she quipped.

Changing the subject obliquely, her tone altered. 'Howard can blow his top, of course. I wouldn't have married a man who was too perfect. He works very hard and he's a softy for serving on committees. The Friends of Chesley Hospital Trust, the Youth Club out at Wharton, the Chesley Supporters Club – you name it.'

She was pulling her dress over her knees, and the grace of her body swamped him. She bent forward and moved a queen on the board then fell back again, her ballerina hair-style framed by the soft rose colour of the wing chair.

'Oh, fiddle-dee-dee, Philip.' She fluttered her fingers under her eyes and waved them limply, brilliantly mimicking the southern belles simpering and shaking their fans in the epic film *Gone with the Wind*. 'Enough of these questions.'

That was it. Sara herself had decidedly put paid to his not-too-subtle inquiries. It would do more damage than good to have pursued it further.

I love this girl – I love her!

Sara Mallory, you are infinitely dear to me . . . The miracle . . . It might have been pre-ordained for this time, this place and this moment! It was as if the ice which had been slowly creeping round his heart for aeons of time had suddenly and gently evaporated. The encrustments of habit which had brought into being something dry, something under-nourished, an emotional ring-pass-not, a boundary he'd never been able to cross since the so-painful first love of Catherine, had dispersed into thin air. Here was the blessing, oh, so infinitely desirable, of a reprieve, a pardon. I love this girl, I love this girl. He repeated it over and over again as though he was slowly drinking a deep draft of hemlock.

'Oh, look!' With a sudden movement Sara leant forward, her fingers darting quickly and decisively over her white squares. She had sacrificed a pawn, and placed a knight in a defensive position; suddenly she saw her chance, bent forward eagerly and took his Queen.

'You're trapped Philip, you can't move – I do believe I've won the game!'

'Well, well, I believe you have!' Philip echoed, laughing and abandoning himself utterly to this new-found, wholly engrossing emotion. She regarded him softly, fondly, all the slap-happy sexlessness of the dinner table melted away.

'You know, Phil, you could have got me earlier on,' she explained reflectively, and he wondered with a deep pang of the heart, whether she was speaking unconsciously.

'Your knight could have crossed my queen over to that black square.' She signified the move as it might have been.

'Your mind wasn't on the game,' she bantered.

I want her in bed. My God, it's what I've always wanted. I want her physically, mentally, spiritually – call it what you like. Then his own mind made a sickening lurch – backwards, six years ago – the rape . . . He was in the darkest labyrinthine depths he had never dare to explore before – that near-rape. Visions rose up of the entire, loathsome episode: the hut in the garden, the deliberate gutting out of the candles, his inexplicable loss of control; the rolling about and entanglement of bodies on the floor; thought followed thought, vision followed vision, as Sara was busily packing the chess board and ivory pieces into their box, chatting about this and that as she did so, and he mechanically replying with his usual wit and repartee with which he'd always been wont to serve her.

It was as if he was in possession of two minds: the one oiled and working well, the other a dreadful groundswell emerging from all the implications of his rapturous discovery – that he adored this girl.

When Howard returned, Philip had to force himself to look squarely into that candid face.

Jesus Christ, we can't help our thoughts.

He was riveted with shame; the treachery, the betrayal, the sheer tawdry meanness of what had been in his mind here in this room; he, the honoured guest, craving to play the part of the lecherous predatory male, chasing after the benighted married man's wife . . . He had utterly failed Howard, his friend, miserably. Despicably he'd failed him.

As soon as good manners allowed, he made his excuses to leave early – that he had work to do at home. 'I'll phone you, Howard,' he said cryptically, and kissing Sara goodnight was a mere peck on the cheek. He could not trust himself . . .

Driving home in the dark, he went once again into deep introspection about Catherine, his first, youthful love. It was proving to be prosaic and undramatic, a kind of artificial respiration in some subterranean fashion had been going on for years. For as long as he could remember, Catherine had been the dark symbol of his love life, demon-angel, harlot mother, regression into infantile feeling and cloying dreams – the High Goddess Hecate had pursued him for so long – it was crazy that to reach dry land he'd had to wade through such miasmic swamps.

Nobody knew that he had bouts of melancholia and depression which required great effort to fight. It was the reason for his busy council world and his perpetual round of engagements. He couldn't stand his own company for long. Hating being alone was his secret.

I'll phone Howard that I did try. He *had* tried to help him, dismal, miserable failure that it was. You can't keep women locked up at home these days, not even a doctor's wife . . .

He scoffed at the notion that he could have been of any use to Howard. They will have to sort it out for themselves, and probably very painfully, was his grim verdict, and he was again overwhelmed by the tumult of love, shame, exultation, in which this evening had so unexpectedly embroiled him.

He garaged his car and when he unlocked the door of his bachelor pad and walked through the empty sitting room to his empty bedroom, and stared at the empty bed — all he could see was Sara lying there, she his mistress, he her lover.

It was the height of irony that he'd freed himself from one sister, only to be captured by the other.

Chapter Ten

Blasted snow and ice, tons of it, how I loathe the stuff. Sara peeped through the frantic wipers of her car; supposedly the street centres had been cleared at dawn, but to very little purpose. More snow had come, browning the two feet high snow-piles pushed up on to the pavement kerbs and spattering the muddy slush up into the wheels as she steered very slowly and carefully towards the gallery.

Howard had only washed it two days ago – he needn't have bothered; all that effort for nothing; she moaned in sympathy for her husband; she could always do plenty of that, she could see his point of view, but the trouble was that she put off and put off and put off doing anything about his soreness, his exasperations, so that he'd ceased to actually *say* anything more.

She was puzzled that a man of Howard's temperament could react so snappishly over what she considered small irritations. After all, there was so much at stake in her bid to straighten out the complex financial affairs she'd been married into.

Removal vans coming and going to the marital home, bringing in and taking out antique furniture, occupying road parking spaces, making a noise, disturbing the neighbours, yes – it was a damn nuisance. But what's the alternative? I'd have to find a room to rent every time I've got an overflow, and that's like looking for gold in Chesley.

Thank God there was a bit of a breather at the moment. Things were quiet before the arrival date of Chesley Antique Fayre later in the year. The best known fair outside London, Americans came, Europeans came, Germans especially came, and there was even a fine trickle of Russians bringing in small items: clocks, samovars, objects they could dispose of quickly for the precious foreign exchange; friendly, handsome, bewildered-looking men and women.

God – you're guilty of plaguing us again! Why can't you keep your snow for picture postcards? She liked to cheer herself up with little drolleries. One had to blame something or somebody for this damned ghastly weather – it might as well be God – and for heaven's sake, why can't something be done about this bloody traffic?

Philip had tried to get the ear of the Public Works department, but to no avail. The traffic must flow, they told him, and here she was, flowing down two steep hills, round unnecesary islands since they were one-way exits and entrances, the flower beds in them now dumps of dead rotting plants, smothered in mud. She flowed into a side street, then up two hills she'd come down on. It's taken a quarter of an hour and as the crow flies it's four minutes, and it'd be a damned slow crow at that . . .

Poor, dear Philip, wasted effort again . . .

Her face softened perceptibly when her mind veered to Philip, and a thoughtful reverie took the place of her frustration about wasted time and effort.

There'd been a very subtle change in Philip's manner towards her lately, in the last three months. She couldn't put her finger on it. Something about the way he looked at her when Howard wasn't there, and their chess games together were a laughing farce as he put himself out to discuss the histories and various schools of painters and painting, particularly the Moderns. Sara's admiration for the brilliancy of Lucien Freud, Philip's hatred of the violence of Francis Bacon, her defence of his menacing suggestiveness, the sheer threatening power of those hanging lumps of flesh . . .

It was all right to flirt a little with Philip when Howard was out occasionally on his night calls, but something more? No, she was old-fashioned enough to want to be loyal to her marriage vows. Perhaps it counterbalanced too, and soothed her troubled conscience somewhat, that certain practices in her business – or rather malpractices, were getting beyond her control . . .

Carefully she parked her car in the place for her in the stone courtyard – a bit of Victorian frontage abutting the gallery, and which she shared with a few other premises, including the Sunlife Insurance Company next door, that *had* like Sara's, a nicely carved old frieze, decorating the wide, heavy, dark oak frontages.

Mervyn as ever was already waiting for her in the central space encompassed as it was everywhere with some beautiful specimens of his boss's splendidly acquired know-how, after four years of experience in the trade.

'Good morning, Mervyn,' Sara acknowledged her assistant with a beaming smile, and he beamed back at her – they were on exceptionally easy and good terms, Mervyn loved Sara as much as he could love anybody beyond himself. Mervyn was suave, very intelligent, obsequious, a great eye-for-the-main chance when it came to chatting up the customers and off his own bat, considerably inflating the prices Sara herself had estimated. And he was ambitious; Sara wondered uneasily how long she was going to be able to keep his services; like Beevers upstairs, he was irreplaceable. She had inherited them both from the previous owner of the business, a Mr Jonathon Fox, who had thoroughly imbued these men about the ins-and-outs of sticky goings on in this tricky business of antique selling; it was not good for their souls, but very good for the gallery. Mr Fox had died suddenly, and his widow, knowing something of her husband's reputation, couldn't get rid of it all quickly enough . . .

'Anything special, Mervyn?'

'Not really, Mrs Mallory. Mrs Shaw-Taylor is coming back about the walnut tallboy – you didn't tell me about the time you wanted it out of your house. Oh, and that bedroom chest-of-drawers, Miss Louisa Elliot . . .'

Sara paused at the foot of the stairs leading to the higher regions. Oh Lord! This would be the second time in two days that she'd disturb the peace of her home, with Mrs Waite fussing about it, and Louella out shopping – both only part-timers. For once a feeling of guilt spread through Sara's veins and settled in her brain as second thoughts.

'I've changed my mind about that,' she smiled sweetly over the banister, 'I'll take them out when I've to take that rosewood secretaire for storage somewhere . . .' She had to be flexible, and Howard was getting rebellious, his patience was wearing thin at times . . .

To her extensive knowledge of painting, Sara had very rapidly absorbed a good working knowledge of antiques and objets d'art, old prints and china. It was a strange combination, dedicated artist and portrait painter, and at the same time a clever, adroit business woman. She often reasoned out and philosophised to herself about money, and the function of money: money is the blood of the world, she told herself grandly; block it, plug it up anywhere, and there you'll find chaos. Business is an act of pure creativity; it's like the bee going to the flower which enticingly offers its nectar; the bee carries it on its back and eventually something that's entirely new comes forth – thick, gluey honey, and that's very nourishing.

It was nice to make a virtue out of necessity, and necessity it was, since Howard was a marvellous GP but had no business sense whatever. His £40,000 worth of capital in her father's struggling, on-the-edge self-employed business haunted her dreams: it was a question of family pride, family honour; and she herself when they married had persuaded him to buy their home on far too big a mortgage – not that he'd required much persuading . . .

Sara knew her limitations, she was a splendid, alert and knowledgeable buyer, but was no good at selling her wares to bland, ignorant, curious or inquisitive customers – they were not like her clients in her studio. No, thank God she could leave all the selling to Mervyn.

She went up the rickety stairs to the high, spacious top floor to reach her tiny office. Here, she came into her own; and here also were rooms put to very special use, for here lived her witch's apprentice, the inimitable, hateful, dirty, perpetual dewdrop-at-the-end-of-the-nose, curse-his-rotten-soul, magnificent craftsman Beevers, Amos Joshua Beevers.

Beevers was the sticker-on of saddle-backs, the carver of ball-and-claw feet and pedestal legs, the sawer-downer of stretchers for tables and chairs; Beevers was the finder of wooden-headed nails and blunt-ended screws, the patcher-upper of worm-holes, the producer of pot-rings, the maker of scars and stains and burn-marks for her antiques. He bleached, he stained, and concocted the formulas which imitated the shell-like tints, colour and patinas of walnut, rosewood, box and mahogany.

For Sara, it had all progressed almost unwittingly. It was a reputable and well-known practice to fill in unsound pieces of wood by panelling taken from other pieces of similar age and period; to repair broken legs by substituting others and of pulling out useless drawers and remaking them.

But there came a time when there were not enough legs or drawers to go round. They had to be made, carved and fashioned from modern stuff; and from thence it was only a step further to reproducing the whole article which looked so good it was easy for Mervyn to palm it off as the real thing. Sara was caught up in the wheels of her own success. One simply *had* to satisfy increasing demands and keep up with one's orders.

Beevers was in his room next door.

What's he doing? she wondered uneasily.

There were days when she loathed Beevers — days when she couldn't accept the startling situation of herself as a criminal — and the cold feeling swept over her that today would be one of them. A strange dance of angel and devil thoughts bemused her, thoughts which made up her peculiar conscience these days, upthrusting fag-ends of biblical quotations:

'Let he who is without sin be the first to cast a stone.'

'Take the mote out of thine own eye.'

'Oh, gosh, my eyes are so full of motes it'll take the rest of my life to remove them.'

It was no good trying to joke herself out of the mess. Her intentions at least had been entirely honourable when she started, if that was any comfort . . .

She opened the door into Beevers's room and flinched visibly when she heard his beastly tobacco cough. He was bending over a particularly fine Regency table, fitting on a beautiful new leg he had expertly reproduced; she saw from his expression that he was gloating over his work. He was a genius. It struck her forcibly that he loved what he was doing, his work was as necessary for his happiness as painting was for hers.

She greeted him shortly and as she silently watched his sheer craftsmanship his enthusiasm rebounded on her. Mervyn would sell it as real, pure antique and, again, terror clove her tongue and dried up the saliva; again, the torment of the damned threatened to throttle the life out of her and again it came over her now, as it so often did, how absolutely dreadful it would be if Howard and Philip and her respectable circle of friends in which they moved, ever found out how far the gallery had gone in perfidy.

The morning sale she attended was quickly over, and the professionals, Sara amongst them, made their way to the dustbins in what had once been a garden. Here, as silent witnesses to the Ring, they were sorting out the lots, splitting the differences in the bidding prices and their real value, the swapping of money exchanges going on swiftly with scarcely a word, even the little Welshman, Taffy Edwards, although he'd bought nothing at all, strolling over to claim his cut for not bidding. Dog does not eat dog in the antiques trade . . .

Sara returned speedily to her office to keep pace with her finances: the ledgers, the credit and debit accounts, the VAT forms and so much else, all expertly kept in apple-pie order. She was, after all, her father's daughter.

But, God help me, when am I going to paint undisturbed?

It came over her, as it so often did, this wild mental and physical urge to feel again a paint-brush in her hand, the exquisite sensation of the first bold stroke on the canvas. Wolfe said that if I didn't paint, I may as well be dead and how right he was. In spite of all the bustling activity, the camaraderie of the dealers and the customers, the enjoyment of making a business woman of herself, right down in the core of her was this sense of emptiness.

I've rigged up a studio here in the gallery – what more can I do?

In one of the spare rooms above the showroom she'd set up an easel, a table for paints and brushes, a sink and a chair and a cheap old mirror on the wall; and here, in any short spurts of spare time that she had, she'd kept her painting going, working on line, perspective, tone and anatomy – all the essential basics.

Oh, Picasso – your *perfect* circles, those curves and squares and oblongs, done just like that, the eye alone, no thought required, just *doing* it. I've forgotten none of it – it's still there. But trying to run two careers in tandem, as well as looking after a husband and a home was very hard going . . .

The day she married, she'd felt like a small, trapped bird, deeply enmeshed in Howard's passionate love, wrapped in inevitability; she hadn't chosen marriage, marriage had chosen her: it was *time* for marriage. Mother Nature, MN for short, calling up her resources buried deep down in every human being, the beguiling call to mate. She loved Howard but hadn't been ready for the institutional state of marriage; her scholarship had been denied her, she hadn't travelled, she was a very incomplete human being.

Wolfe had been as devastated as she was that she hadn't been able to take up the Nash Memorial Art Scholarship she had so brilliantly won; and it wasn't about the reflected glory on himself and his teaching studio, as she'd every reason to know.

Of all things, Wolfe had turned up at Wharton where she was painfully convalescing – driving his own car.

'Good heavens, Wolfe, have you had it long?'

It was a staid, dark blue Austin Maestro.

'I bought it after your acid comments that I spent too much on taxis,' he said dryly, looking straight into her face and daring her to comment further. And straight away she knew it was to do with that secret between them, never ever to be spoken about or divulged to anybody: the tragic unburdening of his soul on that fatal night when he'd described his young wife's death and the manner of it.

Perhaps the grief of telling her, Sara thought later, had acted as a catalyst about motor cars, tied as he was to a locality, and Ledingham of all places, which replaced tying himself permanently to any one woman in his life for ever. Perhaps I did him a bit of good for a change, was Sara's sober summing-up.

In the old manor house, still painfully walking about on crutches, she'd shown him her valiant efforts to clean and restore some of the Mallory ancestral paintings. His white teeth split open in a sarcastic grin but nevertheless he had encouraged her and twice again he'd made the long journey from Ledingham to see her, which was why she had invited him to her wedding, with its pantomimic drama as a result.

Since then, in all these years, Wolfe phoned her regularly and kept in touch.

She sat now in her office, her eyes deepening to a reflective, inward-looking gaze and memory, unbidden, surged in – visions, tiny vignettes, people on screens in past situations and moving about and, very much alive, was Wolfe Falkland, the man with the swaggering walk and the devilish grin deep in a luxurious beard, the man of outstanding virility – Wolfe the artist, the Maestro, Lucifer, his battering raillery and rudeness over the telephone which she'd learnt to counter with her own brand of raillery and wit – it worked, she could give as good as she got.

He said my marriage would last four years. Well, he's wrong, it's lasted five years already . . .'

Recent memory beckoned. 'I don't know what's got into Howard lately,' she wondered pensively. Only the other day they'd had a snarling row, the sound she'd grown up with between her mother and father, lashing the walls and Sara's heart thumping in well-remembered alarm. Now, the atmosphere was repeating itself, her own throaty voice of indignation and Howard's sharp growling protests in return, high and low, fits and starts, the loathsome noise losing momentum by sheer inability to carry on, only to start again, until suddenly she was caught by the silly, uncivilised, bad taste stupidity of it all. In trigger-flash reaction she'd burst out laughing, only this time Howard hadn't laughed in quick response as he usually did. He'd rushed out of the house and slammed the front door behind him.

Her deepest feelings were again stirred by memories of the six months she'd spent convalescing at Wharton after her accident. Wharton with its dreamy air of the mellowed kindliness of civilised aristocracy with its hotch-potch of architecture all blended together like the different trees in a wood, like the inlays of old furniture; and the mutual love of Howard's dear parents which vibrated as strongly as organ music. Sara bathed in it; it had seduced her; she longed to become part of it. Howard was spoilt by love: besides the adoring love of his parents, Darby and Joan, the aged retainer, Emma, the aged gardener, the aged helps from the village, all of them showering love on Howard, the son and heir. Sara's profoundest impression was one of billing and cooing and clucking over Howard; and, as is so often a syndrome of an only child, he was a natural family man, he wanted children.

I absolutely, categorically refuse to get pregnant. That was the root of the matter; she could never rid herself of what she'd seen in the slums of Ledingham: the unwanted children, the abortions and miscarriages, the disorder and profligacy of Mother Nature and the pain she demanded of women.

I'll never let MN get the better of me. Her rebellion was like putting her finger to her nose and waggling it at that omnipotent, greedy deity who used women's bodies for *her* purposes.

She only vaguely understood where the real trouble lay between herself and Howard, whether her role should be that of High Priestess or sacrificial victim in the strange ritual that was performed in bed. She was only too aware of what was going on in her mind, too little aware of the responses of her body; she felt wonderment, immaturity, disbelief.

She'd become wary, worried that in spite of over-elaborate precautions, she'd find herself pregnant; she'd think of the myth of Lilith, Adam's first wife, barren and infertile herself, and always present at childbirth. Lilith, the scream-in-the-night baleful handmaiden to miscarriages, stillbirths and similar tragedies of the bedchamber.

Now, as ever, Sara smothered any misgivings she might have about her marriage, tidied her desk and wore the bright neutral personality of a business woman scarcely touched by a marriage relationship.

The weather was clearing and the damp in the air had given way to a snappy, invigorating, ice-cold tang. Deciding that old Beevers's face would make an excellent pattern for an antique carpet, she left him to his illicit devices and instructed Mervyn to lock up for the night when the time came. She returned to her car, took herself into the centre of the town and had a quick lunch in one of Chesley's many high-class, ultra-respectable restaurants, and wondered dispiritedly whether she might call on her brother-in-law Lester's business of auctioneers, estate agents and valuers. Whenever she could, Sara passed on information about private house sales of furniture to Lester and Lester in turn was supposed to keep out of his sales and give her the chance to buy privately any special antiques or objets d'art which he thought might interest her.

Sara suddenly remembered that in actual fact Lester had, in his vague way, told her about some pews in a disused, derelict old church at the bottom end of the town, some carved wood old Beevers might find useful.

When at last she found the church she was cross and irritable; the traffic as usual was building up in frustrating stops and starts and this part of old Chesley still retained a kind of village atmosphere with narrow streets meandering into little squares and No Entrance signs everywhere.

Damn and blast – I'm lost! She got out of the car and stopped a likely person who would show her the way to St Wilfred's Church. If Howard had been with her, he'd have known the way instinctively, they'd have got there in no time. Strange, she posited, Howard just hates *asking* anybody the way to anywhere, he goes out of his way *not* to ask and he finds it . . .

St Wilfred's Church looked as old as it was, thirteenth century, she discovered. She and Howard had made a hobby of visiting numerous old churches round their beloved Wharton and interest began to assert itself. The railings in front of this poor old derelict monument to ancient piety had already been half-removed and the still deep-in-snow pathway almost obliterated the three steps up to the open stone porch. Thankfully, the front door was not locked but the latch was broken and hanging down and vandalism at once crossed her mind.

She opened it wide. Well, my God – empty! The blasted place was empty of pews, the pulpit, the wooden screen before the altar-place had been hacked out from the damp, mildewing walls leaving pathetic scars where they had been, and the plain latticed windows were broken and missing everywhere. It was obvious that one day the whole structure would be bulldozed.

Oh, Lester, you fool! Wasn't it like him, typical! He never gets his facts right. Someone had got there before her!

All this wasted effort getting here, time always a hump on her back, pressing her down . . .

There was another door at the back of the church and she was surprised that it opened out into quite a large field although it should not have been quite so unexpected, as many houses and buildings merely showed their faces as facades to the streets and behind them was open countryside.

Sara mooched across to a broken-down stone wall to the side of the church where she could just discern what looked like a row of stone steps leading down to an underground cellar door. Always one to explore, irritated and thwarted by her fruitless journey, she teetered down the steps through the slush, getting her trousers wet to the knees, hands freezing and feeling very sorry for herself. Here again the old black, ancient wooden door was unlatched and tentatively she opened it.

Inside, she saw, placed one against each of three sides of the once white-washed, but now grey-with-dirt walls, three stone coffins, cold carved sarcophagi, memorial tombs, once placed proudly and conspicuously within the church, never with bodies lying in them, the bodies always lying buried in the crypt. Sara's magpie mind was full of such scraps of information so, unafraid, curiosity uppermost, leaving the door wide open so that the dimmest daylight could filter in, she pushed her arm right down into the half-open top of the first coffin she came to, her hand feeling through a mound of dead, shovelled-up leaves of long summers ago, mixed with dead grasses and crumbly, dry earth. Ouch! She withdrew her arm as quick as she could, the palm of her hand and tips of two fingers gushing copiously with blood. Curse it, damn it! She fiddled for her handkerchief out of her large shoulder bag, staining everything as she wrapped it round the wound.

Her attention was fired, fully roused by this something on the floor of the coffin. This time she pulled up handfuls of the detritus and, as she was beginning to suspect, there, down on the very bottom of the coffin itself, she could see, even in this dimmest half-dark, a sparkle of bright gold. Very gingerly, she brought up a small shard of stained glass. She took it to the open air outside the cellar door, wiped it as best she could with her blood-soaked handkerchief, spitting on it to make it moist, and swabbed it clean. She bent over it as an alchemist might his crucible, or a scientist his bunsen-burner, and was struck dumb with admiration. She had dragged up a piece of painted glass that had a distinct design, a small diaper of maple leaves, a kind of motif found round the borders which gave the name and origin of a particular kind of glass. She scrabbled out other pieces, some quite large, very carefully holding the fragments between her two hands. She was awestruck by the unearthly brilliance of the colours, lavender, deep violet, amber and glorious emerald green.

Eureka! What have I found? Is it treasure? She said it out loud under her breath, disappointment turning to rising excitement, fever pitch. There's a market for stained glass. God almighty, I'm damned well going to find out!

To her great delight, she discovered that she had no need to risk cutting herself to pieces when she fingered her hands and arms into the other two coffins; neither of them had lids and large pieces of stained glass were more than half-way up to their tops, chock-a-block in the debris of leaves and grass and earth. Evidently the glass, years ago, had been laid where it was, by somebody who did not know what else to do with it.

'I'm going straight back to the gallery. I'll tell Mervyn and we'll fish out those large cardboard boxes in the attic; we'll get shovels and we'll wear thick leather gloves and our wellies for the slush. I'll bring brushes from the kitchen at home. Mervyn, we've got a rendezvous here tomorrow at the crack of dawn before anybody else can get here first or even smell the treasure!'

As Sara sped along the nearly deserted streets back to the gallery as quickly as she could, she began to have some unwelcome misgivings. What was she up to now? She took comfort that she herself had never actually sold a fake to any customer. She'd sat back and watched the skill in doing so which Mervyn had inherited from his predecessor; she had gone along with it, compromised herself, deviated from the straight and narrow path of rectitude!

'Oh dear,' she sighed, 'this is going to mean a lot of work. It puts back my painting farther and farther.' And there was the niggling, disquieting supposition that somewhere in all this, Howard might feel that he was being squeezed out. There was always so much to do, so much to do . . .

A quick vision came into her mind, the great painter Daumier's famous picture 'Crispin et Scapin', the young man with his hand cupped, whispering conspiratorially and very closely into the ear of another young man dressed as a pierrot. She had agreed with her 'gang of four' that it was men who were the natural born plotters and conspirators – you see them, heads together in corners everywhere, and in parliaments all over the world; but in a weird, vivid transformation she quickly replaced the model of the dissembling young man in that fabulous painting; with her own cupped hands she was whispering excitedly in perfect collusion into Mervyn's receptive ear, his face beaming with anticipation and expectancy.

Chapter Eleven

Hard physical exercise, that's what's keeping me sane, more or less sane. Howard showered himself down quickly and put on again his warm pair of trousers and polo-necked woollen sweater, dark blue with thick stripes of red and grey, and brushed both hands through his very wet hair, tidying it as best he could.

'Bye, Howard, I'm off.' Julian Huntriss called out to him from the door of the shower room, squash rackets tucked under his arm, ready to dash to the car park, to home, domesticated wife and an evening meal.

Howard had already been to his own home and come out again, fleeing the emptiness of the house. It was Luella's day off, Luella the Spanish help who had taken the place of Stefania, the Italian one, just as Mrs Waite had been superseded by Edith. This arrangement had held good for some time but Howard no more liked it, or got used to it. The retainers in his own family home at Wharton had been fixtures there throughout his parents' lifetime and he liked to see the same faces around him.

Dispiritedly, he had wandered into the dining room, switched on the fire, sat down and begun to flick his fingers through a magazine, as a grasshopper skips through the grass. His gaze fell on a large pile of books and one by one he picked them up and read the titles: *The History of Stained Glass, Glass Heritage with Particular Reference to Stained Glass.* These books about stained glass littered the place upstairs and down.

Another of her hobby-horses! Good God, she's so damned mysterious about it all. Strange foreign letters arriving by every post, Switzerland, Germany; run-rounds to find interpreters, getting herself all tensed-up, doesn't do for two of us to be like that.

For some time he hadn't felt well. He seemed to have become a being of light and air, luminous, mercurial. He felt that his whole body had taken a narrower compass and he knew he was beginning to feel unequal to the conflict unceasing within him.

To deaden his nightmare he grossly overworked, but for once surgery had finished early and, unable to bear any longer the tantalising challenge of a house which was full of her, though she came and went like a sprite, on a sudden impulse he'd shot from his chair, dashed up the stairs, changed clothes, fished out his squash rackets from the cupboard under the stairs and sought the comfort of his favourite Chesley Rugby Union Supporters Club.

Sara would be home just before seven to cook the evening meal which Luella had prepared beforehand, the cold 'befores and afters' of the meal set out and covered up on the sideboard. Sara was punctilious about this. She was super-organised. And I'm not, Howard frankly admitted. He was more easy-going about household chores and would have liked her to be more flexible but she was so damned taken up with the gallery, her painting career, and now this stained glass business, he had to agree that life would be chaos if she didn't organise it well.

He had the feeling that he was being put through a mincing machine. That hated gallery had made a complicated tangle of their relationship. It was extraordinary how something begun as a dim and insubstantial idea – selling privately the Wharton crush of overcrowded antique furniture and family heirlooms – had soon materialised into a hard, concrete way of life; things become crystallised before one is half-aware.

He'd gone over it in his mind countless times since the bankruptcy, feeling endless guilt that he'd never known of his father's financial difficulties, and had never asked.

If I'd given him Uncle Oliver's legacy it would all have been swallowed up, poured down the drain. What could it have done but shore up a few cottages?

His parents had buried their heads in the sand and Howard had inherited this inborn sense of unshakeable security, whether it was justified or not.

He wanted above all else to have the same sense of security about Sara, his wife.

He took himself to the crowded bar where he knew he'd find friends from his rugby-playing days, the old disorderly bunch of ex-players and supporters, all having long since turned themselves after gruelling study into solicitors, accountants, bankers, public servants and others enriching the mix by not being born with silver spoons in their mouths, Howard noted wryly: working electricians, would-be engineers, artisans, plumbers, men from the Gas Board, all of which pleased him, since he himself worked hard for the club's financial committee and was delighted by this inrush of new members.

But he couldn't feel sociable tonight. There was too much of exasperation and a deep loneliness in his heart. His usual bright, boyish, often jaunty disposition seemed to be slowly seeping away like an overflow of turbulent water seeping into dry earth.

He ordered his second whisky although, apart from parties and social occasions, he was essentially a beer or lager man. He carried his drink into the long, narrow, deep red and blue carpeted lounge and sat on an empty settee in front of the floor-to-ceiling glass wall which overlooked the tree-lined path and garden, the glass doors through which the members could stroll in and out in the summer time, but which were now securely locked against this hurricane-force wind churning up the leaves in the dismal early March weather.

He sloshed his whisky round in its glass and placed it on the long, narrow table in front of him. This blasted hurricane suited his mood; his attention became fixed to his left. One rocking tree, high as the club roof, was being frantically smashed into by the tree next to it. Time and time again, it drew back and then battered itself forward right into the stomach of the other thick-bellied tree, outer branches flaying and clawing and clutching, like a man yelling with anger and frustration at its stoical adversary which bent itself forward and gently slapped it back into place. Time and time again the nearer tree gathered strength between the tremendous gusts of wind to have another go. Howard felt great sympathy for the rebuffed, unavailing, baffled tree; grimly, he associated his own emotional predicament, his sense of impotence and powerlessness to alter things with the battered tree. Sara's super-exaggerated obsessive worries about their financial affairs, some private preoccupation concerning which he felt shut out, never consulted.

He adored his wife as though they'd been married only yesterday.

'I want, I want, I want her to want me as I want her – especially in bed . . .'

He stared into his whisky glass then lifted and drank half of it at one gulp. He worshipped that apple-breasted woman, as supple and lithe as a dancer. Even thinking about it made his senses quiveringly tense. He wished passionately to be the perfect lover.

She couldn't relax in his arms. It was always as though she was terrified of pregnancy; that in spite of every precaution, she feared being taken unawares; and the precautions themselves were off-putting. His eyes returned to those madly tossing trees in the garden. The jaundiced view all stemmed from his wife's unacceptance of Mother Nature – MN for short. He smiled to himself, remembering this added appendage she always gave to Nature, red in tooth and claw, and the careless, uncaring profligacy which led to plagues in the sky, millions of birds swarming and making barren in one night whole acres of man's laborious endeavours to sow crops and harvest them; swarms of locusts, swarms of bats, swarms of rabbits and mice. Nature can only regulate itself by death and disease.

'It needs Man to regulate Nature,' Sara insisted. 'Put the damned goddess in her place.'

She had this tragic view of life – tragi-comedy more likely. 'We are as we are, Howard, we can never jump out of our own skins.'

He sat thinking about it, sombrely protesting, because he saw for himself daily, even though at professional arms-length level, the struggling nobility, the stoical acceptance of incurable diseases, patients doing their best to cope with impossible situations. One's bloody well got to hang on to the idea of Man's redemption, even if we can't believe it . . .

He breathed deeply and stared into the darkness of the night, and drank more of the whisky. I almost envy the 'bachelor state', he mused ruefully – look at Philip, nobody to bother about but himself, not a care in the world, respected by all; he can indulge in every whim that takes his fancy, he'll be mayor of Chelsey someday, a chain round his neck; but there's something about Philip these days, as though he's missed the boat somewhere . . .

And there's Felix, Sara's brother, living it up in Guyana – another carefree bachelor. Felix had actually 'phoned them at Christmas, and half joking, half seriously, asked Howard if he'd care for a spell out there – the plantation had recently lost its doctor, and it was a hell of a job to find a replacement to settle in that isolated, colonial-style life . . .

Howard felt the painful twist of a chain round his own married neck for a moment but then, his senses stirred by his unaccustomed imbibing of liquid fire, there was a sudden outline of Sara in a vision before his eyes: a bachelor? Never! Not on your bloody life! If you missed out on the worries, you missed out on the joys as well. The sheer triumph, elation, jubilation, to have carried off a girl like Sara Nightingale! The love, the laughter, the magic that simmered in his blood! Testily the reality hit him hard: how do you make love to your wife when you reach a high point, her arms tight round your neck or somewhere, her head over your shoulder, and she suddenly starts ribald laughter – giggling silly nonsense – not taking it seriously, and there was always a signal when sex was a very serious business indeed. She'd make a pantomime of it, it was grotesque! It was like a piano symphony when suddenly it goes into a different key, the rhythm and harmony lost in a frustrated maze when he too found himself laughing and it all turned into nothing but a romp! He grinned sourly, the reflections lining his forehead, settling into an unhappy scowl . . .

The acerbic mood strayed into the realm of his profession: doctors running an extremely busy surgery, was getting more and more like a blasted business! All the paper work, the damnable details the partners had to keep an eye on however much you diversified and delegated. The family planning clinic, the maternity care clinic, midwives clinic, their two panel nurses busy running round and all the links to be made with other authorities: the immunisation programmes, Healthy Diet and happy Child sessions; emergencies; part-time women to-ing and fro-ing behind the reception desk, repeat prescriptions and all the bloody intricate finance involved; the over-the-top equipment the nurses had to carry about with them, bottles, rubber gloves, sterilised needles, medical data – the lot!

Perhaps he'd have been better off following the long history of dedicated colonels and brigadiers of his forebears. The thought came to him restlessly, but that wasn't likely these days, and I can't see Sara relishing the prospect . . . He got up and went across to the bar in the next room; carrying his empty glass, he asked the barman to fill it up. Standing glass in hand at the bar counter, a degree of confidence began to return to his usual cheerful optimistic self. Perhaps Sara could organise a 'get together' at home? That's an idea – invite her gang along, and he'd bring some of his own comrades-in-arms – a cocktail party, a bit of fun; ideas about a party brilliantly filled his mind . . .

'You're Dr Mallory, aren't you?' A big, frog-eyed stranger with a double chin and thick neck, a middle-aged rabbit-trap mouth and thick greying hair, sidled alongside and was speaking to him.

'That's right.'

'Mrs Sara Mallory's husband?'

Oh, so that's what I am? A husband of sorts. He looked the stranger up and down and felt his hackles rise.

'That's right,' he repeated curtly.

The stranger licked his lips, and suddenly a large, soppy smile transformed itself into an accusing, disgusted, repulsive leer. 'Clever woman – your wife.'

'Thanks.' Does this add up to all my yesterdays? he wondered grimly.

'I've had business deals with her, palmed a wonderful fake wall-cupboard on me, wedding present, a regular sleight-of-hand.'

The words floated through Howard's consciousness like some vaguely unpleasant smell.

'I beg your pardon?'

A fatuous thing to say. What does one say when someone stands in front of you and accuses your wife of fraud?

The man went on. 'That antique gallery has the biggest reputation in town for fakes. Fabulous! The things I've heard . . . Got a second opinion on my tripod-table, so-called.'

Howard nibbled at these words as a mouse nibbles cheese. Fakes, fabulous fakes, what in hell?

'Oh, I was caught all right, pulled a real fast one on me.'

The man had decided to be cheerful about it after all; be a sport . . . Philosophically, he proceeded to recite lurid details of the many dubious deals connected with Sara Mallory's gallery that he'd heard about since he himself had been made a prize ass of.

Listening intently, silently, Howard was collecting himself; slowly drying up into something stone-cold sober. He smiled when the other fellow smiled, laughed when he laughed, allowed himself to be dug in the ribs, allowed himself to be thought of as a fine smart fellow, perhaps as fake a doctor as Sara appeared to be an art dealer, ignoring his poor patients, smarming over his rich ones, a fine husband for his up-and-coming wife.

He watched his hand clutched round his glass interestedly. It was shaking as though he suffered from palsy. He banged it down so violently a quietness came over the room; men paused, looked up a second later, as of one mind, those nearby sprang from their chairs as an athletic, broad-shouldered figure uncoiled and clutched ferociously the lapels of the utterly taken-aback man next to him. The man was thrown against the bar, scattering glasses, rocking the soda syphon, spilling another man's drink. The cowering figure was shaken like a dog as Howard heard his own voice hissing thickly, 'Repeat that again! Repeat that again and I'll take you to court, do you understand? I'll bloody well take you to court!'

Crazy to commit blue murder, restraining hands were upon him. Dimly at first, then after a few seconds, realisation surged through him, full of agonising realisation of what he'd done. He saw the effects of it on the astonished faces, the alarm, and met full on the staring concern in the eyes and grimaces of his fellow men. He'd lost control of himself, upset the apple-cart, caused an uproar . . . His brain in a scattering vortex as he pushed their hands off him, he muttered thickly something about being sorry he'd done in public what he'd have preferred to do in private and, dazedly turning about, he made for the bar door.

Outside, the hurricane wind got hold of him and at once tried to strip him of his clothes, churning around him as though to emphasise the boiling and churning in his head. Struggling and buffeting his way to the car park, he flung himself into his car.

He didn't know for how long he sat like that, in his car, rigidly motionless. It might have been hours or minutes, he'd lost account of time. Nothing more than he *should* sit like that, absolutely still, rooted, was needed to underline the gross tumult which transfixed him as searingly as though he were undergoing actual physical torture.

The drink-warmth had long since disappeared, leaving an ice-cold nausea in the pit of his stomach which acted as a sort of spring balance to what what was going on in his head, and these two levels of heat and cold brought him to yet a third state, a clear still space, the eye in the storm where existed knowledge . . .

He was dragging up from the Stygian depths a flaming conviction that what that loathsome reptile had said was true, or at least there was some truth in it, maybe exaggerated, but true in essence. Things she'd let slip, the look of nightmare worry he'd caught every so often in her expression when things were supposed to be doing so darned well.

It was surprising how quickly he got there. He hadn't visited that place, that hated place in over two years. He stared at the top attic window brilliantly lit and, with a vicious bang of the car door, he was out and speeding the length of the gallery stairs, amazed to find how easily he'd walked into the private business premises which were his wife's. In the dark he ran full tilt into a body rattling quickly downwards, somebody he knew vaguely – ah! Sara's conspirator, her precious assistant.

'Oh, it's *you*, Dr Mallory.' Mervyn's tone was wheezy with astonishment. 'Mrs Mallory's in the studio, top floor right – we're a bit late tonight . . .'

Beginning to tremble, it took Howard all his time to keep his hands off the man. Astonishment changing to an enigmatic smirk, Mervyn quickly scuttled away.

Speeding more stairs two at a time, knocking himself against the narrow walls, Howard burst in, stopping dead as an animal stops. He was suddenly so weak that he could feel the blood draining out of his face and it was her voice, husky and incredulous, that brought him to a sense of reality.

'Good Lord – it's *you*, Howard! I thought Mervyn had forgotten something! What's the matter, have all the patients died?'

A brush was in her hand, a nearly finished portrait of Mervyn was on an easel in front of her. It was like the rubbing of salt deep into his mortally wounded self-respect to have that ridiculous face smiling down at him.

Howard's mouth opened and he found the words.

'In God's name, what d'you think you're doing?' His voice shaking and fury mounting, the accusations streamed out in violent jets of scorn.

Christ, how vilely cheap could she get? Did she deny she'd palmed off fake furniture – swindled poor unsuspecting men and women? How long had these filthy, disreputable, underhand dealings been going on? Was she still up to her neck in it? If so, let her bloody well get out of it damn quick or he'd know the reason why. Choking with fury, he cursed her money-making mind, branded her with outrageous selfishness, verbally thrashed her until he was exhausted, and all the time he felt that he was speaking from a great distance and he wasn't getting it across and somehow he discovered he was getting off the track.

All this bitter tirade, this loud denunciation was but a prelude, a bell-weather bagatelle, a puerile nothing compared with the dark inimitable fact he was hammering away at her, that she hadn't co-operated in bed.

'I've had enough,' he heard his own voice crying wildly, 'I'm a damned nuisance to you so I'm off.'

The dagger had been prised in his breast for too long; the livid wound would never heal.

'I'll fix things up.'

He found the strength to become briskly, arrogantly businesslike. 'The bank account can go on as before, I'll phone David tonight about a locum until other arrangements can be made, and wherever I'm going it'll be a helluva long way away from here. You can make what excuses you like.'

Mervyn's face gleamed wetly down from the portrait, his nose only just emerging from its primary button. God! For two pins I'll pick up a paint pot and blot the bloody thing out of existence. But no, I can't. Not even now could he do anything to hurt her, really hurt her. As a parting shot he returned inevitably to the pain that had lain so deeply buried.

'I never realised,' he said bitterly, 'that sex was so uproariously funny . . .'

And he had acquiesced, played it as she wanted it; the soft words, the tendernesses she knew so well how to bestow at other times, were missing from the bedroom . . .

She did not speak, made no attempt to defend herself and he saw in her eyes only astonishment for his uncontrollable torment. The wildness. The feeling of anger so intense that he thought he *would* jump out of his own skin, was mixed up, to his horror, with the stinging tears he could do nothing about.

He turned his back on her and stumbled back down the stairs. From then on he was an automaton, wired up inside to do what he was doing.

It was a total rejection of the downward path he and his wife were remorselessly following in their married life. He was as utterly taken aback as much as she was that the confrontation had taken the turn that it had.

Battling through the storm and back at home, he went straight to his small study where he saw his private patients, snatching up from the hall table Sara's telephone address book. Then he got his passport out of his desk drawer. It was amazing how quickly he got directly through by telephone to Felix, his brother-in-law, still in his office because of the difference in time zones. Making no preamble whatever, he asked Felix bluntly, could he find him a job – any job – anywhere, which he was qualified to do?

Felix practically fell on his neck. Asking no questions, he joyfully and thankfully offered him on the spot the job of reorganising and rejuvenating the moribund health clinic for which he, Felix, was ultimately responsible. Apparently, the new doctor who took it over had taken to drink in a big way, something not unknown on a remote sugar plantation, and then, nearly a month ago, the man had abruptly disappeared, no one knew where, leaving chaos behind him, since when Felix had been unable to replace him.

Next, with the grimmest possible deliberation, Howard phoned David Gascgoigne, his partner in the practice and trusted friend, announcing categorically that he intended to answer his brother-in-law's SOS at once, he didn't know for how long. Would David get hold of Hedley Whitlock quickly? Hedley was their favourite locum doctor. Yes, David thought he might be available, otherwise old, retired Dr Haycraft might be glad to fill in for a while and yes, Jean – Jean Harries, their new woman doctor, could take on some of Howard's patients.

David was sensitive to the tenor of his partner's agitated voice, or guessed that something was decidedly wrong; like Felix, he felt that the telephone was not the right instrument, or the time was not right, to ask for better reasons than the one he had been given.

With acute deliberation and foresight, as though he was looking after the requirements of a going-abroad tourist patient getting ready for a holiday, Howard tucked his head back into the storm and drove to the surgery. There, he inoculated himself against malaria, cholera and yellow fever. From the surgery he got through to Heathrow and Gatwick airports and inquired as to the time of the next flight to the Caribbean, to Guyana via Trinidad.

It was all falling into place like the devil in the pantomime having his way without let or hindrance from the fairy godmother. He was horrified to note that there was an extraordinary exhilaration in what he was doing. There'd been a peculiar male esprit-de-corps, so quick and easy had been the responses; he'd been calling up the cohorts, battle had been joined, war had been declared. Vital decisions had their own anodyne . . .

He returned home, packed a bag, phoned Sara, informed her of what he had done, that he didn't know how long he would be away. His voice curt, his heart pounding, he put the receiver down.

He took a taxi to Manchester and caught the last train to London.

Chapter Twelve

'Do what you want to do, and pay the price for doing it,' Sara said it out loud to herself viciously. 'Since Philip couldn't take me, I shall take Mark. He's to be my escort and that's that.' She imagined painfully the gossip amongst her gang of four girlfriends and sister Olivia, and brother-in-law, Lester, and Uncle Tom Cobleigh and all . . . But she didn't care.

Everybody who was anybody would be there at the theatre tonight, the last performance of Gilbert and Sullivan's popular opera, *Iolanthe*, proudly produced and presented by the gifted mother, the beautiful Mrs Diana Nightingale.

Sara was ready, waiting in the drive as Mark, the Canadian whose portrait she had been commissioned by him to paint, drew his large Rover car up and opened the passenger door for her and it purred its uninterrupted way through the quiet, for once, Chesley street.

They had scarcely time to take their seats in the stalls before Act I commenced and, as she expected, five pairs of eyes and five lots of raised eyebrows and five inquiring smiles greeted and watched them both as they pushed their way across their knees.

Sara loved this early Edwardian repertory theatre which Chesley grimly clung on to when all around were losing theirs.

As always, she was already sketching in her mind the so-satisfying oval shape, the ornate and elegant white and gold fronts of the boxes with their mysterious shadowy-red interiors, the domed ceiling painted in contrasting deep blues and amber and the bright golden lights, now dimming into black as Act I began.

She and Howard had been part of the audience so often. Oh, bloody hell! She was not going to think of that just now . . . She soon felt Mark's large hand gripping hers and his knees touching hers in the dark, but she concentrated on her mother's production and what was going on on stage.

Private Willis, resplendent in Grenadier Guards uniform, turned his large back to the audience, roaring with laughter to see that he'd sprouted a gaudy pink pair of wings between his shoulder blades, whilst the mortal male chorus in gowns and gaiters were intermixing and gambolling with the female chorus fairies; the Earl of Mounterat and Tollere, the long curled judges' wigs, the lights full on their bald heads, pates and grey hairs. Off-stage, Sara judged that both of them must be at least sixty years of age, and how she applauded them as they danced together with exquisite comic timing. The audience went mad with thunderous applause when the whole large company turned their backs and each and every one of them had sprouted fairy wings. A wonderful time had been had by all!

Olivia, who adored parties, hasd arranged for supper to be laid on for the ten of them in the refreshment room and they first gathered in the bar for drinks. 'Do congratulate your mama, it was marvellous,' Hilary enjoined the sisters, sipping their wine.

'I'm afraid we won't see her – it's their backstage party for the cast,' explained Olivia.

'The whole production was marvellous,' Sara broke in, her eyes shining with pleasure. Her mother had not been exactly a Rock of Gibraltar in her daughter's present troubles, but Sara felt no resentment whatever on that score. Her mother was her mother – a lady who had always done her own thing – and had paid her price in a poor marriage. George Arthur was not there, he was away on business . . .

As seemed inevitable at theatre bars, the five men had separated themselves from the females and were grouped together a little apart. The girls were longing to know more about Mark whose existence she'd kept warily secret.

'He's from Ontario. He's been in England for the last three months buying new machinery and getting business for his company in Ontario,' she explained. 'He'd seen one of my portraits on sale in the gallery – one of the market porters I'd got to sit for me years ago when *I* had to pay *them*, not the other way round!' she laughed. 'What's he paying you?' sister Olivia whispered inquisitively.

'One thousand pounds,' Sara told her, laughing with relish. 'He thinks it's cheap. He'd have to pay much more in Canada. He wants it, he says, for when he's president of the board in ten years' time. He's anticipating. He's got a canny Scots background.'

'Is he your lover?' Olivia asked her later, agog to know more about that tall, gangling, inclined to red haired man, not taking much part in any conversation. Olivia's lifted eyebrows and roguish smile was not in any way malicious, but she was a good digger-out of maggots . . .

'No,' Sara lied shortly. 'He's middle-aged, he has a wife and a family. I know extremely little about him.'

She would not tell Olivia that she wasn't prepared to tell Mark anything about *her* background, so very pointedly she had not asked him for his. He seemed to guard his secrets as well as she did.

'Philip would have brought me but he had a long-standing engagement to give a talk at a painting seminar in Winchester; those very scholarly articles he wrote for *The Country Forum* about Leonardo da Vinci's life and works have paid handsome dividends – he's now on the lecture-circuit list – *and*,' she laughed, 'what do you know! Who else is going to be lecturing at the same weekend school? None other than my dear ex-tutor, Wolfe Falkland. Remember him at my wedding?'

'Remember him! How could we ever forget him!' They all laughed joyously.

'He does these seminar dates now and then – gets him out of Ledingham for a change, one can't blame him.'

'Do you ever see him?' Hilary asked curiously.

'No, but he keeps in touch over the phone,' Sara replied airlily. She did not add that Wolfe loathed the idea of her turning herself into an astute business woman and neglecting the gift she was born with. The gallery was a forbidden subject between them.

She wondered as she saw their expressions change whether they were all busily assessing the truth of his prophecy – the failure of her marriage.

'And Philip?' Olivia asked with a twinkle in the same dark black-lashed, dark green eyes as her younger sister's, and almost with a nod and a wink in addition to the twinkle.

'Philip? Oh, he's fine,' Sara replied enigmatically. She was very uneasy talking about Philip to Olivia who was greatly intrigued by the six-year friendship between the two, especially in view of his passionate affair with Catherine which seemed to have sealed his fate forever.

Sara loved Philip, she always had; but she told herself that she loved him as a woman loved a priest; her love, she felt, was on a higher plane. He was distant, unattainable but it would devastate her if he went out of her life for ever. He phoned her to see how she was, he took her out almost weekly to little restaurants where they dined and talked; her ideas about art and painting and Mother Nature and mankind and womankind; and very warily on both sides about Howard. Philip seemed to have appointed himself as her unofficial guardian.

After the uproarious meal in the small theatre restaurant just beyond the bar, with Mark sitting next to her being politely interested in this very English gathering of friends on such good terms with each other, knowing each other's backgrounds, marriages, births, deaths, business affairs – it would have been discovered that they knew very little about Sara of the observant eyes and listening ears and inner thoughts, she of the great surface charm, her hard inner realities and confused emotions . . .

In great spirits and camaraderie they all kissed each other goodnight and made their way in separate cars to home and bed.

Sara, extremely sensitive to the exchanges of knowing looks and curious glances, under-the-breath remarks and muttering, took her place next to Mark in the car he'd bought in England for his business use. He hated the idea of living in Manchester, headquarters for his work connections, and thought the journey to Chesley well worth his while, although he was very vague as to actually *where* he lived in Chesley. 'Which of the many hotels?' Olivia had asked at the bar, and Sara had to confess that she had no idea . . .

His hand at the wheel, they purred swiftly through the empty Chesley streets so late at night in this balmy September evening,

I hate being a man's mistress, Sara frankly acknowledged the fact to herself. I hate the *idea* of it; his fancy woman, his doxy. It nagged her. If you don't do these things *before* marriage, she reminded herself, so you do after marriage what you didn't do before!

The thought did nothing to assuage her guilt. And it was *she* who had initiated it, unwittingly, it was true. The gallery commitments being as they were, she could only paint portraits of adult men and women at evening sessions at her home. Mark seemed such a lonely man, obviously missing his family away in Canada. Her soft heart went out to him – he was nice, decent – on impulse she'd put her hand on his shoulder, reached up her face to his and kissed him. The alteration was dramatic, the sudden hungry, pleading look in his eyes, his taut, tight sweep of arms around her, and she heard the voice of her friend Muriel from her hospital sojourn of years ago. 'Men want to eat you when it comes to sex.'

Pity overcame her. Why not? What had she to lose? Grief and rebellion overwhelmed her on impulse. The emotion over which she thought she had complete control, her caution, had deserted her. She took him upstairs to the large double bed in the guest room and they'd taken off their clothes, got into bed and made love. Nobody could have been more astounded than Sara.

Now she took Mark straight to her beloved new studio and gave him coffee. She still had an enormous thrill every time she set foot into what had once been a cold, concrete-floored garage for one car and was now resplendent at twice its length with its two large windows facing north, a properly laid on sink, floor covered by means of long, dark, glossy wooden boards, and to the eternal pleasure of her dreamy artistic eye, in the far corner she'd had made a lovely copper-canopied small red-brick fireplace and hearth fitted with a black iron antique fire-basket. An old ship's bucket banded by copper with a rope handle was filled with logs and placed on one side and, next to it, a small, old walnut table with a shaded, old, bulbous glass lamp. Here, whether she was painting or not, she could sit and dream. A lean-to car port was built outside to take two cars. Howard's was still there and Sara meticulously drove it every other day.

'All paid for by my stained-glass treasure trove,' she told her friends in laughing glee; her hunch had proved splendidly right but what a nightmare of worry that had been. Advice to be sought, litigation avoided; Sara had learnt her lesson; to have everything strictly above-board, no Mervyn or Beevers shady tricks.

She researched stained glass every step of the way, made arduous trips to London, winkled out esoteric authorities and guided herself through red tape. The precious glass was pieced together by experts in the city of York. The find proved to be a small haul of fifteenth-century Swiss glass; a specialist dealer bought it and Sara was the richer by £40,000.

Tonight, Sara preceded him upstairs to the guest room. She let Mark out of the front door at 2.30 am, a happy and contented man.

The next morning had been a very fruitful one for Sara; she'd gone to the studio at once, put up the easel with Mark's two foot two by two foot three portrait on it and retouched the eyes; plain background, shoulders and arms slightly forward, head slightly back.

She threw down the mahlstick and picked up a fistful of small brushes, the sound of them scuffling and clicking as with assured suddenness she changed them, darting down onto the canvas and each time the brush continuing upwards as though the stroke was recorded in thin but durable air; feverishly, she dipped into the paints on her palette and on the table next to her like a witch over her brew; then the sure strokes on the canvas; and every so often she up-ended the brush and pressed the blunt end hard in. With panther-like grace she drew back, then moved right back into the canvas alarmingly tilted forward so that she could work above her subject. Fingers down to the hog-hair, she was painting 'blind', by feel and touch alone like a boxer in-fighting.

It was a demonstration of white-hot alchemy, the creative impulse a glowing furnace within. The portrait was still not quite finished to her satisfaction.

Soon after eleven pm it was the acme of bliss to run a hot bath and lie full length in the bubbling foam, her senses as voluptuous as the Queen of

Sheba's must have been in her bath of asses' milk. Climbing out, she took a towel and wiped away the steam from the full-length mirror on the wall of the spacious old-fashioned bathroom, giving an infrequent and inquisitive appraisal of her body from top to toe.

'Well, not bad. Everything in the right place!' The gleaming, satiny skin pleased her for its texture – odd that she'd always been strangely perfunctory about her own body, in strongest possible contrast to her absorbent interest in everybody else's.

She slipped on her white Victorian-style nightdress and her feet by natural habit took her into her own bedroom, the connubial bedroom with its single beds; the room she and Howard had once shared, oh so long ago.

Outside of the dissembling love scenes, Sara had to concede frankly that Mark was not exactly her type; he was monosyllabic, had little conversation, his hobbies were bird-watching and mountaineering, about which she could contribute very little, and there were few outlets for her own wit and natural gaiety. He was grave, solemn – he wasn't fun. Mark gave the impression that he desperately wanted female company after a hard day negotiating difficult problems about computer machinery. Sara thought with cynical amusement that this dear, most attractive-looking man desperately wanted to be entertained; she was being called upon to play the role of a Japanese geisha girl . . .

It was Dr Jean Harries, the new partner in the practice, who had taken Sara in hand; this was the simplest explanation. She had merely invited Jean home one evening for a chat and advice about a perverse cough – she'd never looked after her health as she should – it had always been Howard and his no-nonsense approach and come for a walk and get some fresh air attitude; she'd absolutely handed over such health problems to Howard.

Jean was the motherly sort and, to her own amazement, she found herself pouring out her dread of pregnancy, her fears about the pill, and Howard's wish for a family, which did not match hers.

'Not much wrong with you physically, my dear,' Doctor Harries informed the tense, on-the-edge-of-her-chair patient, after a thorough examination of her inner hiding-places, her heart, her blood pressure and everything else. 'I'll put you on a stress pill, but leave it off as soon as you can, they are effective up to a point. But Sara, this fear of pregnancy is not uncommon – on the contrary: it isn't so much children, the responsibility, the bringing them up; it's the fear of *having* them, and let's face it, it's nine months of hell for some women – you're imagination is too vivid!'

Sara felt she was always too busy, she shied away from giving herself time for any real self-questioning and self-analysis: we make mistakes, we should do our best not to make the same mistake twice; we've got 'blind spots' we never see and so they are never put right. This was her simple philosophy.

'Life is a short span for we mortals,' Jean finished kindly, as Sara got up to go, 'we should make the most of it whilst we're here, shouldn't we?'

Well, was Mark the answer? Speeding home Sara pondered the question for once, and felt decidedly culpable, flawed and delinquent. In spite of the initial excitement, it was a messy area in her life, she concluded candidly and scornfully – a man's mistress, what was that? Life should be simple, straightforward. Her deepest need was to be able to detach herself, give people their own space to be responsible for themselves, teach themselves not to need help in the first place. But she was always finding herself embroiled, attached, bedevilled by other people's affairs; her father, Wharton, what she'd inherited at the gallery, the intimate confidences of her models in the studio, her own life locked away in secrecy . . .

In bed that night her eyes deliberately focussed on the bed beside her own – and bloody well empty these last four months! At last the tears came, it was like the bursting of a dam; she lay back on her pillow exhausted by weeks of feverish activity and dreadful bouts of stifling uncertainty . . . I ought to be better, a better person, she admonished herself desperately. I wish it was as easy as wiping out a mistake in an oil portrait – too much light here, too much shadow there. Oh God! I give up, we are what we are, I am what I am.

Joylessness seeped into her very bones; she felt the guilt of the damned; being another man's mistress was sacrilegious, impious profanity. I am a normal woman with a normal sexual appetite. There was grief and deep rebellion in this protest and now, as the harvester rejoices when he gathers in his precious load against all odds and hostile elements, slowly and deliberately she relived what had gone on in the guest room with Mark, recapturing the whole of it, savouring it, receiving in retrospect the dazzling heights of sexual fulfilment: with Mark – not her husband. She'd called a truce with MN.

She gazed at the empty single bed, so cold, devoid of human essence. From the outset of their marriage it had been agreed to sleep in separate beds, what with her restless insomnia and sometimes the urgent necessity for him to dress quickly and get out of the house for a vital night call. It amazed her that, before she could put a side-light on to see what was happening, Howard had done his vanishing trick and was gone.

Love Howard? Of course she loved Howard! Loving Howard was as natural as breathing. If you stopped doing either, you were dead. She'd never questioned it – you don't talk about breathing, you just do it. Howard was April sunshine and flying leaves and sparkling liveliness; when Howard entered a room it seemed that the windows opened of themselves, no stuffiness anywhere . . .

And he's bloody well left me! Was she to live in this large stone house by herself for the rest of her life? Living alone was an art she had not mastered, even though her self-forgetting sessions in the studio was an undying compensation: widows, widowers, old people coped, and some made an art of it, but she fell into none of those categories, she was neither fish nor fowl.

How long was this practice to go on – of only communicating with each other via Felix or Olivia? If this was to teach her a lesson, a last ditch attempt to save the marriage, the ultimate catalyst, a doctor's life-or-death medical treatment for a serious heart condition? Sexually at least he had at last succeeded, but scarcely in the way he would expect . . .

The one thing Sara hated, had always dreaded, was failure. Failure was something she could never come to terms with and, of all things, she'd miserably failed in her marriage.

Her mind jerked to Philip. 'You're getting thin, Sara,' he'd warned her bluntly. Oh, my dearest Philip, the one anchor she could cling to in such a tumultuous sea! Philip always seemed to be on the verge of divulging some solution of his own for her marital problems but he always hesitated, held off, and the moment passed . . .

She needed some practical solution, some quiet balm for her unquiet spirit. The gallery, even her on-coming painting career was not enough. She was beginning to realise that she wasn't quite as self-sufficient as she thought she was.

In the pitch dark of her bedroom she at last fell into troubled sleep. In a dream so vivid, so sensational, she was certain she actually heard Howard's footsteps coming up the stairs and he was singing in his fine baritone voice, in ringing tones, one of his favourites, the haunting aria *La donna è mobile*. He was singing it in translation:

>   Woman is fickle and born by the breezes,
>   Her thoughts will wander, ever deceiveth,
>   Fond of variety
>   She is beguiling
>   Frowning and smiling,
>   Never the same,
>   Never the same.

The final aria rang out with a tremendous flourish. Then with his quick, growling animal vigour, he was in the bedroom, his arms were around her, hugging her, rocking her, his floppy fair hair and her wavy dark hair all tangled together. In deep, profound trance they were swimming underwater in a small lake not far from Wharton; so close together were they, like two floating amoeba; like vague plants; like twins in a womb, conjoined, undifferentiated, utterly relaxed in each other's arms, no more striving, or grief or nerves, her body soft as tissue, pliable and inert. Totally relaxed they rocked slowly, remorselessly upwards and broke surface into multi-coloured light, mackerel waves. An outpouring of pure joy rushed through them both.

In bed, Sara found herself half awake, immersed in a wretched feeling of self-loathing and dejection; disordered; nothing was ever going to be right between herself and her husband, and so long as there was this heavy sadness, there was a listless disinclination to spring out of bed and make for the studio. Instead, as a kind of aching solace, she reflected, as she so often did, on the question of *mouths:* mouths could tell her so much more than eyes about the human psyche. Thick lips, thin lips, good teeth, bad teeth, gaps in the teeth hiding in and out of mouths, and the diverse shapes they twisted themselves into – sneering, leering, snarling, thrusting, then the wide-open smiles and laughter. The strange sounds that emitted from the back of those mouths, kissing, whispering, hissing sounds.

No face is 'ordinary' Sara mused . . .

She was sitting bolt upright in bed, and to her amazement, tears were streaming down her face, and she'd never been a crier.

Her tear-smudged eyes looked down on the floor, and she saw herself as a dark shadow in a pool deep, still, clear water.

She thought she heard the echo of Howard's voice, but she could hear what he was saying.

Chapter Thirteen

Mervyn is getting too big for his boots; he's not taken kindly to the brake I put on him. When it came to selling what she had bought, Mervyn was *too* good. It's his fertile imagination, Sara mused, and he's ambitious. I could never replace him . . .

It was a worry; and old Beevers had not turned up for work this morning; his wife had phoned that his bronchitis was killing him.

Mark was away on business. He wouldn't be coming in this evening so that she could not add the finishing touches which would finally complete the portrait she'd painted of him between the sessions of love-making. By and large she'd had a tedious day . . . Sitting in her drawing-room in front of the television screen, her supper tray on one side, she felt dispirited and tired.

I'll have an early night, she promised herself without enthusiasm, and went to bed at eleven o'clock, determined not to think of Howard as she so often did before belatedly dropping off to sleep.

The shock of being awakened suddenly, leaping from bliss to acute tension in a second, hearing the slap of a gate and a bang on the front door, Sara's nerves were torn to shreds. Oh God, what's that? Oh Lord, what is it? She was out of bed and at the window before she knew how she got there, dragging on a dressing gown, staring through the glass, the pale light of the street lamp illuminating the outline of two men. Good Lord! It's Wolfe – it's Philip!

She ran downstairs in screwed-up agitation, hearing a bellow like a dog baying at the moon, followed by a peculiar, snickering laugh. Sara switched on the light and threw open the door.

'We're drunk!' Wolfe bawled, teeth flashing. He was propping up Philip with both arms, Philip giggling like an insane schoolboy. She was too dumbfounded, too grossly flattened to speak.

'And he's drunker than I am!' Wolfe thumped Philip's shoulder affectionately and they staggered into the hall. She ushered them into the studio; Philip, his impeccable grey suit crumpled and the worse for wear, Wolfe, his shoes as dusty as though he'd walked the Sahara, red shirt, belted jeans; Wolfe the buccaneer and painter with a vengance, his black eyes glinting, bushy eyebrows raised . . .

'We've come to shee your pitshures, Sara, shee wot yer 'rupt to —'

She ushered them straight to the studio; Sara switched on the electric fire in the hearth and Wolfe carefully let Philip fall limply into her high-backed model chair, his eyes closed, head rolled to one side.

She glared hotly at Wolfe. 'Wolfe, you devil! *You* made him drunk!' she cried in horror. Never before in her life had she seen Philip even slightly inebriated; such an extraordinary fall from grace was inexplicable. She sat on a stool next to him and held his hand whilst Wolfe's massive tallness swaggered about the room, Roman nose and arched nostrils much in evidence.

'Wolfe, you devil!' she repeated helplessly. 'I don't think he's drunk at all; he's putting on an act to keep his new friend company.'

Sara guessed rightly: Wolfe had done all the driving. She sat and she watched, holding Philip's hand at four o'clock in the morning, her eyes fixed on her ex-tutor's face and thrusting beard as he poked them into her framed pictures on the walls and finally, with a deep sigh, sliding down on to the floor and pulling out unframed pictures and sketches that were neatly piled into the corner.

Picking them up and putting them down, as painter to painter, she could see how he was appreciating the gradual shift of styles and subjects as she'd progressed over the last ten years.

Other paintings of her Ledingham days she'd fondly preserved: bits of washing like old flags hanging from the stark tenement balconies; action paintings of scruffy young urchins shinning with spider precision over the roofs of disused warehouses, small spindly electrical human rods. Especially, she'd tried out her colours on the living rooms: the acid mauves and puking purples of cheap goblets and vases and bric-a-brac; the ox-blood wallpapers rocking the retinas; the wilting artificial flowers and the stuffed newspapers filling up gaps in the walls. As she sketched, she'd suffered the good-humoured bawdy jokes of the idle bystanders and wizened harridans sitting in their box-like balconies with their air of endless leisure; and once she'd watched with breathless wonder the sun entangling itself in Pontillist lights — the golden hair of a fabulously beautiful young girl, the 'lily on the dust heap', Sara's mind gushing with analogies from Fra Filippo Lippi and Crivelli — the matchless painters of old. All had been grist to her mill.

Wolfe paused and sympathetically turned it round full on to show her her best portrait of Old Joe, the little man she entertained in her secret bohemian digs; Old Joe, who lived in the little cupboard-like space he'd fitted out for himself under the roof rafters.

Old Joe was dead now, he'd been dead for some time . . .

'Christ, woman!' Wolfe roared a mighty bellow of laughter. 'Must you always wallow in degenerates like these?'

He was carefully investigating her catalogue of her 'second period' in style and content, and she stood up and came across to him. These were her old, treasured canvases, symbols of hope, frustration and achievement.

'I pulled them home by the forelock out of Chesley market. I paid them their fees and they asked no questions.'

'I suppose this one is a biting comment on contemporary social society?' He was grinning widely at the canvas in his hands. It was a portrait of Odette, a gargantuan woman who worked on the sweet stall. All Odette could talk about was food: food boiled, food braised, food underdone, overdone, done in white sauce. Food and fat even waddled out of her voice . . .

Wolfe put the portrait down and got up and bent his great height to Sara. 'We can't love anybody, Sara, unless we first learn to love ourselves.'

He'd seen that she'd progressed from her protesting idealistic Ledingham period to this second one of disillusion and grim humour. But there was no time for her to work out any pertinent implications as she watched him, fascinated, as he picked up from under the windows, one after the other, portraits of two girls and one boy — schoolchildren from ages ten to twelve; these were her latest. Sister Olivia had guided some of her richest friends to the studio for these excellent likenesses of their darling sons and daughters, to be given as birthday presents to their up-and-coming ambitious husbands, to hang upon their sitting-room walls and remind them of their duties as fathers. And portraits of the mums themselves were soon to follow. Sara had to admit that MN had done her job thoroughly with those strapping kids. She reciprocated Olivia's help in kind, promptly appointing her as her agent and giving her a generous share of the fees as commission. Olivia's beloved son, Bobbie, got the benefit of it, being now a boarder at Giggleswick School, one of the best public schools in the North.

It all seemed pretty small beer to Sara after her hopes of fame and fortune. She'd been side-tracked by the gallery and her passionate intent to buy Howard out of her father's business and repay the mortgage on this large house with its prestigious stone facade which she'd persuaded Howard to take on when he'd only just set up his partnership GP practice.

Although she would never admit it, the gallery, much as she still enjoyed snuffling out bargains in antiques, was becoming a drag. These children came with their mums and sat for her after school hours, so more and more she was having to leave it to Mervyn to lock up at night, yet she couldn't afford to give it all up.

'I like painting children,' she confided. 'I like painting their innocence whilst they've got it.' She didn't go on to say that they had to learn all about Mother Nature, then they'd lose their innocence all right . . .

'Oh, indeed?' Wolfe bent his eyes piercingly to look at her. 'And what fees do you charge, if I may be so bold as to ask?'

'Oh, enough commensurate with my honour,' she answered grandly, enjoying the fact that she probably charged as much as he did for similar work in Ledingham.

'Honour! *You* speak of honour! Oh, come off it, Sara.' He bared his fangs in a flashing mobility of jaw. 'Your honour is a trail of little snowflakes all round the antique business in the whole county, one can't catch up with your honour.'

Oh God, he knew about the scandal . . . She'd begged Mervyn to pipe down, to be more circumspect in his descriptions and not to inflate prices beyond human gullibility; other antique proprietors might admire him for getting away with it, but he went too far.

'People buy my furniture for the joy of looking at it,' she excused herself. After all, Amos Joshua Beevers was a genius and she could do nothing about that.

'I grant you,' Wolfe answered genially, disposed to be friendly. 'I hope your husband's enjoying himself in Guyana,' he said pointedly, black eyes staring at her quizzically.

Damn him! He's thinking of his wretched wedding prophecy. Sara remembered shivering. With the greatest agility she flinched away from the dangerous subject of her husband.

Wolfe continued to mooch around the studio, calling out to her with fair partiality all that he found to praise or blame. She could see that he was impressed, even excited, and her mood softened. All I know, he taught me; went out of his way to help me; made me his assistant, she remembered sentimentally – guiding her and going over to Wharton to encourage her to make a proper start.

He made his way slowly to the end of the studio where Mark's portrait stood on its easel in splendid isolation. He'd clearly seen her trepidation, and deliberately prolonged the agony by turning over the pages of a sketch book placed carelessly on a chair, before casually placing himself in front of it. Anxiety gripped her until she felt she could scream.

Suddenly Wolfe threw back his magnificent head in a baying laugh. 'Now this one sucks!' he crowed, gazing questioningly at Mark, and she understood with the greatest unease that he was studying it now, no longer as a portrait but sizing up the man. He bent his head comically to one side, squinting at it, cupping his chin on his hand.

'Personable, no doubt; well-satisfied with himself.' He walked up and down, closely regarding the model.

'He has a secret life, you've painted it in his eyes!'

'What do you mean, a secret life?' Pleasure as an artist and apprehension as a woman were equally alert. 'I wanted to redo the shadows at my next sitting. I thought I'd finished,' she mumbled uncertainly.

Wolfe lowered his voice. 'I can see he's your lover,' he replied very quietly.

Oh, the fiend! How could he possibly? Had he been prying into *her* mind, or the portrait's? Had she lost the art she fondly thought she had of controlling her expressions and concealing what was going on in her mind?

'Your imagination runs away with you,' she said coldly, her manner becoming very distant as she braced herself to resist the satirical baiting. He roared with laughter. 'It's in the picture, you can't get away from it!' He was taking his time, staring and absorbed.

'Oh, he's odious,' she fumed and fidgeted, her hands tightening.

She'd used a new free-stroke style, Mark sitting back in the depths of the hugely winged brocade antique chair with ball and claw feet, the same chair in which Philip now reclined, completely comatose.

A strong hard-nosed face stared back at them both: a sensuous mouth, auburn-red hair and straight eyebrows, neck well set into the collar, arms with large, capable hands relaxed and folded across his chest, an air of authority. It was a portrait from waist up, no legs visible. Mark looked what he was, a fine specimen of the Celtic race, of the typical Highland Scot whence his ancestors came.

Sara stood side by side with Wolfe.

'We're all copulating all the time, aren't we?' he rubbed it in. 'The birds and the bees and the cats and the dogs, and plants and flowers. Think of it, Sara, there are male and female *flowers*!'

'Don't forget the whales and the elephants,' Sara said sourly, bemused that she'd been rudely rumbled and was past redemption.

He left her side and viewed the other pictures scattered about. 'Who cares anyway,' she heard him mutter. 'It's of no damned consequence.'

Oh God, she wondered tiredly, why do the feathers fly? Why are we always at each other's throats? I don't enjoy arguments at four o'clock in the morning . . .

He returned to the portrait, gazing at it keenly and critically for a long time; Sara retreated to the stool and held Philip's hand.

At last he spoke. 'This *must* be exhibited.' He murmured it slowly under his breath. 'You know, Sara,' he went on with infinite kindness and proprietorial pride, 'you are a female Prometheus – think of that! A truly free spirit. You've flown to heaven with your little twig; you've stolen the fire and brought it down to earth.'

Sara's heart thumped. He was in full tutorial, garrulous flood. 'As you know, my dear, Prometheus paid for it dearly; a vulture pecked at his liver every day. There is a price to pay for freedom, Sara. You don't need me, or your missing husband, or this old chap here,' he nodded indulgently at the supine figure slumped in the chair.

She took in silently what Wolfe was telling her about herself. She made the startled acknowledgement that this great big uncouth fellow artist *knew* her; knew the secrets of her innermost soul; secrets about her which she scarcely knew herself. To Wolfe she was no mystery; she was part of the great mystery of Art, the Art that supersedes the artist who is merely her tool, her instrument. It came to Sara with relish, a revelation, what Wolfe was saying was an anticlimax. She knew her own worth, no need to fuss about it; at last she was independent of his opinion. She shrugged her shoulders indifferently.

'I'll exhibit in my own time,' was her lofty response.

'Uppity!' he mocked. '"I'll exhibit in my own time." Get yourself to London, woman, and exhibit there. Get out into the world and stand up to it, girl. Stop being Chesley-bound or you'll never taste the ripest fruits.'

Sara wondered. Time itself could grow wrinkles in the interval between high enterprise and its execution, so swift was the one and slow the other. She wished passionately that she could have twelve arms like the Hindu gods so that she could paint with each one of them.

'You know, Wolfe, that it takes two years to stage an exhibition and I notice you haven't had one yourself in London the whole time I've known you; you always make excuses.'

Attack, she decided was the best form of defence.

'Ha! Waspish! I've thought about it,' he said noncommittally.

A sudden movement by the fire alerted them both. Philip gave a loud groan and his hands thumped the sides of the chair like a marionette's.

'I think he's going to be ill, Wolfe.' Sara seized on it thankfully, feeling weak and with nothing left to say. Swiftly, Wolfe was across to him and in one movement he'd pulled the moaning man into a sitting posture and with another had him on his feet.

'You're right,' he chortled, 'he's going all colours.'

Philip slumped, almost fell, and Wolfe came to a quick decision. 'I'll carry him.'

With a heave, he had him in his arms and watching, an appreciative sparkle lit up Sara's artist's eye as silently she compared the two; the rough-surfaced Henry Moore statue extruding enormous dynamic power, holding effortlessly a Praxiteles sculpture, ravishing the senses with its relaxed and pure classical profile.

She followed a couple of yards behind them as Wolfe made for the front door. 'It's round and round the mulberry bush,' she exclaimed to herself with laughter. Philip was her troubadour: his eyes spoke love, his voice never mentioned the word. He was like the troubadour of old, singing of his love underneath her window and then his impulse was to pick up his lute and steal away.

And if Philip was her troubadour, Wolfe was her toreador, her matador, picador. He slighted, insulted and baited her, her Svengali, phoning her, making her *do* things, keeping her up to scratch, pushing her in the direction of the changing wind.

And Mark – who would be calling on her tomorrow – what was he? He was like a flashing meteor on the scene, come from nowhere; a gift from heaven sent to educate her in physical love. Her thoughts raced on as she went ahead, opened the front door and, clad only in nightdress and dressing gown, opened the rear door of Philip's car where very gently Wolfe deposited his burden into a sprawled heap along the back seat.

'Do stay overnight with him. Do look after him,' she pleaded as she bent over Philip and kissed him as though she was kissing an over-large baby, and she slammed the door to.

She wanted to thank Wolfe for his praise of Mark's portrait, she wanted to be generous, but she had no words to say it. She shivered in the cold night air and at once his great arms were around her, she felt his beard warm on her cheek and she didn't mind. She found herself dissolving happily in triumph and wonder and knew that she only had to beckon and he would come. He'd even tried to sell himself in instalments – five years at a time – it being too much to expect that she'd take all of him in one go.

Oh, at all costs she must switch off this current between them. God forbid if sex became an appetite, to be got anywhere, as if she were a prostitute. I'm glad I was never one of his many; he can't tick *me* off his list . . .

Instinctively, she struggled against him and abruptly he released her, conscious that she had gone away from him, his face massively brooding, his eyes gleaming into hers. Strangely, they had in them an underlook of sadness, of valediction, and for Sara there was nothing left but an aching consciousness of roads which they would never travel together, obscure, equivocal, unknowing, might-have-beens . . .

He put himself soberly into the car driving seat and in the moonlight his beard seemed a little ragged. Sara thought she saw a hint of grey in it; his bulk, she noticed, was thickening; there were slack muscles round his waist, evidently the large consumption of alcohol was beginning to tell; weariness creased and lined his forehead; why, she thought dejectedly, he looks fifty!

It came over her as a great shock, that that would be his age.

Chapter Fourteen

'What a hell of a noise the frogs are making tonight,' Felix said lazily, both arms resting his neck as he sprawled in the wicker chair.

'Perhaps it foretells the imminent arrival of the rains,' Howard replied hopefully, 'I can't wait.'

Felix, the boss, had invited him to dinner and now they were seated outside the verandah surrounding this large spacious bungalow, imbibing more downers before putting in an appearance in the recreation room. It was obligatory that they join the group of lonely overseers and staff whose families, because of the educational needs of their older children, were forced to make their homes in Georgetown. They did their best to entertain each other as best they could in between their leaves and occasional weekend getaways.

'We are but little knots of semi-consciousness in the ocean of Time,' Felix remarked with exaggerated seriousness, 'and one has to admit that unknotting our knots enough to walk up the road is an effort even for an old-timer like me in this heat.'

Since he came here nearly six months ago, Howard had the feeling that he was wading painfully through exhaustingly resistant swampy ground. Sitting here was a waste of time; *work* was his saviour. Without his obsessive interest in his work, this constant, overpowering heat would have driven him mad.

Both men were dressed in the proverbial shortjak and shorts. The veranda was wide-open to a purple limitless night, swarming with iridescent stars, the moon cradled on its back in a nimbus of milky blue.

Mallory's ears buzzed, his eyelids itched with sweat, his whole body felt like flaky clay which would crumble if anybody touched it; the rains had not yet come . . .

'Wart – you outrageously beautiful hare-brained scut – come here!' Felix's yell was hideous, like a Red Indian about to scalp, and it carried itself to the kitchen beyond the dining-sitting room.

'Yassir, coming, sirr,' came the reply, like a weak far-away train and Wart appeared, two vertical wrinkles creasing each side of his thick lips as lazily as a black serpent rippling through an oily sea.

'Get the piano open in the rest-room,' Felix's euphemism for the recreation room, 'and see to the drinks there, Wart.'

'Yassir, of course, sirr.'

'Y'know, Wart, you look so fat and healthy, if it wasn't so damned hot we could salt and make some juicy steak out of you!'

'We could mince him,' Howard suggested helpfully.

'We could!' Felix began a clinically detailed account of the parts of Wart he'd like to eat: tonsils could be specially picked *à la* black pudding; eyes could slip down whole like oysters; more intimate parts should be served with brain flavourings, except of course there was no brain.

Every meal was the occasion for some tête-a-tête with the household staff and who but Felix, with the possible exception of his sister Sara, would have thought of perpetuating nostalgic memories of his own native land by planting the names of all the English flowers he could think of on the hapless heads of the household, his field hands, their wives and all their born and unborn children in the house, the clinic, their own houses – no barrack-like quarters but rather rickety family structures – one and all perched high on stilts like birds nesting among the trees.

Howard found himself in a burgeoning garden of Tulips, Fuchias, Red Hot Pokers, Jonquils, Hearts-ease: a troll, this one! Their less beautiful male counterparts rejoiced in humbler nomenclature: Dandelion, Bladderwrack, and the uncomplimentary nomenclature of Wart, Compost and Weed for the houseboys, most of them black Africans or Portuguese.

For fifty years and more nothing much had changed in the routine of this remote corner where sugar could successfully be planted, cut and transported on to the Esquibo river and thus to Georgetown. The cane-cutters all loved this crazy boss, Nightingale, who said and did mad things, often going just that much too far than they knew how to take. 'Going too far' had been Felix's grievous undoing in England, responsible for his many jobs and falls from grace, but here he had so fitted himself into his exotic background, he was indigenous with it, he would never return home.

Wart's coal-black face, working somewhere between laughing and crying, for he didn't know quite what the occasion demanded, decided on laughter and hurried away to do the boss's bidding.

'We've reached the danger stage, Howard. The married men are finding it jolly hard to work to satisfy their thirsts *and* their wives. For myself, thank God, I'm a bachelor. I take things easy and wait for the cool season. You notice I contrive to have my leaves when the heat of the day and night has departed.'

Howard laughed. He knew by hearsay of his brother-in-law's leaves: the fantastic menage he was supposed to keep going in Georgetown and up the coast to Demerara: rumours of bizarre harems which, if they were true, would rival in numbers and variety those of the most prolific Arabian desert sheiks. He supposed that there might be a tiny grain of truth somewhere; when challenged, Felix neither admitted nor denied, he merely chuckled knowingly.

'Howard, I must talk to you about Mimosa,' he said. He looked at Howard squarely; all the Nightingales had the same liquid green eyes: Sara, Olivia, Catherine, Diana their mother, now Felix . . .

'It's time Mimosa got married, she's eighteen, getting on, you know. Shamrock's lined up for her, he'll make her a good husband. Of course, this doesn't mean *you* need be without. Poppy is casting roving eyes on you, I notice. They could easily be – er – diplomatically diverted. She likes white men and I can't see there's much to choose.'

Cheerfully, Felix went on, summing up with brief logic the comparative sameness of Mimosa and Poppy, and Howard felt himself going red at this so-casual reference to the stark fact that he – Howard – had in no time very gratefully accepted Mimosa's favours.

Immediately on his arrival, Felix had engaged Mimosa and her mother as daily housekeepers to do his cooking and the household chores and look after his comfort generally.

Mimosa had gone further than that; Howard smiled thinking of her; she was like a pretty piece of pottery. She stood about immobile. She knew how to stay put in one place, then trotted off in little spurts.

Mimosa blew away the sexual misgivings Howard discovered he had been storing up about himself: the fearsome awe that he was taking part in some adulterous mystery. Women, as Woman, the opposite sex, becoming a subject in his mind fluffed and blurred, he could now think of calmly again. Half-thoughts had become thoughts, sexual emotions were crystallised. He knew the outline again, the landscape; it was astonishing to think that to sort himself out in that direction he'd had to come from the other side of the world and find himself a young girl of glowing, dark mahogany skin . . .

Like the majority of cane-cutter families on the estate, Mimosa was of Indian stock; her mouth, her nose, and chin were small and delicate, her face oval; yes, he owed so much to Mimosa, she deserved a good husband.

'You know how much I owe to her.' Hearing his own voice, Howard was surprised how emotional it sounded.

Felix nodded understandingly. 'I'm a great sower of wild oats myself,' he said caustically. 'What you feel for one, you feel for the lot!' he added with a rake's cynicism.

Howard smiled. At least he knew better than that. Felix was incapable of real love; there never could be a substitute for 'the one'; if there was, I'd search the world . . .

'Not to worry, Felix. Mimosa and I haven't – er – cohabited for quite some time. I don't feel the necessity this hot weather.'

'She and her mother will, of course, continue to look after your household chores,' Felix assured his brother-in-law cheerfully.

'Oh yes, they serve me very well, I've no grumbles that way.' Howard felt his facial muscles tightening imperceptibly. Felix and Sara were alike: they were both good, natural judo performers and each had a gentle, skilful way of using their own weight to push back their difficulties: use them and come out better; whereas he, when he got his bearings recklessly barged in, regardless of consequences, right up to his bloody neck, for good or ill . . .

They got up from their chairs and sauntered outside along the pagoda walk to the recreation room which was fenced in by a short path and flowering bushes. Inside was a billiard table and a small raised platform at the far end with an old upright piano on it. Wart was behind his makeshift bar – an old shop counter, the shelves behind stacked with bottles of whisky and spirits and a large barrel of beer with modern machinery to serve it properly – Felix's only concession.

Some of the overseers and staff were already there: Robert Leathley, the boss's deputy, the little Welshman, Trevor Davies, with Martin Chalmers who was an old school friend of Davies, thus making them blood brothers, and Bengt Almgrist the Swede. Others drifted in later. No females; the younger men with wives and children stayed at home. After a few drinks, Felix moved to the piano: a little Strauss, a few bars of Beethoven. He played well; Felix did everything well. The lighter wayward green of his eyes reflected the less concentrated character compared with his sister Sara. He liked to do something for a little while, then move on to something else. He boxed, fenced, played the banjo and the guitar, he was a 'man of parts'.

Mallory was aware of noise and laughter around him, peered at the bunch of males who'd been his close companions for six months and felt an enormous longing to change the scene. If only, by some charmed distillation, he could find himself seated in a red plush comfortable seat in the Chesley Assembly Hall! Enigma Variations, Delius's Koanga; the conductor, Soltisari, standing there on the rostrum playfully tossing about the music as the wind tosses balloons . . .

They all settled down to steady drinking. Soon they'd be nicely drunk, though not Felix; Felix never was. He was in such good form tonight that he decided the party needed an uplift.

Mallory knew that bland, innocent, looking-around look. Smallish, slim-hipped, with not a spare ounce of flesh on him anywhere, with a brilliant smile and quick as lightning, Felix whipped off the tablecloth from a nearby table and, discarding his shorts, he bunched it round his middle in a lacy ballet-skirt. Unceremoniously, he snatched Howard's towel from his lap; Leathley switched off all but one light and the long wooden room at once assumed the dimensions of a shadowy stage.

Turning to the piano, Trevor Davies cleverly improvised on an 'In a Persian Market' theme, and Felix skipped lightly in from the wings, mincing light as gossamer on naked toes, the towel gently flapping, arms gracefully stretched and fluttering, he pirouetted, shook himself like a tambourine, tangoed with an imaginary partner then with raised behind he reverted to the bandy-legged inelegance of an aged ape, muttering gibberish, eyes rolling in idiocy, hairy legs sagging and sagging, antics becoming weak and eccentric, scratching his chest and brisking his back with the towel; skipping and hopping like a little girl, undulating like a duck, his tutu fell off and, completely naked he rippled his muscles in expressive regret and carefully retied it amidst the wild thunder of the piano.

In madder and madder excitement, Felix twirled the towel round and round his head in cowboy lassos, made a flying leap for the chandelier, thank God missing it and, unabashed, the born dancer skilfully floated down, delicately quivering and twitching the rag towel until, at last, the dying swan sank exhausted in low obeisance to the floor.

The guests were collapsed in their charts, wiping the dripping sweat from their eyes, their tongues hanging out for a drink.

It was an amazing performance; nonchalantly, Felix retrieved his shortjak shorts . . .

Wart began to dispense gallons of beer, the atmosphere from tobacco smoke could be cut with a knife, and Howard, who'd been trying desperately to break the smoking habit, was sorely tempted to restart.

God, I must get out of here! Suddenly, wildly, Mallory stood up and was tearing out through the heavy mosquito curtain, down the veranda steps, fighting to stop the violent hammering in his brain, down the short path and reaching for the wooden fence for support. If he didn't have some fresh air, he'd die . . .

It seemed only a few minutes passed before Felix came down the steps to join him, but he'd lost account of time, so utterly was Sara occupying every fibre of his being, Sara his wife who wouldn't be shut out any longer.

Howard turned wearily to this so self-contained man next to him. 'How can we think we are honest, Felix, even in matters of love?' These last months, like a snail he'd been forced to carry his past around with him, and who was he to judge what Sara had been doing in the hated gallery?

'I've had plenty of time rotting here to question myself – you can't keep the lid down *all* the time – I lent her father, your father, money, did you know that? I was a partner in your father's business and I dressed it all up, even to myself, that I was merely giving a helping hand to somebody who needed the capital more than I did. But the fact remains, it was the Nightingale family, and I grabbed it. Also, I got her to spend months on end at Wharton after her accident; grabbed that too; Sara felt *obliged* to marry me.'

'I fear I'd find your kind of love a hell of a restriction, ole man. I tell you what – life is mysterious, miraculous, transient and ridiculous; above all ridiculous. We perceive a thing, we get pleasure or pain out of this, they drift in and out, then, if we're not too lazy or too damned hot, we cease to think, we find ourselves dancing. Life's just a dance of relationships, with some people you waltz, with others it's a foxtrot or a bloody energetic Scottish reel. I suspect that between you and Sara it's a tango. You know what can happen in a tango.' He left the thought enigmatically unfinished. 'You're a bloody good doctor anyway, Howard,' he finished consolingly over his shoulder as he made his way back up the veranda steps to the rest room.

Moodily immersed in dejected self-questioning, Howard made his way back to his own home, reflecting that after a heap of correspondence with their joint bank in Chesley, he'd discovered that Sara hadn't touched a penny of his own salary that had been passed on to her; it looked as if she'd severed all connection with him: then via Olivia he'd learnt that every penny had been expertly invested in profitable shares. He was told too something about a sideline in stained glass – all those books that were lying around when he so abruptly left the marital home; it was all beyond him. Sara didn't want to be looked after and protected from the slings and arrows of outrageous fortune; he knew that she'd be coping, and that at least was a comfort – like whistling in the dark, or clutching a golden charm in your pocket. But deep down, nobody knew better than Howard himself, that he was a man who needed to be needed, an outlet for his innate tender loving care – a family man without a family . . .

Next day he was up early and quickly made his way to the low brick building which was an up-to-date, comparatively new accommodation for the clinic which the company owners and the Georgetown powers-that-be financed between them, under the easy control of Felix Nightingale, general manager of this large sugar plantation. The clinic served not only the needs of the plantation, but those of the surrounding villages and a host of outlying hamlets. Howard's excellent gifts for easy relationships, his close ties with his brother-in-law, and his rapport with all and sundry of staff and overseers, right down to the field workers and village families, eased his path considerably; if *work* was a dance, as Felix postulated, then he could dance all right.

His first object was to set up a voluntary rota of any of the men's wives who lived on the estate, be they black, white or brown, to help him reorganise the antenatal child surveillance, welfare and immunisation scheme. The female volunteers were invaluable in soothing fractious infants, supplying toys for the new creche, and generally making themselves useful.

Next, Howard arranged to take groups of urgently needed blood donors to the prescribed hospital in Georgetown; henceforward, it was to be on a regular basis and twice he had driven the busloads, the donors ranging from Felix himself down to the lowliest field worker. They were very popular social occasions; they all loved to feel that they were doing something useful.

How often did these mercy-promoting sessions remind him of that very private, heart-stopping occasion when he'd sat and watched his own blood slowly dripping into the barely alive body of his future wife. Now not a trace of it remained inside her; her own revitalised blood cells had taken over long ago. Their separate blood, their separate lives, there was nothing, no signal he could grasp, that the well set-up antique dealer and extremely talented portrait painter, Sara Mallory, had any need for him whatever.

An experiment which went down very well in the social life of the plantation and another escape route which gave him a little relief from the hideous wearing-down of nerves in that hot climate, was the organising of two cricket teams: overseers and staff versus the cane-cutters, the workers. It was something which Felix had not attempted; playing cricket was a too hot and rather boring pastime for his taste.

Mallory was given an old field, a makeshift hut was built and furnished with tables and deck-chairs, underground water and gas pipes were tapped, a tiny kitchen complete with drinks and tea urn was laid on and the womenfolk let loose in it. Nets for practice were rigged up and Mallory assiduously coached them all.

The doctor was proud beyond measure of their growing prowess in the game. It was of special delight to hear these lithe-of-body Indians and the black, very black, cane-cutters ringing the air in his own English language which to him always seemed something of a miracle – the age-old, nostalgic, stilted phrases of 'Howzat' and 'Oh, good show, sir,' and 'Well caught, sir'.

Howard gave his all to the venture and it became a splendid social focus point, but not for one minute did it ease the bleeding pain, like an unhealed ulcer that was going on inside of him.

When things got especially bad, he tried his hand at cane-cutting. This indeed was an eye-opener. To the laughing and giggling perplexity of the watching workers, this crazy doctor hacked and thrashed at the cane with such vitriolic, fiendish concentration almost of the set purpose of killing himself, sweat dripping off his back, and suffering aches and pains beyond belief.

At the weekends when the clinic closed, Howard and Christopher Dent, a truly dedicated overseer who was most efficiently in charge of all the transportation arrangements of this large plantation, took themselves off to the beautiful hinterland of Guyana.

Dent was a calm, quiet, uncomplicated man. He had no idea of his companion's monstrous secret, that he had separated himself from his wife, and Dent was not inclined to pry.

On his arrival, at his first interview, Howard felt that he *had* to tell Felix something of the circumstances in which he'd so hastily left Chesley; about the gallery, Sara's preoccupations; all but the bed part; *that* he could scarcely bring himself to think about; *that* part he kept to himself.

In the boss's old car, with thoughts of Sara like a thousand demons baying behind him, he drove from village to village and hamlet to hamlet, injecting malarial sufferers against the disease which was endemic in Guyana, visiting patients too ill to attend the clinic and lending a sympathetic ear to the poor womenfolk grappling with their hoards of children. And, one and all they loved him.

Today at five o'clock he broke off all work for once. It was too damned hot to do any more and there was nothing now urgent enough that couldn't be left until tomorrow.

'Goodnight, sir. See you in the morning.'

'Goodnight, John. It's been a hard day.'

John Turner was his young medico assistant whom Felix had wangled from Georgetown, doing his year's practical work with the clinic. Felix swore that never again would he find himself in the position of having no doctor to fall back on and, up to now, John was proving his weight in gold.

Howard, restless, anchorless, was in a grim mood, bitter at the incongruity of finding his work so bound up with making arrangements for midwives serving outback hamlets bringing babies into the world, when he himself was thirty-one and not a father, and Sara in England didn't want babies at all. 'It's a mockery, bloody stupid burlesque . . .'

He was desperately tired. In addition to babies and anxious mothers, the clinic had battled all day long with minor to serious accidents, machete cuts and sprained and broken bones, the common lot of cane-cutters doing a difficult job.

Well, one can either burn away or rust away, I suppose. He hurtled the old Ford car Felix had lent him towards the beach only half a mile away from his bungalow and, parking it on the wet sand with no other soul in sight, tore off his shortjaks and sweaty, short-sleeved shirt, and rushed naked into the glamorous blue, blue, sea, swimming furiously overarm, getting the sweltering fatigue out of his body and salt into his eyes.

Cruising slowly towards his home afterwards, he felt better able to withstand the itching bug in his mind: this battle, this war, this passionate obsession that his wife must make some move to convince him that she wanted him in her life, that their partnership was so moulded together, there was no room for secrecy, masquerades, concealments.

He ran up the four wooden steps of his bungalow, went straight to the bathroom and showered, got his disobedient fair hair into shape, clothed his deeply tanned, well-shaped, vigorously renewed body into a cotton dressing gown, strode to the veranda and flung himself into the cane easy-chair. Mimosa and her mother were busy in the kitchen preparing his evening meal.

His relationship with Mimosa was so ambivalent as to make him feel almost schizophrenic. Within a month of his arrival at the plantation she had shyly offered herself to him. His whole being a turmoil of ice within and heat without, he'd made little resistance when she'd crept into his bed. But now all that was over. He'd castigated himself endlessly; enough was enough. He found that it had merely exacerbated the perpetual hunger and thirst of spirit; the guilt; the remorse, the inner questioning as to why he'd found it so heart-rendingly complicated with Sara and, to his amazement, all so natural and easy with Mimosa.

She brought him his meal and he gave her the very warm and friendly smile she expected. She handed him the aerogram and sleepily departed.

Who would be writing to him from England? The address was typewritten and he turned it over to read the sender's name and address. He found that this had been rubber-stamped and all he could clearly read was 'something Chambers'. The writer's signature was unknown. He suddenly realised that his heart was pounding as though a dagger was at his back and his throat was dry.

It had come then at last? He knew that all this eternity he'd been dreading and supinely waiting for was ended. This was the answer to his spiritual inertia, the feeling that he was of the walking dead. She had made the first move, and now what? What were his intentions, would he be prepared to give grounds for a divorce? That would be juicy. He said it aloud with a mirthless laugh, 'with Mimosa as co-respondent.'

He noticed that his fingers were trembling as, with intense haste, he opened the letter and he looked down stupidly when three newspaper cuttings fluttered down on to the floor like dirty snowflakes. He ignored them, his eyes travelling at once to the signature at the bottom.

Philip! By God, Philip! He controlled his mind to read.

'My dear Howard, I got your address from Olivia and I'm taking it upon myself to let you know, as you are nominally her husband at any rate, that Sara has been ill with a severe infection which kept her in bed for nearly a month. She is now up and about and improving daily.

'Although enclosures are supposed not to be allowed, I am risking sending you three news cuttings (there are several others) about her London exhibition. They will speak for themselves.

'I think it was a very fine gesture of Falkland's to make over to her so much of his space at the Laronge and I, for one, am immensely proud of her. Incidentally, she has given up the gallery.

'My real purport in writing is to tell you that I have prevailed upon Sara to come away on holiday with me to Switzerland. We shall be flying to Zurich on the 27th of the month. In the circumstances, I cannot promise not to sleep with her; it relieves my conflict of mind that you should know this.

'I can only hope that your own health, and what you are doing, pleases you, Howard.

'Do, please, remember me to Felix.

'My kindest regards, Philip.'

Christ, in God's name! He felt the stinging tears behind his eyes; heaven have mercy; here he was, banefully keen to look after his own health and Sara's . . . The pores all over his skin were opening as though some mysterious tap inside had been turned full on. He pushed his fingers through his damp hair and loosened the back of his collar as though something was choking him as he slumped back in his chair.

He became conscious that Mimosa was picking up the cuttings, looking at them as a child might look at a picture book, turning them the right way up so that the black type of the article headings showed at the top.

Howard was touched by it. He could smell the peculiar yeasty smell of her; 'baking bread', he called it, fecund and earthy. He held out his hand and the great velvet-brown eyes with the infusion of red in them, lit up in a wide smile. She gave him the cuttings.

The *Connoisseur*, the *Sunday Telegraph*, the *Observer*; he read through them, racing over the print to reach the conclusions. They were by no means uncritical, but none of them damned by faint praise.

'A remarkable collection, Hogarthian in their vigour; she paints quaint characters.'

'Some of it flamboyant poster-work, but . . .'

'Amazing sureness of touch in the technique she favours. We shall be hearing more about this young artist.'

All seemed to agree that here was a hitherto completely unknown young painter who had arrived with a decided flourish. They praised Wolfe Falkland for his perspicacity, his discerning patronage in allowing her name to be linked with his, for having found her . . .

On her knees, Mimosa stretched her long, full throat upwards, her long arms downwards, her brain loosened its hard casing, the thinking syrup slowly dripped out. She pointed to the letter in his hand.

'Good?' she asked. Even her inherent simplicity had seen that the tragic, chasing expressions on his face bespoke some crisis.

'I don't know, Mimosa, I don't know.'

'The 27th of the month!' And the airmail had taken six days to reach the plantation. The centripetal force of a whirlwind was spinning within itself and rampantly rushing through his veins. The wildness in his face was matched by a hurling of his body into his bedroom and the frantic putting-on of his clothes.

For him, all these months, Felix had been like a beacon light in a tomb – a special being – because, as Sara's brother, he was the link, he hadn't entirely lost contact with his wife. Now at last he must face it: the last leap. Now he knew what to do, by God, now he bloody well knew . . .

Outside, he saw dimly the young black frame of the houseboy and he cried out to him as a dying man for a priest, 'Dandee, Dandee, where's the Boss?'

'Cross field Four, doctor, field Four.'

Dusk was changing to darkness so rapidly that Mimosa's puzzled eyes could scarcely see the racing figure dissolving into the black steamy mist . . .

Chapter Fifteen

Sara wasn't disposed to let herself into the frightful emptiness of her home just yet; slumping behind the wheel of her car on this icy afternoon was not conducive to good health following on her exhausting bout of flu.

The carport outside was at least somewhere where she could sit quietly and think . . .

What a staggering surprise! She'd savoured appreciatively the good lunch her father had provided for them both in the pink and white wedding-cakey atmosphere of the Chesley Royal Hotel, the most elegant hotel in this conference town of many good hotels.

In one of the lounges afterwards waiters flitted about from table to table, dispensing trays of coffee, manfully displaying the hierarchy of their trade: white shirts and dark trousers for the commis, white shirts plus white jackets for the 'higher-ups', right up to the very formal black jacket, black waistcoat and striped trousers of the head of the tribe, the restaurant manager himself.

Here, sitting opposite each other at a table for two in the midst of it all, George Arthur Nightingale delivered his bombshell: that he had arranged, through Howard's solicitors and his own – Howard's consent of course to be obtained – to take into his business a new partner. Furthermore, a man prepared to invest his own capital into it, the recession in his view having definitely lifted. George Arthur's precious Huddersfield and Halifax cloth was already creeping into the nooks and crannies of the European Common Market.

George Arthur was off on his high horse, his enthusiasm quite undiminished; his small but solidly respectable business was due to expand enormously.

'It hasn't been a good investment for Howard, Sara, I know that and I deeply regret it.' His voice trailed off, his face becoming flushed and embarrassed; he stopped, giving his daughter time to collect herself, and Sara wanted to ease his pain.

'What's the new partner's name, Dad?' she asked.

'Gaunt, Mr Ian Gaunt,' he replied.

It struck her forcibly that Gaunt was an apt surname. Poor Dad! Being completely his own boss was an unfulfilled dream and from now on he was to be only half a boss; Mr Gaunt was to be an active, not a sleeping partner; George Arthur's dream was only half a dream . . .

Neither her father, nor Howard, nor Philip, nor anybody truly understood her frantic inner anxieties: Howard's legacy being at risk; her deepest fears that the warehouse would remain crammed full of unsold merchandise, business being so erratic and downright bad; family pride in such an intimate matter was uppermost.

I had reason to cling to the gallery, she comforted herself, but at what price? Howard was a damned fool to put his money in my father's business – whether he intended it or not, it put a hold on me. It gave her a sour feeling and she suddenly felt very cold.

Now I can pay off the mortgage in Howard's name. I'll see to it somehow; or he can bloody well buy gas shares, or water shares, or something bloody well safe, and I'm going to Switzerland with Philip in two days' time and that's flat . . .

Promises were promises, they had to be kept . . .

Sara turned her mind away from following up these vital implications; swiftly, her thoughts turned back to her father's parting remarks before they got into their separate cars and went their separate ways.

'I'm glad you've finished with the gallery, Sara. You can get on with your painting now; I'm very proud of you, my girl,' he said simply with a catch in his voice and, to her surprise, she was proud that he was proud. She hadn't realised how much family approbation meant to her and how nice it was that Olivia and Catherine and her mother had been so fulsome in their congratulations on the success of her first exhibition in London.

And the gallery . . . A surprise of surprises; the greatest surprise of the lot. Barely a month ago now, out of the blue her chance had come and she seized it without having had a single thought about it beforehand.

It was all over a drink with a stranger in the bar on the important occasion of the Chesley Annual International Antique Fayre. A Mr Byron Masters had politely introduced himself since they were standing next to each other, then he offered her the next drink and they moved to a table. There, he casually told her that he was looking round for a good antique business in Chesley since his wife had fallen in love with the town and they wanted somewhere: a place where they could happily retire and live when the time was right.

'What about mine?' Sara heard herself saying, almost before she knew that she'd said it. She realised now that for a long time, especially after her strenuous stained-glass period, that a small, underground rebellion, antipathy, was getting hold of her, although she was always too busy to think about it or sit down and analyse it. She was overworked; the serious flu illness was on its way and brought it all to a head. Painting the portraits of small children, shutting out the world in the confines of her studio, and now the steady flow of adults making their inquiries and commissioning their portraits took up all her time. It had just happened; she herself had planned none of it.

Before Sara knew where she was, Mr Byron Masters had bought the business lock, stock and barrel. Philip and her solicitor had done all the conveyancing and the goodwill and accounting between them; it had been amazingly easy and for a fleeting moment a smile appeared in her eyes and hovered round her mouth.

I hope to God Mr Masters can make an honest man of Mervyn, which was more than I could do . . . A real wide smile appeared, altering her expression and lighting up her whole attitude as she prepared to get out of the car at last.

And as for that old reprobate, Amos Joshua Beevers, I hope he can retire before that loathsome spitting cough carries him off. God rest his soul! Whatever the local gossip and scandal, let's face it, other antique dealers in the town could only envy the brilliant team of the three of them.

Philip always said I plan too much. I don't know how people manage if they don't plan their lives. Perhaps we are all born to be coded to a plan by Mother Nature. We are inoculated against certain things happening to us, otherwise they happen.

'You've got a siege mentality, my dear,' Philip had rejoined. 'You're not the great optimist you pretend to be.'

As she got out her latchkey and let herself into the square-sized, high-ceilinged hall of her home she was glad of the warmth and, divesting herself of her outdoor clothes and leaving them there, she fought against the inroads of after-flu depression, made herself a cup of tea, took it into the sitting room and thankfully sank down into the large, comfortable, modern-style easy chair.

Mark! Oh Mark! The full measure of all her recent surprises, one after the other, struck her hard again. What a hell of a surprise that had been. And the blinding memory of it rushed in as though it happened yesterday instead of a bare three months ago, it seemed aeons, so quickly had she recovered.

Mark disappeared from her life as quickly and as mysteriously as he entered by replacing her husband in bed.

She drank her tea and recalled vividly the pensive refrain that invariably ended his last few visits and she squirmed at the thought of the unknown reason for the intervals between each visit becoming longer and longer, and the visits themselves becoming shorter and shorter in time and length.

'Sara, I must go.'

'Yes, Mark, you must go.'

Towards the end there was no time even for an after-drink before he hurriedly left. His eagerness for love-making seemed as hungry as ever but, let me remind you, she giggled, weakly, his final visit lasted a bare twenty minutes from running upstairs to bed and his going out again through the front door. Humiliating, but hard not to see the funny side; it was just like nipping into the pub for a quick one before lunch.

Mark's final telephone call was as dramatic as it was unexpected. 'Sara, I'm flying to Canada tomorrow and I'm not coming back. Something has cropped up – very urgent – and I can't even collect my portrait.' He did sound very sorry.

'I'm deeply sad that I can't say goodbye,' he added very quietly under his breath, as though somebody was in earshot, and Sara had the distinct, instinctive feeling that it was his wife.

His wife! She'd been living in Chesley all the time, Sara was certain, and not all that far away. Strange things, small in themselves, like his anxiety about his car standing in the road outside for all to see, and at last his insistence that he hide it behind hers in the carport. And he – a man oozing power and authority – why did he care so much?

'I'm putting my cheque in the post. If I gave you my office address in Toronto, could you send it there?'

Sara felt she was being taken by storm. All the old feelings which such an emotion used to give her roared back and turned into instant resolution.

'Listen, Mark,' she heard herself lying easily. 'The portrait isn't quite finished, but in any case, would you mind terribly if I kept it? I'd like to keep it in memory of you; I don't want the cheque.' She swallowed this part of the lie with a gulp, her voice as low as his; she was being fey and skittish; not for the world would she let him know that discarding his mistress in such an abrupt manner was hurtful.

I suppose I'm as full of original sin as ever I was, she credited herself with a sigh after the hurried, clandestine conversation came to an abrupt end. He seemed to have lost his controlled, confident air.

Men think it's their *duty* to make passes, to try it on, with every lone, reasonably attractive woman they come across, Sara concluded loftily. After all, MN sees to it that they get their oats from *somewhere*, and he succeeded with me, she gulped dejectedly.

Going upstairs, the huge emptiness of the house was suddenly invaded by Howard. Howard was everywhere. She distinctly heard his voice coming from the study, talking quietly to a patient, then striding into the kitchen. Sitting on her single bed in the bedroom, she heard his footsteps bounding up the stairs two at a time, and banging the bathroom door . . .

'God in heaven, Howard,' she whispered aloud, 'you've a way of making your presence felt, but I'm going with Philip to Switzerland in two days' time; I've promised, and there's nothing you can do about it.' Sitting there, in *their* bedroom, hers and Howard's, her mind reverted to a plan.

Philip was right; she was so addicted to planning outside of her passionate release from it all in her painting that she didn't know how to arrange her thoughts otherwise.

I *could* do it; it *could* be done. The dining room could be the main bedroom, the fireplace would have to go. The house could quite easily be converted into two self-contained flats; it was simple. The lounge could have a dining-alcove and the morning room, which had been so seldom used, might become a second bedroom. The kitchen, larder, laundry room and wood storage room in this pleasant, grey-stoned 1890 vintage, comfortable old house could remain the same downstairs and my studio is sacrosanct, so the ground floor will have to be mine. Somehow in her imagination it was taking on a grey tinge as she battled on.

Upstairs, the junk room could easily become the new kitchen; water can get through it from the bathroom next door and Howard's study will have to be the downstairs bathroom and, oh, there will have to be an outside staircase to the upper floor; that will be a hell of an expense . . .

Between the two flats, her plan wasn't going to be that easy, after all . . . Disconsolately, she paused on the landing outside the junk room, opened the door, and looked in.

Oh, damn you, Howard! He was beside her, his arm was round her waist, they'd just been married. Howard's voice -

'It'll make a fine nursery, darling: triplets at least!' He teased and kissed her.

What a farce! What a joke! And she with her new skiing outfit already packed for Switzerland.

Go away! She couldn't stand these visions and flashes of memory. Suddenly she felt so physically weak, she put her hand on the landing wall for support . . .

'I can't do it! I don't *want* to do it; I can't tear the heart out of this lovely old home; and just as it's no longer needed to be used as a second storage place for the gallery.' Her plan was in tatters.

Feeling altogether bemused, Sara wandered uncertainly and disconsolately into the sitting room, returning to her chair by the unlit electric fire.

Switzerland... Philip... The gossip, pertinent questions from her gang of four being asked; conjectures from all and sundry! The ennui of spirit that she'd been trying to combat for three weeks engulfed her again. She hated her privacy being invaded by gossip. She'd had enough of that with the goings-on at the gallery. Now there'd be another feast of gossip: the public figure, Philip Carver, is taking the wife of the well-known Dr Howard Mallory for a holiday in Switzerland; Dr Mallory is in Guyana...

She knew of Philip's dark side. He'd made the confession to her alone; his fits of melancholy, how his own company frightened him, and why he'd taken to public life as a cure of sorts. The pressure on her heart was heavy with doubt; supposing the holiday didn't go well? In all these years their unique relationship had been wholly dependent on each being unattainable to the other – Eloise and Abelard – the priest and the nun; in each other's company, thrown together for ten days, that particular relationship might become very fragile indeed. I'd be clinging on to happiness by the skin of my teeth. I might turn temptress and find myself Philip's mistress, an astonishing thought...

In a daze of unhappiness and soul-searching, she closed her eyes and through sheer brain exhaustion might have gone to sleep. She had no idea how long she'd been there. It came to an abrupt end with the strident buzz of the telephone. Bemused, it might have been ringing for some time.

'That'll be Hilary.' She was expecting the call.

'That you, Hilary dear?'

'No, it's Howard.'

The clear, familiar voice went on without let or hindrance. 'No ifs or buts. I've booked a plane to Manchester, I'll be home within the hour after that.'

There was dead silence at both ends. It seemed an eternity. Then his receiver was quietly replaced on its hook and Sara, turning like a sleep-walker, found herself sitting bolt upright on a dining-room chair, hands clutching the table end. The unexpected pouncing on her again! She'd never had a plan in her mind to meet this situation; Switzerland was enough.

At the height of the flu fever three weeks ago she'd lain in bed and faced squarely the thoughtless, unspeakable selfishness – or rather thoughtlessness – her careless acceptance of Howard's devoted love for her and her provoking life-style that had driven him three thousand miles away, six months ago.

The truth hurled itself at her. He wants a divorce! He's coming back here for a divorce! Sitting quietly, at last she found the time to consider. I *had* to do the things I did. She couldn't see how she could *not* have done them. The financial mess following on the feckless Mallory bankruptcy leading to the gallery and all that it entailed, Howard's involvement in her father's business, her painting career, the stained-glass episode; and what sort of wife had she been in bed? Playing the fool, scared stiff of Mother Nature?

I was always so damned occupied. Howard merely filled the gaps, and had been allowed to look after her health . . .

Sara was at rock bottom. So much, she felt stiffly, the indomitable, irrepressible, bright spirit: Sara Mallory née Nightingale, that everybody thought she was; the flu had certainly taken its toll.

But we did have so much fun together, she protested in turmoil. I don't *express* love very well, she painfully admitted.

What's he going to say when I tell him that I'm off to Switzerland the day after tomorrow – with Philip? That'll make grounds for a juicy divorce! It'll make it easy . . .

It was a nasty, nagging, bitter reflection.

Her inner gaze slowly cleared as she fastened on Wolfe's picture on the opposite wall; it was her favourite. In its Gauguin-style setting of oscillating yellows, blue-greens, strident violets and soft red landscape blazing down so vibrantly, it was as though he was sending her a direct message; her fantastically loyal Toreador and friend. It burned like an arrow into her whole being to be followed at once by remorse stabbing her with its devil's hook; she'd let him down too!

Wolfe had asked her especially to exhibit Mark's portrait with the dozen others for the space he'd so generously given her in his own exhibition, arranged luckily and quickly for him by the owner of the prestigious Laronge gallery in London.

And I didn't send it! Mark's portrait was too personal. Wolfe had guessed what that secret look was all about; the eyes, the sensuous mouth, that portrait was for her alone. She'd given up a good fee to possess it. How marvellous of Wolfe to have made the gesture . . .

'God damn it, woman. Can't you see I'm doing myself a good turn? The critics will buzz; you're something new, my little Nightingale. As well as coming to see *my* pictures, they'll get a bumper harvest looking at yours.'

Wolfe, her Hercules, her Toreador, so magnificently putting himself out to serve her . . . Even if she wanted to, how could she withstand that enormous combustible magnetism? She'd done as she was told, gone to

London, received the plaudits; Sara and Wolfe together, side by side, and her husband knew nothing about it . . .

The vibrantly charged message from the picture on the wall brought on a surge of practicality. Get a grip on yourself, Sara, stop behaving like a cretin!

She sprang from her chair, made a headlong rush for the kitchen, forced herself to eat a sandwich and swallow a large mug of coffee and, racing upstairs, she tore off her clothes, had a quick shower and then, moving into her bedroom, she paused. What does one wear for a divorce announcement? she asked herself savagely, her hands reaching blindly into the wardrobe, her fingers finding the softest, least severely cut black skirt she possessed. Its silky folds clung to her figure contrasting beautifully with the loose-sleeved saffron-coloured blouse with its faintly jewelled front. She put on a simple pair of gold drop earrings to match and let loose her swept-back ballerina-style hair, vigorously brushing its shiny darkness down to her neck and shoulders. A quick touch of lipstick and she was ready to meet this man who was her husband.

I'm like a cat on hot bricks, but I'm ready . . .

Her movements became mechanical; before leaving the bedroom, she turned the central heating full on, put an electric pad in each bed and switched them on by means of a central switch to low.

She stared torpidly at Howard's bed, not slept in for so long. Oh, my God! He can't sleep here; he won't *want* to, how could he? He'll arrange to stay at the Chesley Arms after I've told him about Switzerland, and I'm not going to retract, ever . . .

Somehow, the very thought of Howard sleeping anywhere but in his own bed seemed obscene beyond relief, and the superhuman effort to keep the lid on her imagination as to the role she was very shortly to be called upon to play all brought her down to earth with such a jolt that, again through sheer physical weakness, she sat abruptly on her bed.

She sprang up again at once. Damn it all, I'll ask him to sleep in the guest room –

The cold emotional floundering, the stinging hurt of it all; she could only send up a fervent prayer that she'd meet this crisis in her life with some degree of dignity and on no account whatever allow Howard to see how his flight to Guyana had affected her.

She straightened her shoulders, tossed back her hair, and marched firmly into the guest-room next door and placed there, too, between the sheets, an electric pad, and switched it on low.

This was the bed where she and Mark had sported and loved. She stared at it with the deepest concentration as if she'd never seen it before. Beevers had made the surrounding baroque bedhead from her own design; it was unique and she'd had it photographed and displayed in the gallery but, when it came to it, she'd refused to have it duplicated. Like Mark's portrait, it was hers and nobody else's . . .

Sara looked at her watch. Oh, for heaven's sake, still two hours to go, and she shivering with nerves . . . Ah, but there was one place, her refuge and her strength, one place where she could shut out the world and be damned. She rushed to the studio, finding strength every step of the way.

Switching on the lights nearest to her easel, she first took down from the hook behind the door the old white coat she had commandeered from Howard years ago, and carefully covered up her impeccable outfit.

Visibly relaxing, she all but strolled across the darkly varnished bare boards of the floor to the small brick fireplace in the far corner and picking up the efficient most modern metal fire-lighter, she thrust it between the logs piled high in the basket grate. With the utmost satisfaction, she knelt by the brick hearth and watched the dry-as-bone logs quickly burn. Sara was in her natural element; with surging confidence she was up and over to her easel, preparing her palette of paints from the trestle-table full of paint tins, jars, brushes, cloths, oils, varnish and paraphernalia essential for her craft.

In the last few weeks Sara's style had altered. The stresses and strains, her grieving sense of aloneness, her ill-health, had paid dividends in the artistic depths of her soul; portraits now were for business purposes. There were new insights, new attitudes, a heightened awareness of life, of Mother Nature's surprises in − her new, symbolic, abstract paintings, new experiments she was trying out.

Contriver of her proudest peace, her never-failing antidote, the blessed world of Art opened up and lovingly grasped her to itself. Imaginings were transformed onto canvas, into shapes frosted in moonlight, shapes the winds of the desert had blown over for centuries, circles into squares, squares into circles, dancing diamonds of light, brilliant splashes of luminous acrylic paint, suggestive Dionysian joy and meaning; the aches and pains of the body were forgotten; the slaying of the spirit melted away.

Sara lost all sense of the passage of time; time stood on its head.

A loud noise in the hall; the sudden tremendous jolt to her heart; people's voices; concentration smashed to smithereens . . .

'Goodnight.'

'Goodnight, sir.' The sound of a taxi driving away.

He was there − in the hall.

Sara scrabbled off her white coat and she was standing opposite him wide-eyed, stiff, stomach muscles squeezed in knots.

'Hello – I never travel light, do I!'

Bags of every description were in his hands, under his arms and on the floor. All the flotsam and jetsam of a quick air flight surrounded this sturdy, athletic-looking man. His new, thick winter overcoat was open and flowing, his hat was at the back of his thick tousled hair and the striped tie hit her with its multi-coloured brightness.

'Let me help,' she heard herself saying; what prosaic words to offer a husband after an absence of nearly six months; the man who'd run away from her, couldn't stand what was happening to their marriage.

'These bags.'

He freed his arms and hands of them, putting them down at his feet, and quickly divested himself of his coat, revealing underneath a rough brown tweedy country-style jacket and trousers to match, all evidently bought near the airport, off the peg, she guessed.

'Presents, Sara!' he said, the words accompanied by an extremely hesitant expressive smile. With slightly shaking fingers, he opened the zip of a bright blue canvas bag, bringing out and unwrapping small parcels one after the other, laying them on the lid of the small, antique, carved oak chest against the wall, bereft of its usual plants and bowls of flowers because the day after tomorrow she was off to Switzerland with Philip.

'Presents? Presents?' she repeated. Disbelief and incredulity were stamped all over her. He was carefully placing little presents on show: a small tool-leathered purse; a pair of exciting native slippers; curious beaten-silver dishes; delicately carved five-inch high wooden images; little stooping figures of young and old men and women with bundles on their backs . . .

'These,' Howard explained, fingering them with deep appreciation, 'all these were carved by our field workers on the estate. I thought you might like them.'

Presents! Sara felt – not herself; that somebody else was occupying this taut body, this stretched mind; queer sensations of total incomprehension . . .

He made no attempt to kiss her, and she had no idea what her response would have been had he done so. He saw her astonishment and self-consciously grinned.

'Well, it's near enough to Christmas, isn't it?'

He's putting on an act: a tactical move as he might have done on a rugby football field . . . That absorbed intaking of his blue eyes as he looked at her; she knew it so well.

This is me, he was saying . . .

Sara would have loved to have gone on being not herself, but somebody else, as though she was looking down on this scene from a great height, but no, she jumped tight back into her own skin and became a high-tension, alert spring of practicality.

'Have you eaten? There's things in the fridge – I could cook something – it wouldn't take long.'

'No thanks, not now.'

Faint beads of perspiration were on his forehead; he had something to say, he wanted to talk – urgently . . .

She opened the studio door with a dramatic flourish, stepping aside for him to see into it, savouring to the full his astonishment at the striking change in the old concrete-floored garage; this was *his* surprise.

'The final result of my stained-glass treasure trove,' she explained airily.

'I didn't help at all, did I?'

He visibly flinched, she'd never seen such an expression on his face before. A good studio was what he'd so wanted for her and she'd got it without his help, thank you very much . . .

'I never asked you, did I?' she said with a wry smile. She seemed incapable of asking anybody for anything. Wolfe, her Toreador, had told her so with great vehemence many times. It never entered her head to actively *seek* advice until the exhausting research into stained glass, which in itself had been a salutary lesson.

She walked briskly over to the small, red-brick fireplace in the far corner, switching off ceiling lights as she did so, and switching on the old Victorian glass-shaded lamp on the little antique walnut table placed next to the hearth and showing off the copper-canopied chimney piece with the black basket grate firmly back-centre overshadowing the warm, cheerful, red hearth.

She put more logs on the fire and, turning round, she saw her husband was at the north window, pulling aside a chink of the plain purple unpatterned curtains she'd drawn together before she began her painting session.

Howard was staring into the blackness of the garden; patches of light from the street lamp outside showed up the drifting snow; thick layers of ice were already on the window sills.

He went in a storm – and he returns in one . . . Sara brooded with deep foreboding as to what was to come.

'You know, Sara,' he said huskily, coming across to her and seating himself in the large wing chair next to the fire, 'in the taxi, I realised I was passing through what was once all Mallory land; my grandfather, great-grandfather, and *his* father, and *his* father before that – right back for two hundred years, and do you know – I swear I saw badger-tracks at the crossroads this side of Wharton – isn't snow fabulous stuff!'

Sara descried only too plainly a deep sense of proprietorship in his bearing; whatever else, he was going to stay here in Chesley; he was home and so glad of it – and she was off to Switzerland in two days' time . . .

She dragged down onto the floor in front of the hearth one of the plum-coloured seat cushions from the sofa facing it. Mervyn had got for her this prized old sofa, necessary for the mums to sit on whilst their offspring sat for their painting sessions. With her inborn grace, she sank on to the cushion, the sofa resting her back.

The scene was a small, red-lit oasis in that long, darkened room. Wide blue eyes stared steadily into the dark green, deeply questioning eyes of his wife. Howard rested both arms on the chair-ends, deliberately allowing his gaze to travel slowly all over this inexplicable figure at his feet.

It was she who broke the silence. 'How's Felix?' she asked him hurriedly, conscious that he saw that she'd lost weight, was very pale under her light make-up. The professional gaze of a doctor was mixed with that of a stricken but determined husband.

'Felix?' Howard raised his eyebrows and his expression altered, reflecting both fondness and pain whilst she tried to visualise this mysterious brother of hers she'd seldom seen: the manager of a strange sugar plantation in far-away Guyana.

'Felix is terribly like you. I was out of the frying pan into the fire, wasn't I!' he told her with a short, grim laugh. He did not give her time to digest this.

'I'm giving up the practice, Sara.'

Oh my God, this is it! A preamble to a divorce; scandal; ignominy . . . What could she say?

'I phoned David from the plantation. He consulted Hedley straight away and phoned me back. They both agreed that Hedley should take my place in the partnership – the financial side will be all right and, after all, Hedley's been locum for six months – he's dug in.'

More extraordinary changes of partnership: the gallery, her father, now this! Sara averted her face to the fire, trying to take it in. The Fates were shuffling the cards like mad; it was becoming a dance . . . She remained silent, expressionless.

'Oh, I see – ,' was all she finally managed to say.

Howard's tone was even and enigmatic. 'David told me about a new opening at the County Hospital in Manchester and I phoned them from Guyana straight away. I've an appointment with them in two days' time.'

'I see,' was all Sara could think of to say again helplessly. Her voice was very quiet, her face expressing utter blankness; she was beyond surprises.

'I came to the conclusion when I was away,' he told her casually, 'that I prefer hospital work; the new drugs interest me. They're tremendous – new drugs for transplants. The county has set up a new team and I want to get my nose into it in the early stages. Genetic engineering – it gets right to the source, the mind boggles – it's perilous knowledge, Sara. We've simply *got* to find the cure for these incurables, like Alzheimer's, these disgusting diseases.'

It struck Sara as infinitely remarkable, quite incongruous, that they should be talking like this in such a husband and wifely way, when she had yet to break the news that she was going away with his one-time friend and family accountant, Philip Carver.

'There isn't the scope in general practice,' he was explaining.

Sara sat and listened, the tension between them lessening perceptibly. She could feel the ache inside of him; emotions, the suffering centre solely in her own mind, she could transfer to his, it was mutually shared. She was beginning to understand . . .

It was high time she said something about herself. 'My paintings have been exhibited in London, thanks to Wolfe. He allotted me some of his space.'

She told him so off-handedly, so casually, she might have been having an admired exhibition every day of the week, but the effect was somewhat dimmed when he answered at once, interrupting her before she could tell him more.

'I know, Sara. It's brilliant, wonderful! It was what I hoped for all along.' And, of course, it was . . .

Even Howard's powers of persuasion had failed dismally when it came to Sara making quick money and establishing herself as a very successful business woman; the two careers hadn't mixed.

'I've sold the gallery,' she said, looking at him squarely and challengingly, as if to inform him that she'd only sold it because her portrait painting of children had taken off so suddenly, and now the adults were quickly following.

'Yes, I know, Sara.'

It was almost becoming a refrain. Olivia must have been very busy telephoning Felix to put Howard in the picture. She hurriedly glossed over this one great bone of contention between them. Her interest had been sagging and, now that it was sold, it may as well never have been . . .

Watching Howard avidly watching her, it struck Sara forcibly that he looked older, more mature; his whole attitude testified to the fact that in Guyana he'd cleared the ground, made a new foundation for himself, reshaped and rejuvenated himself against all odds.

She saw that in spite of his travel-tiredness he was strong and alert and his fair skin was healthily tanned whilst she had become less gay, blithe and ebullient as the weeks dragged into months. The aloneness of the house coupled with the serious bout of flu had got her down; she felt fragile, more vulnerable to hurt; only her Art had saved her.

He knew about the stained glass episode, he already knew about her exhibition, he knew about the gallery. But now she really *could* surprise her husband because she'd only heard about it this very morning.

The secret, shadowy part of herself was enjoying this. She told Howard in great detail of her luncheon appointment with her father at the Chesley Royal Hotel, and the imminent disclosure that Howard's contract as the sleeping partner in the business was to end, and of the arrival of Mr Ian Gaunt on the scene. She even ventured a little joke.

'It's a cinch!'

'It's up my sleeve!' Howard rejoined at once. They were actually laughing together! It was unbelievable . . .

The buzz of the telephone in the hall startled them both.

'I'll take it, I'll take it.'

He was up from his chair and striding out of the room as he'd always done, before she could collect her wits. Her husband was back with a vengeance.

It *will* be Hilary this time, Sara assured herself, sitting alone on her floor cushion and staring into the glowing fire.

'I could paint him! I could paint him!'

She knew at last how she could paint this familiar yet so unfamiliar man's portrait — when it was too late. She'd got into the heart of him; everybody had a revealing secret look for a fraction of fleeting time, if one was able to grasp it. Howard's secret look had been plain for her to see years ago but she'd never bothered to register it in her mind . . .

Howard returned slowly back to his chair, settling himself quietly.

'That was Philip,' he said.

'Philip?' Sara echoed stupidly.

'He didn't seem surprised that I was back. He wrote to me, you know, about your London exhibition, and that you'd sold the gallery, and there were news cuttings about your stained-glass find as well.'

Philip! God Almighty, it was Philip! Not Olivia, not Felix — it was Philip who'd stolen her thunder and robbed her of surprises and triumphant announcements as to her fortunes of the last six months either because of, or in spite of, a runaway husband.

'Philip wrote to me that he intended to take you to Switzerland.'

It was out. Philip had done it all. This, at least, he'd made easy for her. Yes, in two days' time; and Howard knew – had known it all along.

'And he told me that he intends to sleep with you when you get there,' Howard went on relentlessly, giving her the whole of it.

'What! Philip told you that?'

That was another damned surprise! Not for one minute had she any intention of breaking that precious bond that held together the unique relationship with Philip over the years, especially this thread between them of the last six months; their unobtainableness physically, one with the other, Philip's loyalty to his friendship with Howard, had been the very essence . . .

She was stumbling, baffled, incredulous.

'Philip loves you, you know,' Howard said simply.

How long had he known? If he'd guessed, it was something her husband had kept very silent about, in his heart . . .

In what manner did Philip love her, Sara asked herself now. She'd been very content to lie in the cradle of his unobtainableness for so long.

Staring into the fire, in a flash of real understanding and speaking very thoughtfully and calmly, she explained to Howard, and at the same time to herself:

'Philip loves me in the centre of his bachelordom; he loves me like a pressed flower in an old book; like a pinned butterfly he can look at when he's depressed.'

Philip was bound, she decided, to write that letter to Howard; his very love demanded that he try and bring husband and wife together. Was it self-preservation on his part? She ought not to have been surprised – taken off her guard.

'Sara,' Howard straightened himself, his look became stony with self-control as he spoke with brutal directness.

'Before we go any further, I must ask you whether you want me to stay tonight or pick up my bags and go.'

He told her about Mimosa very graphically, holding nothing back. He described what had taken place between himself and Mimosa in bed. His expression as he finished turned into a terrifying uncertainty as to whether he was to receive punishment or absolution.

'I finished it because I only wanted more – I can't do it without love,' he explained. 'I had to tell you, Sara.' It wasn't something he could hold back: a secret . . .

It's his temperament, he couldn't *not* tell me. It would be on his conscience for ever . . .

Sara understood. To her, what was done was done – couldn't be

183

undone. She became vividly aware of Mimosa and the background to the scene: Mimosa of the red-brown eyes and mahogany skin cooking for him, *serving* him in more ways than one. Feeling confused, unable to look at him, Sara hugged her knees and turned her face to the fire. She still had *her* secret.

She felt foolish, shamed, abashed. Howard was so upright, honest; she was in the predicament of whether or not to confess her own sinfulness. She wished Howard had never told her about Mimosa. She'd never even considered enlightening her husband about Mark; now – was it incumbent on her – was she being fair?

Suddenly, with instant resolution and bounding grace she was up from her cushion and crossing to the farthest wall of the studio where half a dozen of her framed pictures were lined up, their blank canvas backs facing outwards. In spite of herself, a nervous, impish merriment was bubbling up inside of her. Now she *had* something new to tell Howard: it was a form of judo-reaction, the timing was right; action, not words . . .

She chose a picture and, returning to the hearth, she bent over Howard's chair and placed Mark Seager's portrait into his hands.

'My answer to Mimosa,' was all she said.

Mark's face, with his secret look and sensuous mouth, stared at Howard, and Howard stared back, flabbergasted, dumbstruck.

At last, sitting back in her place on the floor with the sofa behind her, Sara took the portrait from him and, kneeling across to the fire, her silky black skirt ruffled up and showing a great deal of the black tights underneath, pale saffron soft sleeves falling back to her elbows, she very carefully and forthrightly pushed the portrait deeply into the back of the iron basket and the spurting, crackling logs. The flames leapt up, devouring the oil paint. Mark's handsome, craggy features were obliterated in a frenzy of sound and smoke.

Sara watched silently and, stupefied, mesmerised, Howard gazed long and hard, slowly digesting the implication that it was this man, not Philip, who'd gone to bed with his wife. He refused to allow his imagination to go further. He must suffer the same electrifying fact that, within a mere six months, he and Sara, both of them, had each been unfaithful, one to the other . . .

Sara's thoughts raced in memory. There you go, Mark, up the chimney in sweet-smelling smoke: a sacrifice to some goddess of rectitude on high . . .

Physically now at ease, leaning back half-propped up by the plum-coloured sofa, dark hair outlining the broad, high cheekbones, she was stifling a desire to laugh. 'That was my best portrait,' she murmured regretfully to herself.

Howard, spellbound, continued to watch, fascinated by the performance which he knew put an end to all speculation on his part. It was her secret, and she'd divulge it to nobody.

He sat back at last, relaxing in the enveloping chair, and only now did he feel that he could deliver Philip's message.

'Philip – er – suggested over the phone that I – er – that I change places with him and take you to Switzerland in his stead. He says it can all be arranged quickly, the plane isn't full.' The frank face flushed and he looked embarrassed but hopeful, longing and expectant. The look seared into her heart and into her mind.

It said it all: this is the look she would paint.

Well! Yet another surprise! She was becoming inured to surprises, and how far was a divorce from all this . . .

The decision seemed natural and normal, going on holiday to Switzerland with Howard her husband, not returning home as Philip's mistress.

She took the poker and, leaning across the hearth to the fire, she stirred into a red glow the logs mixed with the dying ashes of Mark's portrait. Sitting back again, relaxed, her mind made up –

'Yes, Howard,' she promised quietly, 'we'll go to Switzerland.' Then – she didn't know why she said it, or even precisely what she was saying – it was spontaneous, unintentional, out of the blue –

'Wouldn't Philip make an ideal godfather!'

With an exultant cry, Howard was there beside her, all over her, pulling at her skirt, her blouse, smothering her neck in his tweed jacket, raining kisses with pent-up abandon on her cheeks, her mouth, in her hair, everywhere; and she was responding fully and, strange to tell, none of it was a surprise . . .

No need now for electric pads in each of their single beds upstairs; no need for the electric pad warming the sheets in the guest-room.

On the floor! On the floor! For a brief moment Sara's mind travelled back to a little hut in her mother's garden; but memories become very thin ghosts in the passage of time . . .

Sara thought she heard a noise coming from down the chimney: a real chuckle; a jubilant, rejoicing, I-told-you-so chuckle . . .

That, she concluded gaily, happily, that will be Mother Nature, MN for short, running all the way to the maternity ward.